THE SLAUGHTERED LAMB BOOKSTORE AND BAR

SEANA KELLY

The Slaughtered Lamb Bookstore and Bar

Ebook ISBN: 9781641971546

KDP POD ISBN: 9798689235776

IS POD ISBN: 9781641971591

NYLA Publishing

121 W. 27th St., Suite 1201, NY 10001, New York.

http://www.nyliterary.com

For Gregory, who never tires of
discussing which drinks should be paired with
which books at The Slaughtered Lamb.
He might have a spreadsheet somewhere.

ONE

Wherein a Werewolf, a Wicche, a Vampire, and a Demon Discuss the Likelihood of a Zombie Apocalypse

No one can sneak up on you if you keep your back to the wall. No one can hide in the shadows if you never turn off the lights. No one can hurt you if you never let them touch you. Trust issues? You bet. I have my reasons, but we'll get to those later.

"Give me a break, Sam." Owen, my trusty boy Friday and wicche extraordinaire, smirked.

"All I'm saying is that zombies have undergone more of a transformation over the years." Hiding a grin, I blew on my tea and watched the waves hitting the glass wall of my bookstore and bar.

"Speed, maybe," he said as he stacked glasses under the bar.

Perched on a stool, I sipped while Owen checked the liquor bottles, replacing empties. Tables were scattered throughout the bar, green leather chairs surrounding them, with small stained-glass lamps topping most. I scanned the room, checking if anyone needed a refill, but it was a ruse. Clive, a certain ridiculously handsome vampire, drew me like a zombie to brains.

"Nuh-uh," I continued. "Remember the whisperers in *The Walking Dead*? Speech requires thought."

"I beg to differ."

Ignoring him, I forged ahead. "In *I am Legend* they could reason, and in *28 Days* they were wicked fast. No more shambling around and bumping into trees for modern zombies." I paused. "You know what, I've changed my mind."

Clive sat at a corner table, lost in shadow. His eyes felt like a soft caress and an unfamiliar shiver ran through me. Swirling the tea in my cup, I allowed myself a quick glance in his direction. He took a sip, watching me, his storm-gray eyes crinkled in an almost smile.

"Are you shitting me right now?" Owen dropped an empty whiskey bottle into the recycle bin and pulled a fresh bottle from under the counter. Owen's hair glinted in the light, a natural black liberally streaked with electric blue. Or maybe it was the piercings in his ears and eyebrow. The boy sparkled. He reminded me of a shiny Chris Peng.

What were we talking about again? Clive scattered my thoughts without even trying. He was Master of the City, the highest-ranking supernatural in town. He'd show up once a month, have a drink, and I'd start considering things I had no right to consider. I was not good romantic material. Still, Clive made me wish things were different, that I was different.

"Sam?" Owen waited for a response.

"No, what I mean is, I don't think zombies have changed the most in pop culture; I think women have." I totally had this argument in the bag.

Clive leaned forward and cleared his throat. "You believe the depiction of humans has changed the most?"

Clive never joined our reindeer games. I sat stunned for a moment, his voice a decadent rumble in the quiet room. Shaking it off, I said, "I was just messing with Owen on the zombies. He's terrified of—"

"Who wouldn't be? They're zombies!"

"Here's the thing, though. In Romero's 1968 *Night of the Living Dead,* Barbara is worthless. She's a walking cliché. Weak, childlike—"

Heavy footsteps pounded down the stairs into the bar. I could have kept arguing, but I'd clearly already won the argument. Clive and his stupid sexy face were making it difficult to hold on to my thoughts.

"Nice tee." Dave, my half-demon short order cook, came behind the bar, interrupting the excellent point I forgot I was making. He stared intently at my chest. I was wearing my zombie survival guide tee today. It was what had prompted the argument with Owen over the depiction of supernaturals in pop culture.

I hid beneath shapeless, sexless clothes to avoid attention. Seven years after the fact, and I still cringed when I noticed gazes drift to the scars trailing out of my sleeves or collar.

I used to be considered pretty—long, wavy brown hair, green eyes, a thin, athletic build. That was before. My efforts at androgyny, though, were wasted on Dave. He enjoyed fucking with people too much. My issues made me easy prey. He smirked, knowing his scrutiny was making me sweat. Grabbing a bottle of cinnamon schnapps, he poured himself a glass.

"Glad you like it," I said. "You can never be too careful. It pays to be prepared for the shambling undead."

Dave made a dismissive sound in the back of his throat. "Please. They're only as dangerous or as focused as the demon who calls them. Most will give out before the fight gets interesting."

I never knew how seriously to take Dave. He was a good guy, albeit one with deep red skin, pure black eyes, and occasional bouts of uncontrolled anger. But no one was perfect.

"I swear," he continued. "Most demons have ADD. Just when things start to get good, they wander off to start some new shit. It's why they never get anything done."

He winked at me as he walked toward the kitchen.

I spoke to Dave's massive back. "I'll have to remember that. Thanks."

Clive, impeccably dressed in a dark suit and snowy white shirt, tapped a long finger on the table. "'Weak, childlike…'"

"Hmm? Oh, yeah." My brain went on hiatus while I watched him take another sip. The man gave good swallow. "Um." And that British accent did funny things to my stomach. Clive was stupidly handsome, with dark blond hair, intense gray eyes, strong jaw, and broad shoulders. It was good he only dropped in every once in a while. I'd never be able to interact with him on a daily basis.

"Sam?"

How did a single syllable undo me? "Barbara was weak and childlike, tripping and falling. She's almost comatose with fear in the 1968 version of the film. When Romero remade it in 1990, Barbara was a warrior. She strapped on the ammo and started blowing away zombies."

He tilted his head, studying me. "Better to be fearsome than fearful?"

"Yes." Seven years of battling back the fear that wanted to swamp me, wanted to pull me back down into the dark, pushed the harsh sound from my lips.

Nodding slowly, he stood. "I'm glad to hear it. Good evening."

Like a slavish zombie to a juicy frontal lobe, I watched him climb the stairs and leave. What was it was about today's conversation that prompted the normally brooding vampire to speak? Zombies? It felt more like it was women fighting back that had piqued his interest.

The sky tonight was a brilliant purple, the water almost black as it crashed against the windows. My bookstore-bar was nestled into a cliff face at the waterline. During low tide, waves swirled around the bottom of the window. At high tide, the window-wall was almost completely submerged.

My home lay hidden beneath one of San Francisco's scenic spots. Land's End had a long stairway that led down to an over-look. When humans reached the bottom of the steps, they found themselves on a platform that overlooked the meeting of the Bay and the Pacific Ocean. When supernaturals walked down the steps, they passed through a magical entrance and kept going deep underground to my bookstore and bar.

As much as I thought the bar was a work of art, it was the view that got all the attention. It was also why I'd decided on dark wood throughout. When you had an uninterrupted glass wall looking out on the ocean and Golden Gate Bridge, additional eye-catching décor seemed pointless.

To the left of the stairs was the bookstore. An old-fashioned pub sign, The Slaughtered Lamb, hung down from the carved entrance. It was an exact replica of the one in the film *An American Werewolf in London*. It was my nerdy nod to being an American werewolf behind the bar. The Slaughtered Lamb was for supernaturals only. After all, everyone needed a strong drink and a good book.

"Samantha."

Looking up, I found two bright yellow eyes staring intently at me. "Ule, it's nice to see you." His cup was full, thank goodness. "I see Owen has set you up this evening." The concoction smelled foul and I had no desire to refill it. Owen brewed some kind of rodent tea for customers like Ule, an owl shifter. "Do you need anything else?"

He gazed down into his cup for a moment, before his large, unblinkingly eyes found mine again. "No."

I tapped the bar and smiled. "Good talk."

Something large thumped against the window.

"Oh, dear." A wicche's concerned voice drew the attention of the room. She was staring out the window at the black, teeming water.

An object was drawn away with the tide before rushing back and smashing into the glass again. A body. Female, naked, and torn up. I came around the bar, horrified. Well-hidden scars burned in recognition. The tide slammed her back into the window, and I jumped.

The body jerked in the swirling water in a kind of grotesque ballet. Closing my eyes, I felt my gorge rise. I couldn't leave her out there alone. I knew what it was like to be torn up and alone.

Turning, I looked for one of my regulars, a selkie. He was slight and dark, with translucent hair and brown, sealskin-colored eyes. I gestured to the window, hand trembling. "Will you get her, please?" Her body slammed into the window, and I recoiled.

The selkie hung the modesty robe back on a hook by the water entrance, wrapped his sealskin around himself, and dove out into the ocean. We saw him seconds later, navigating through the strong tide, pushing her body toward the square of water in the floor of the bar. It was held in place by a magical membrane. Ocean nymphs and other water fae could cross back and forth, but the water never broke the barrier.

He nudged the body towards the entrance. Leaning forward, I grabbed her and pulled. She slid a few feet across the floor before rolling onto her back.

Milky eyes stared sightlessly up. Her body was blue and bloated. Bloodless slashes exposed muscles, ligaments, and organs. The cuts were ragged. Who knew how long she'd been in the water. Her injuries might have been the result of rocks or sharks. The extent of them, though…my own hidden scars flashed through my mind.

Grim, an aptly named dwarf, offered the blanket I kept behind the bar.

I nodded my thanks, unable to speak. Shaking out the blanket, I covered her with it.

"Do you know her?" Owen asked.

Voice unsteady, I responded, "Not sure. She's a wolf. I can smell that under the seaweed and brine. I'll call my uncle, see if he has anyone missing from his pack." Alone, lost in the cold, dark ocean. "If she's not his, I guess I'll have to contact the Bodega Bay pack." How had the woman ended up here of all places?

Owen rested his hand on my back. "Can I help?"

I stiffened. I didn't like being touched, not even when I needed it. Maybe especially then. It had been seven years since I'd been attacked and turned. Werewolves, like many other supernaturals, weren't supposed to age. I'd been seventeen when I was turned, but I looked older now. Being the lone wolf in San Francisco meant I hadn't had anyone to teach me fact from fiction. Maybe the books were wrong about werewolf aging. Regardless, my body might be a horror, but it was that of a strong, healthy twenty-four-year-old. Emotionally? Well, there were some things you never recover from.

After getting the dead woman photographed, wrapped, and placed in the far corner of the cold-storage room, I sat in my office. Breathing deeply, I tried not to remember the soft pop the knife made as it broke the skin and sliced through my body, the harsh intake of breath as teeth tore and claws ripped. *No*. It was better to be fearsome than fearful. I wasn't going down that path again.

Sitting up straight, I scrubbed my face clean of tears. Enough. I willed my pulse to slow. I needed to call Marcus. I barely knew him, had only met him right before I'd been attacked and then had been pushed away afterward. He reminded me of too many things I've tried to keep hidden.

I hadn't realized it growing up, but the reason my mother never allowed me to see or speak with Uncle Marcus was because she knew he was a werewolf. Right after she died, when I was seventeen, he reached out, wanting to get to know me. I didn't remember my dad. He was gone before I was able to form and keep more than the vaguest of memories. No matter how I asked, Mom wouldn't talk about dad, saying it was dangerous to give the dead too much of ourselves.

Even though I had promised my mother never to contact Marcus, when he sought me out at her funeral, it felt like a second chance at family. He seemed kind, but I should have listened to Mom. I'd agreed to visit him on what I'd later learned were his pack grounds. I'd been attacked, tortured, raped, and turned by a werewolf he couldn't identify and never found.

Staring at the Degas postcard on the wall of my office, I forced my mind to think about delicate ballerinas in blue, letting them take the place of suffering and humiliation. When my hands had stopped shaking, I uploaded the photo of the dead woman and sent it to Marcus. Maybe he'd know who she was. If not, I wasn't sure what to do with her. We never handed over our dead to the human authorities. The less they knew about us, the better.

The phone rang six times before a voice clicked on, asking for a message.

"Marcus, it's Sam. I fished a dead woman out of the bay in front of the bar. I just sent a picture of her to your email. If she's not one of yours, I'll contact the other Bay Area pack."

Hand clenched, short nails digging into my palm, I struggled with how to continue. "I guess I just didn't want her to be alone." I cleared my throat. "Anyway, could you let me know if you recognize her? I'd appreciate it." I let the receiver fall into the cradle.

AFTER CLOSING, I DECIDED TO GO ON A RUN. I NEEDED NORMALCY and control of my own body. Exercising to exhaustion helped me sleep. I refused to let the memories isolate me from the world again.

Jogging up the stairs, I inhaled deeply. Cold, salty wind skated off the ocean as I stretched at the cliff's edge before heading out. Muscles warm and relaxed, I sped up, running hard and fast, away from open ground and through the woods. Fallen pine needles carpeted the ground. A muffled foghorn bellowed in the distance. It should have been calming, but I couldn't shake off the feeling I was being watched. A rustling in the trees brought me up short. I scented the wind. Stilled to listen. Nothing.

Running again, I carved my way through the long beach grass, swirling in the high winds along the bluff. The waxing moon glowed in the gathering fog. A couple of miles from the bookstore, I scented a wolf and skidded to a stop. I was the only wolf in San Francisco. There were no packs in town. It was part of the reason I lived here.

Heart thundering, I couldn't stop thinking about the woman we'd fished out of the bay. I desperately wanted to shift, to protect myself, to have claws and fangs. It would take too long, though. I'd be vulnerable to attack until I'd completed the change. Tipping my head up, I scented the wind again. It was stronger. The wolf was closing in and I was out of time.

I tore back towards my cliff. A mile from home, the sound of paws pounded the sandy dirt behind me. Would anyone hear if I screamed? The fog swallowed screams. I raced headlong toward the trees, frantically looking for a weapon of some kind. I wouldn't let anyone overpower me, hold me down—not ever again. Paws thundered on the path.

Ahead, I saw the silhouette of a woman. I ran to her. Moonlight glinted off a swath of blonde hair. I felt momentary relief, thinking I had help. Then the hatred rolling off her hit, and I realized too late that I'd been herded into a bigger threat. I didn't know what she was—the wolf's scent was too strong—but I knew she wasn't human.

Understanding that death loomed before and behind, I pivoted to the right and ran toward the brush growing at the edge of the cliff. I felt the wolf's fur brush my ankle as he passed. He skidded, spun, and started after me again. Out of options, I sprinted to the cliff and threw myself over.

My heart stopped on the free fall. I had three or four seconds to question the sanity of my plan before I was plunging into freezing seawater.

Plummeting down, my body cracked against the slanted cliff

face, deep underwater. I kicked off, fighting my way to the surface before my lungs burst. Breathing was difficult at the surface as waves capsized over me, pulling me under. I spat seawater. Knowing I couldn't be far from the bar entrance, I swam, hoping the wolf hadn't followed me over the cliff.

Like a ragdoll, I was tossed, pulled down, and then shoved back up by the teeming ocean. Something brushed across my cheek, something long and flat that I hoped very much was kelp. I caught only a glimpse of it before I was knocked sideways by another wave.

The seaweed or whatever it was scraped against the back of my neck. Cringing, I batted it away as I was yanked under again and again, fighting the relentless undertow. I sputtered to the surface and realized the vine had encircled my neck, squeezing tighter as my body was spun in the churning waves. Treading water as best I could, keeping an eye out for jagged rocks, I scanned the darkened cliff face, looking for the bar entrance. It was hidden from view, glamoured to look like nothing but rock, but there was a deep groove bisected by a forty-five-degree slash that almost made an X-marks-the-spot landmark. The bar entrance was right beneath that X in the stone.

Sputtering water, I yanked at the vine that had begun choking me. It moved and constricted once more. When I pulled, it undulated in a way plant life didn't. The scream stayed trapped inside my head as my larynx was crushed by what I hoped, by all that was holy, was not an eel. Sentient underwater seaweed was less terrifying to me than an eel wrapped around my neck.

Needle-like teeth latched onto my hand. I froze in horror for only a moment, but it was enough to drag me back under the freezing waves. Fingers numb, I tore like a wild thing at the creature encircling my neck. I felt bites on my neck and hands, but I didn't care, so great was the cringe factor. With a final rip, I snatched the now inert pieces of God-anything-but-an-eel from my throat and let them drop from my bloody hands.

A wave crashed, and I was under again. Eel parts floated away, but it was the shiny thing dropping straight down that caught my attention. My hands flew to my neck. It was bare. My mother's necklace. I'd ripped it off when I'd killed the eel. It was all I had, my only link to her. Diving down, I grabbed with unfeeling hands, but somehow managed to catch it by the stone pendant before it sunk into the murky depths of the bay.

Eel-free and clutching my mother's necklace, I swam toward the bar's entrance. Even though I was preternaturally strong, it was a slow and arduous journey. Thankfully, the wolf hadn't followed me over the cliff. When I finally found the entrance, I dragged my exhausted, battered body in and lay there, panting and shivering on the barroom floor. Who were those two up top? Were they connected to the dead woman?

The Slaughtered Lamb was warded to high heaven. My wards, a kind of magical security system, were set with me as the key. Over time, they had begun to respond to my intentions as well as my words. I locked them down and dragged myself back to my apartment to take a long, hot shower.

The black stone pendant hung limply from my injured hand. I couldn't explain it, but not having it around my neck was causing my head to throb. I would get it fixed. The first chance I got, I would get it fixed and back around my neck. I'd been little when my Mom set out the jewelry making tools and made it for me, when she made me promise to never take it off.

Even after a steaming shower, I couldn't stop shivering. Later, dressed in my warmest sweats and burrowed under blankets, I wished for a cup of cocoa and a hand to hold. Instead, I fell into a restless sleep as my mind cycled through trauma, past and present.

TWO

We Now Join this Nightmare, Already in Progress

The sheets twisted around my kicking legs, as I dropped back down into nightmares.

RAIN SPLASHES ON THE PRISTINE MARBLE HEADSTONE.

Bridget Corey Quinn
Beloved Mother.

I overhear a murmuring of voices, but I can't tear my eyes from the evidence of my mother's death. Sobs catch in my chest. I'm alone in the world. Seventeen and completely alone. I hear a strange growling sound and then a blinding flash of light in the sky. There are gasps and mutters, but I can't tear my eyes away from the headstone. Loss, crushing inescapable loss, takes me out at the knees. I drop into a shallow puddle of mud atop the new sod. A crack splits the stone, a jagged scar between Corey and Quinn. My tears mix with rain. My necklace throbs in time with my breaking heart as footsteps sound…

My traitorous subconscious plucked through memories for the next stop on Sam's Repressed Horrors Roundup.

Footsteps crackle on pine needles. It's past midnight as I walk in the inky black, flashlight forgotten on my uncle's entry table. The cabin I'm staying in isn't far. I have my phone if I need a light. A breath of sound behind me and then blinding pain. Nothingness. I awake to suffocating fear and unimaginable agony. Blindfolded, arms strain over my head in scalding, metal handcuffs. The passage of time is marked by screams turning to breathy croaks. Slick, sticky blood runs down my body, dripping off my toes. The tickling of fur against my skin signals his change. Part of me is happy for the blindfold, that I don't have to watch this monster tear me apart. Teeth shred my skin. Claws dig under my ribs. Does the blindfold make it worse? Faceless, he becomes every man. Liquid washes over my abdomen and legs. Slashes burn anew. I kick out again and connect. I'm in hell, the torture never ending, but I'm still fighting. The long, serrated blade slices through my chest as he continues to carve in the dark…

The memory faded, tension leaving my body with it, until my mind plucked out another one to torment me with.

It's night again. The Slaughtered Lamb is under construction. I'm doing my best to ignore the angry vampire whose name I don't remember. He stands in the corner of the cavernous bookstore and bar. Helena, the wicche I've been staying with in the months since the attack, says that Clive assigned guards for me. I don't understand why. I'm no one. Looking through catalogs of book titles, choosing what to stock, I try to ignore the dark, resentful eyes peering out of the shadows.

Working, lost in my own thoughts, I miss something important. Hours pass. Fog blankets the ocean, obscuring the moon. There's a strange, wet sound. A great, shaggy shape stands out against the gloom. I search the bar's corners. The angry eyes are gone. Have I fallen asleep? A large, black horse shakes himself, water dousing me. A soft plip, plop *echoes in the silent room. Reaching out to him, he snarls, teeth snapping. Blood drips. A shocked scream breaks the dream-like quiet. I'm running, a monster at my heels. Hooves thunder in the empty rooms. I race through the back and around to the huge, free-standing bookshelves that were delivered earlier. Hiding, hunkered down between wood and wall, breath held as my heart races, I make myself as small and silent as possible. A gust of hot air hits the top of my head. When I look up, blood-red eyes skewer me. I flip myself over and kick out at his muzzle. Broad shoulders shove the bookshelves away as powerful jaws snap down on my leg, crushing my ankle. He drags me toward the water entrance, toward death.*

Fighting, kicking, leg shredded, shouts hoarse, I claw at the floor, desperate to escape. My foot drops from its mouth as the fae horse rears up, slamming down on my stomach, crushing my organs. Why have me live through that werewolf's torture just so I could die now, as I was learning to hope again? Teeth scrape bone, as it drags me toward the inevitable. Unspeakable pain like fire bathes me. I twist and writhe, but his hold is unbreakable.

Eyes screwed closed against the pain, a wail on my lips, I kick again and again. My mangled leg drops. Clive is standing over me. Gray eyes take in my battered state as he yanks the jaws of the kelpie open. A sick, squelching pop sounds as Clive tears them apart. He throws the carcass toward the water entrance and then is kneeling in blood and seawater, gentle hands ghost over me, pulling away the pain.

And then the darkness pulled me under again.

SHOOTING UP IN BED, I AWOKE WITH A START. THAT DAMN KELPIE. Kelpies were magical water creatures that took the shape of horses and lured people to the water before attacking and snacking. If I had known there were freaking kelpies in the San Francisco Bay, I'd never have put in a water entrance. I was destined to end my life as chum.

The kelpie attack had taken place over six years ago, when the bookstore and bar were under construction, and I still had nightmares about it. Thankfully, not as often these days. I guess the dead woman, the wolf, and the scary blonde were too much for my subconscious. The kelpie had sensed my fear and decided to haunt my dreams again. *Bastard.* Dreaming about Mom was odd, though. I rarely ever dreamed about her funeral and the freak lightning storm. That day was a blur of pain and fear.

Details were missing, but perhaps that was normal, given how my life had changed so completely.

Clamping down tightly on the other part of the nightmare, the part I refused to think about, I turned on the bedside lamp. No more darkness. Pulling up the covers, I flinched, my arms stinging. I rubbed them, assuming I'd cut off the circulation, and yelped in pain. Slowly pulling up my hoodie sleeves, I saw long, livid scratches running down my arms. How the hell had I done that?

This was no good. I'd never fall back asleep. Grabbing a book off my nightstand, I pushed into my bunny slippers and shuffled into the living room. After pulling a soft ocean-colored throw from the back of my couch, I padded through the bar's kitchen, picking up a plate of snickerdoodles Dave had left me—for a demon, he was a good guy—and wandered into the darkened bar. I worked the knobs and buttons on the espresso machine. Cocoa, that was what I needed. With marshmallows. Snickerdoodles, *Pride and Prejudice,* and a cozy blanky were the perfect antidote for tortured nightmares and mysterious injuries. Sitting at the corner table next to the window, I turned the lamp to its lowest setting and read, erasing the ugliness.

Suffering along with Lizzy through Darcy's 'not handsome enough to tempt me' declaration, I sensed unnatural movement in the water. I'd become used to the rhythm of the ocean, the ebb and flow as the dark waves hit the window at my side. The tide was high, so the waterline was far above my head. Turning off the lamp, I peered into the swirling bay, trying to locate what had inexplicably sent chills up my spine.

Please, don't let it be another dead woman. I didn't think my psyche could take too much more tonight. Finishing the last of my cooled cocoa, I watched the silent swirling beauty, the cool weightlessness of the water, pressing in on all sides. It could buoy and it could sink. Life and death. Tonight, though, it seemed to be watching me.

A dark, massive tentacle struck the window, right where I

was sitting. Leaping back, I fell off the chair, slippers tangled in the blanket. What the… In all the years I'd lived here, I'd only ever seen a handful of octopuses in the bay. Whatever this giant tentacle was attached to was not native to San Francisco.

Suckers spread on the window, and then the tentacle pulled. The window bowed but held. A piercing squeal had me clamping my hands over my ears as the monstrous tentacle dragged its suckers down the windowpane. The ocean churned. Something huge was displacing water.

Holding my breath, I slowly withdrew, trying not to draw its attention. I rounded the bar and grabbed the phone. No dial tone. I wasn't sure what was out there, but I knew I didn't want to have anything to do with it.

Impossibly long tentacles slammed against the window again. They covered the ten-foot-high window and then some. Bluish suckers as large as my fists stood out against the almost-black tentacles. When they convulsed, the window rippled. Adrenaline spiking, my stomach dropped. I slid along the back of the bar toward the stairs. Fangs and claws were no match for that thing. What I needed was a harpoon.

The beast's vast, dark body rose in the water, obscuring the bay. A gigantic, glowing yellow eye found me, hiding in the dark. My blood ran cold, as death stared me down.

Colossal tentacles convulsed again, and a seal on the window broke. Water ran down the inside of the glass, pooling on the bar floor. *No, no, no.* The eye moved closer, the suckers constricting. More seals broke. Seawater sprayed the bookstore and bar, cascading down the window. My bunny slippers were drowning. Another squeeze and the water gushed freely, rapidly filling my home.

Trapped in the monster's glare, my brain was sluggish. Why wasn't I moving? I couldn't think past the glowing, yellow eye staring into my soul, finding me weak and wanting. I should give up. It wasn't as though anyone would miss me, scarred, damaged, abomination that I was. Alone, hiding with my stupid books.

Like the nightmare earlier, my brain couldn't stop cycling through every horror I'd survived. The psychic assault kept me rooted to the spot. *Worthless*. Head throbbing, I realized those weren't my words. The voice in my head was dark and cruel. Knowing it wasn't me, that while I might think poorly of myself, I'd never disparage books, helped me to distance the pain of those words, helped me to think.

Shit. I knew what this was. I hadn't been hiding in a bookstore for seven years for nothing. I'd been researching and studying, learning everything I could about the supernatural world I was now a part of. Slamming my eyes closed, I broke the connection.

The Kraken ensnared its victims, keeping them docile as he ate. Eyes closed, I splashed for the exit. Tripping on the bottom step and pitching forward, I slammed my knees against the stairs, righted myself, and then raced up. I almost knocked myself out when my head hit the immovable ward sealing the entrance. My wards were keyed to me. It was impossible for one of my wards to refuse me. And yet, I realized as I ran my hands over the solid barrier of the ward, one had. I screamed and pounded. "Open! Open!" It didn't give way. I was trapped.

The tunnels!

Frigid seawater hit me far sooner than it should have. By the time I made it to the barroom floor again, the icy water was at my waist. Eyes still closed, I slogged as quickly as I could through the water and headed toward my apartment.

I stepped on a bottle and it rolled, dropping me into the rapidly rising flood. Scrambling, getting my feet back under me, I stood. The water was chest high now. Sliding my feet along the floor so as not to trip again, I kicked another bottle out of the way. I was sure the eye was still on me. I could feel it watching, like a cat tracking a mouse. It was playing with me.

Something grazed my leg. *Please be a fish. Please be a fish.* Spinning, eyes opening against my will, I peered into the dark water, too afraid of what might be in here with me to worry about the eye. A tentacle had pushed up through the ocean entrance. It was searching for me. I jumped out of the water and landed, crouched on the bar. Shaking, soaked, I ran, sloshing toward the door to the kitchen. The tentacle slammed down on the bar right in front of me, cracking the wood and almost knocking me off my feet again. Leaping over it, I dove for the swinging door.

Wrapping around my knee, the tentacle dragged me back, pulling me under the water. My left hand slid down the kitchen door, trying to find purchase. A shard of wood tore open my palm, but still I held on. Another hard yank had me racing toward a window just as it shattered. A wave of ocean water pushed me to the floor. I grabbed the side of the bar, trying to yank my leg out of its grip before I was drowned or eaten, but the tentacle tightened again and pulled with far more strength than one werewolf possessed. My shoulder popped out of its socket, and I was again being dragged through the water toward the monster.

Two more tentacles wrapped around me from chest to knees, pulling me above the water. One short panicked breath and I was eye to eye with the Kraken. My home was flooded, books and bottles floating, washing out into the bay. It was all gone. My home, my dream, destroyed.

Pulled down, deep into the water, the Kraken tightened its tentacles, driving the breath out of me. Ribs splintering, lungs like cement, I was sucked down deep into the water. The Kraken's maw loomed, a razor-sharp beak waiting. I was going to die. Given my life so far, it was probably inevitable that I'd die badly. The tentacles constricted again, crushing bones.

As it tore my flesh in big meaty bites, I tried to scream. Bloody bubbles foamed from my mouth and then there was nothing, but a beak covered in gore.

THREE

Wait. We're Using the Word Demon as a Metaphor, Right?

Punching, fighting like the cornered animal I was, my arms shot out and hit something hard. The sound of a grunt had me doubling my efforts. I was being held down. *No!* Not again. I opened my mouth and screamed, but only a whispered gasp met my ears.

"Sam. Stop." Gray eyes shone in the murky light, blocking out the Kraken. Clive? Holding in a sob, I wriggled away from him. Sitting up, I turned, my eyes darting around the room. I was in the bar. My bar was still here. How?

"Ms. Quinn?" I flinched as a dwarf I didn't know stepped closer. "I'm Doctor Underfoot. Mr. Fitzwilliam called me when he couldn't wake you."

I stared at the two of them, uncomprehending, willing the panic down. Eyes darting around the room, I tried to take it all in. I was dry. On the floor of my bar. Which had not been destroyed. My gaze finally landed on the doctor who stood about four feet tall, with short dark hair, ruddy skin, and an impressively bushy beard. I didn't know what was going on, but as I wasn't being digested by a monster, I'd hear them out. Backing further away from the men, I tried to assess the situation.

"Who's Mr. Fitzwilliam?" My voice was a painful croak.

Clive stood and said, "I am."

"I was—it was a dream?" Studying the unbroken window, searching for a telltale rivulet of water, I ran a hand over my body. "I wasn't eaten?"

"Is that what you were screaming about?" Clive tunneled his fingers through his hair, before crossing his arms and studying me. In all the years I'd known Clive, I'd never seen him display any emotion. He gave the impression of one who had seen and done it all, someone now bored by everything. The stiff, jerky movement made me focus on him more than I would have at that moment. And that was when I noticed his left sleeve was unbuttoned and rolled up. Blood stained the crisp, snowy white of his shirt.

Heavy footsteps pounded down the stairs. Dave came into view, concern clear on his face. He pulled Dr. Underfoot aside and spoke in a low voice while I tried to avoid Clive's measuring gaze.

Though my legs were shaky, I stood. Being stretched out on the floor while men looked down on me was uncomfortable on many levels.

"Are you all right now?" His voice was low, just for me, and I appreciated the discretion. He wasn't trumpeting my fear to the room.

Breathing deeply, I nodded.

He turned to the window and stared out. We weren't touching, but he was close enough to catch me if I collapsed. Which was nice, though unnecessary.

"Um. Could someone tell me what I missed and how you all got in?" My heart was still beating a mile a minute, but it was over. I kept telling myself the danger was over. I sat in the chair I'd occupied earlier, the book I was reading still on the table.

"You were screaming," Clive said again. "I was—it doesn't matter. I heard you screaming. Your wards were open, and I found you sitting right there. Eyes wide open. Screaming. I couldn't get you to stop. Couldn't wake you." He gestured toward Dr. Underfoot. "Neither of us could."

I'd locked my wards down. I knew I had. How… I'd been trapped by my wards in the vision. I'd yelled again and again for them to open. They must have heard me.

Dave walked over and crouched in front of me, staring into my eyes, sniffing the air around me. "Eyes are dilated and she —" He sniffed again. "You smell different."

"Yes," Clive said. "I noticed that, too. Beneath the terror, she's different."

"Demon," Dave said.

Dr. Underfoot moved forward to discreetly sniff me.

"I stink?" Nothing like having three men stare at you and tell you that you reek.

Dave picked up my cocoa cup and breathed in the scent. He picked up my book and blanket, searching for something. Looking down at my feet, he paused and shook his head. "Nice bunny slippers."

Something had happened to me. I'd lost control of my own body. Someone had made me see what wasn't there. My hands started to tremble again. I stuffed them in my hoodie pocket, afraid to consider what could have been done to me. Again.

"Nah, Sam, not you. Whoever was here, either literally in the room with you or more likely the magic that was sent to ensnare you, is what stinks." He touched my head in a brotherly, affectionate way. "You do smell different, though. It's strange, more complex—"

"Yes, exactly," Clive interrupted.

"We can deal with that later, though. Right now, we need to figure out if a demon has taken an interest in you or if someone has piggybacked on a demon's power to take you out." Dave turned to Clive. "Why am I smelling your blood on her?"

I flinched at the hard edge in Dave's voice.

"I told you," Clive said, rolling down his sleeve and

buttoning the cuff. "She wouldn't wake up. Her heart was racing like a hummingbird's."

"It's true," Dr. Underfoot confirmed. "We couldn't wake her. Her heart was about to give out. Mr. Fitzwilliam did what he had to in order to save her."

"You gave her your blood?" Dave sounded outraged.

"Would you rather she was dead?" Clive shrugged into his suit jacket. "We couldn't find anything physically wrong with her. I thought it might be a psychic attack. I'm immune to that. I took a chance and fed her some of my blood."

"That was a hell of a chance you took with her life."

"It worked." Clive glanced at me, making sure I was still conscious. "She's strong. She's out of the vision and alive."

Clive gave me vampire blood? I ran my fingers over my lips. A streak of crimson stained them. Stomach gurgling, I wiped my fingers off on my pajama pants. That was the least of my worries. If it hadn't been for Clive, I'd still be trapped with the Kraken.

"Thank you."

He blinked, surprised. Expression softening, he nodded.

"So." I cleared my throbbing throat. "When you say demon, you're not using that as a figure of speech, are you? You mean an actual demon just tried to kill me." What the hell did I do to piss off a demon?

Dave strode back to my small table, pulled out the other chair, and sat down across from me. "I smell sulfur, which is a dead giveaway. There's a different, underlying magic entwined with the sulfur, which is why I think someone is using a demon to power a spell targeting you."

Dr. Underfoot pulled a pocket watch from the vest of his three-piece tweed suit and checked it. "As Ms. Quinn seems to be better, I need to get back."

"Yes, of course." Clive shook the doctor's hand. "I appreciate you getting here so quickly."

"I wish I could have been more help." He nodded to me and then Dave. "Goodnight," he said, before turning and leaving.

Clive pulled over another chair and sat on my left side, shoulder to shoulder with me. The emergency may have been over, but having them on either side of me helped quiet the tremors.

"So," Dave said, drumming his fingers on the table, legs spread as he sprawled in the chair. "Piss off any demons lately?"

A laugh bubbled up. "Other than you? Not that I'm aware of."

Clive crossed his legs, appearing completely unconcerned. His shoulder was still against mine, though, giving me a place to lean.

"Is there anyone in town you might have access to?" I asked Dave. "A family member, someone I could talk to?" I needed to know what the hell was going on.

Dave tilted his bald head back, thinking. "Thankfully, my relatives are rarely on this plane." He blew out a breath. "I guess I could talk to Tara. She's a succubus I've known since—well, a long time. She'd be safe enough. She works at the Tonga Room."

"The Tonga Room?" I said. "As in the Fairmont? Tiki torches, cocktails in coconuts, a band that floats in a lagoon, thunder showers every fifteen minutes, that Tonga Room?" I *loved* that place!

Dave smirked. "That's the one."

"Huh. I figured a succubus would get more business as a stripper or a hooker." You learn something new every day.

"She's done that, too. She says she actually gets more action from the married businessmen in town for conferences." He shrugged. "Don't ask me to explain the ways of cheating men on the hunt for pu—"

Clive cleared his throat.

"Companionship of a carnal nature," Dave finished.

"Can I go talk with her?" It was a delicate balance, wanting to feel a connection to Clive but not wanting to make it obvious that I was leaning on him. It was hard to explain. He treated me as though I was capable but had a shoulder at the ready if I needed it.

"You? No. We? I guess." Dave stopped drumming, a thoughtful expression on his face.

"You'd go with me?" I asked, breathing a sigh of relief. "No insult to your kin, but I'd feel better having you at my back when I meet a demon." No matter how much it scared me, my life and home were being threatened. Fearsome, not fearful.

"No guarantee Tara knows anything, but I'll call and see if she'll meet with us. You should check with Owen, see if he can cover. If we're both going out tonight, he'll need to be here." Dave pulled out his phone and scrolled through contacts.

He left a moment later, phone pulled away from his ear as a cranky succubus screeched about being woken up.

Once stomping boots and tinny screams had passed through the ward, the bar became uncomfortably quiet. Clive's shoulder pressed against mine. I knew he could feel me trembling, but I'd died horribly just moments ago, and I hadn't yet reconciled my relative safety with the gnashing beak that had been stripping the flesh from my bones.

"I *am* alive, right? This isn't some mind-shielding hallucination as I'm being swallowed and dissolving in stomach acid, right?"

I heard a chuff of laughter before he leaned across me and grabbed the arms of the chair I sat in. He lifted it and swung it around, placing me directly in front of him. My knees touched the edge of his seat, his legs on either side of mine. He didn't touch me, but his steady gaze helped to settle my nerves.

"You're a survivor. Regardless of what was attempted tonight, you made it through. They only win when you give up."

I nodded. "They're not going to win." I felt my nerves settle as I said it. It was true. I may have been shaking, but I wouldn't give up.

"Fear is good. It can help you survive." Clive paused,

gauging my reaction. "Don't give it the power, though, to keep you from living. You're stronger than that."

A small flicker of pride warmed my chest.

Pushing back, he stood abruptly. "It's almost daybreak. I need to go."

"Of course," I said as I got to my feet.

He stepped close, his eyes traveling over me, as though assuring himself I was still in one piece. His hand rose slowly, giving me time to react. When I didn't flinch away, his fingers brushed softly over my cheek. His fingertips warmed me in ways I couldn't explain.

Clearing his throat, he dropped his hand. "Get some sleep." And between one blink and the next, he was gone. Damn, vampires were fast.

I locked up my wards—again—and walked back to my apartment. Unsettled, I stopped in the bathroom to splash cold water on my face. There was no way I was going back to sleep. My home had been compromised, my mind breached. Safety was an illusion. I'd get dressed and sit in the bar with a baseball bat in my lap. If someone was coming, I was ready.

Leaning over the sink, cold water dripping from my nose, something shiny glinted in the light. Mom's pendant. I thought about why my scent might be different. The only thing that had changed since Dave and Clive had last seen me a few hours ago was Mom's necklace. I'd never taken it off before.

Drying my face, I considered what it meant. I didn't remember a time my mother wasn't anxious. She'd jumped at unexpected noises and never slept through the night. Dad was gone by then. I had only the vaguest memories of them laughing together, as he danced her across the kitchen floor. After he was gone, Mom had lived her life looking over her shoulder, shuffling us into the car in the middle of the night.

It hadn't been a question of avoiding rent. We had some money. Not a lot, but enough to put food on the table. She'd spent her days peering out windows, checking on me, reading old books, and crying over photos when she'd thought I was asleep.

We'd moved around a lot, never staying in one place more than a few months, often only a few weeks. Different apartments in different buildings, yet all the same. Seeming more agitated than normal, she'd worked late into the night on the pendant. Something very special for me, she'd said. I'd fallen asleep on the couch, watching her hunched over the wobbly table, as she mumbled to herself, an open book and her jewelry making supplies spread out before her.

She'd woken me in the middle of the night, hung the pendant around my neck, and told me we needed to leave. It was beautiful, but I didn't care. I was tired and didn't want to move again. We'd only been there a couple of days and there was a park across the street. She'd hushed me, said we weren't safe, and packed the car, as she'd done countless times before. We drove through the night, headed for yet another nondescript apartment.

Picking up the pendant off the bathroom counter, I studied the stones, the design. It needed to be cleaned after my dunk in the ocean and the chain needed to be repaired. I couldn't get over the feeling, though, that without it around my neck, I'd been exposed to who or what we'd been hiding from all those years.

FOUR

Werewolves: Serial Killers or Misunderstood Furries? Discuss

I needed a jeweler to fix my necklace but had no idea where to find one I could trust. So, lucky man that he was, I called Owen. The phone rang a few times and then went to voicemail. Not one to be foiled that easily, I called back.

"What?" Owen's voice was both slurred with sleep and annoyed as hell. It was impressive.

"Morning, Sunshine!"

"I'm hanging up now."

"Sorry, sorry. Don't hang up. I need your help." I heard the sounds of movement and then another deeper voice grumbling. Damn. Owen's date stayed over, and I'd just woken both of them up. "Super sorry!"

"What do you want, Sam?" He sounded a little more awake, which was good.

"Okay, two things: I need you to work late tonight because Dave and—"

"Are you seriously waking me up at…4:58 in the morning to discuss my work schedule? Hanging up now." Less sleepy, more pissed.

"Wait! Please, Owen. That's not the main reason I called. I was just easing you into the conversation. And I've been up for hours pacing, waiting until a decent hour to call and this was as decent as I could get. I almost died last night. Twice actually. Dave thinks a demon is involved in the attacks, so we're meeting with a succubus tonight to try to get info. That's why I need you to stay late. The main reason I'm calling, though, is to ask if you know a good, reliable jeweler who can work with a very important piece of jewelry."

Silence reigned.

"Are you still there?"

"Run that back. A demon tried to kill you. Twice. What the hell did you do?"

"Why does everyone keep asking me that?" Seriously, they acted like I made a habit of calling up demons and them jabbing them with forks.

"Honey, are you okay?" Aww, there was my Owen.

"Rattled but fine. So, can you stay late?"

"I have a date, but..." Low voices rumbled. "Yeah, sure."

"Any jewelry store recommendations?"

"Send her to my family's shop. My sister will look out for her," the deeper, grumbly voice said, and Owen murmured his agreement.

"Go to Drake's Treasures on Marina Boulevard at Beach. It's near the East Harbor. Little place in an art deco building."

"Great. Thank you. Go back to sleep now." After hours of sitting in the bar, not knowing if my thoughts were truly my own and checking my wards obsessively, it was good to have a plan. I'd get the necklace fixed today and question a demon tonight.

"We're awake now."

"And think of all the lovely things you can get up to now that you're both awake." I heard deep chuckles as the phone went dead.

Waiting until the shops opened involved more hours of stress pacing. At nine, I ventured into the city, exhausted and jumpy. My hand strayed again and again to the front pocket of my jeans.

Feeling the reassuring lump helped me to relax for a few minutes before I was compelled to check again. I had no idea if I was right—that the necklace had been spelled to protect me—but as Mom had told me never to take it off and when I had I was attacked by the Kraken, it seemed like a good idea to put it back where it belonged.

San Francisco was my home now, but being out in the open, especially this morning, made me uneasy. Owen liked to tease me about hiding in my hobbit hole, but in comparison to the safety and predictability—until recently—of The Slaughtered Lamb, the world could be overwhelming.

The jasmine-scented sunrise of the Marina District had me striving for calm and normalcy. There. Just as Owen had said. A jewelry store occupied the corner of a beautifully maintained Art Deco building. The plaque hanging over the shop's door said the jewelers had been in business since 1906.

A brass bell chimed as I entered. The shop was dark and quiet. The carpet, a threadbare velvet in a fading cobalt blue, showed the traffic pattern from the door to the middle case and then down the row to each of the other cases. The walls were papered in a silver and gray Deco floral pattern. The dark wood display cases were glass-fronted and topped. A large crystal chandelier hung from a center medallion in the ceiling, illuminating the cases, sparkling off the glass, yet leaving the work area behind the counters dim.

Hand straying to my pocket again, I approached the center display case. It was filled with antique wedding ring sets. A bittersweet tug had me crouching down for a better look. They were unbelievably intricate, these shining reminders that love and fidelity were a timeless reality for some.

"Getting married?"

I jumped out of my skin before a warm hand patted mine, keeping me from tipping backward. I shot up and pulled my hand away. The touch hadn't frightened me, but I still didn't like it.

"What?"

A woman, no more than a hair's breadth taller than me, with brown skin, long, curly black hair, and bright hazel eyes watched me. A worn, red flannel shirt strained at her broad shoulders. She exuded a preternatural calm, and I would have bet every penny in my anemic bank account that she wasn't human.

"Shopping for wedding rings?" Her expression remained neutral, but I could see her chest expand. She was breathing in my scent, no doubt trying to determine what I was.

"No. No. I'm just—no."

"That was a lot of denial in a few short words." A corner of her mouth kicked up. "I don't blame you. Not for me either. So, if not rings, how can I help you?"

I reached in my pocket but paused. Should I give my necklace to an unknown supernatural to work on, even one recommended by Owen? Someone was trying to kill me, and this woman had an odd reptilian scent.

"Trust is an issue, huh?" Nodding, she pulled over a stool and sat. "I'm Coco, at your service. Now, as you're a female wolf living in our fair city—if your scent is any indication—I'd guess you were Sam, owner and proprietor of The Slaughtered Lamb." Winking, she asked, "How'd I do?"

"You've never been in The Slaughtered Lamb. I'd remember." She had a calming presence that helped to quell my nerves.

"Thank you for the compliment, and no, I have not. I gave up drinking years ago, and I read on my tablet. My brother knows someone who works there, so I've heard all about it." Leaning back, demonstrating excellent strength and balance, she picked up a coffee cup from the shadowy desk behind her.

"Can I touch your hand again?" Sometimes I got quick impressions of people when I touched them. Sometimes.

She held out her hand to shake mine. She had a strong, warm grip. The image of fire in a dark cave flitted in and out of my mind. Scales undulated on a massive body, wings stretching out and obliterating the light. It didn't frighten me. On the contrary, it filled me with a sense of longing and comfort. Pulling the necklace out of my pocket, I decided that and the fact she was Owen's beau's sister were as good of an assurance as I was going to get.

I placed the pendant on the glass counter for her to see. Tilting her head, she stared at it for a moment before picking it up and placing it in the palm of her hand, closing her fingers over it.

"What have we here?" she mumbled to herself.

I watched, waiting. Her eyes took on a speculative light as she tilted her head further. It was as if she was listening to the necklace.

"Who made this for you?" She reached for one of my hands, and I let her take hold of it. I guessed she needed a connection to me in order to read the necklace properly. Or she just wanted to hold my hand. As it felt nice, I let it go.

"My mother. When I was a child."

Nodding, her chest expanded again. "This is the first time you've taken it off?"

"Yes."

Opening her hand, she studied the pendant. "She used protective stones. Each one of these—black tourmaline, labradorite, fluorite, black obsidian, blue kyanite—has been spelled separately and then again as a whole to cloak you and keep you safe."

"Spelled?" I shook my head. "My mom wasn't a wicche."

Raising her eyebrows, her gaze traveled from the pendant back to me. "The necklace says different.

EVEN THE CHAIN HAS BEEN SPELLED," COCO'S EXPRESSION softened. "What do you need me to do?"

"I fell in the ocean yesterday—"

"Fell?" The hand that held mine, gripped me harder.

"That's the story I'm going with." I pulled my hand out of

hers and continued. "An e—something got caught around my neck in the water. When I tugged it off, I accidentally ripped the necklace off as well. I need the clasp fixed. Can you do that? Repair and clean it without stripping the spells."

She nodded. "It'll take some work. The clasp is easy enough, but I can't do anything that works against the spells or the necklace might fight me. If it lets me, I'll try to strengthen what I can."

"Thank you."

She studied the broken chain again. "She soldered it closed." She studied me a moment. "What's been happening since you took it off?"

Staring down at the wedding bands, I shrugged. "Nothing good."

Making a sound of understanding in the back of her throat, she studied me. "I can fix it for you, but it will take time."

I started to protest, but she stopped me by wrapping her hand around mine again.

"I'm feeling—" Shaking her head, she stared at our joined hands, dark and light. "I don't know what this is I'm feeling, but I think…being without it is a danger to you. I can push back my other jobs and start on this now, but it will take a few hours."

"Oh," I sighed in relief. "Sure. I can handle a couple of hours."

"I have a backroom." She gestured over her shoulder. "You could wait there while I work."

I thought about how often my fingers strayed to the lump in my pocket this morning. "Can I stay and watch? Will it bother you to have me in your workroom?" I didn't want that necklace out of my sight.

"Sure. Drag my desk chair in. Can you flip the closed sign, turn the lock? This is going to take concentration. I can't stop halfway through." Coco went into a back room and wiped down her worktable, chanting something under her breath. Magic filled the air as she pulled my necklace from her pocket and placed it in the middle of her workspace.

Holding her hands over the necklace, eyes closed, she sang an atonal song in a language I didn't recognize. It sounded ancient and called to mind bonfires and circle dances, long hair swinging in the moonlight while the fair folk presided.

I hadn't realized that my eyes had drifted closed until her song changed, rousing me from a doze. I checked the wall clock. She'd been at it over an hour. Sweat clung to her forehead and neck. I needed caffeine if I was going to stay awake for the repair, and she needed some water. I didn't want to interrupt her, so I quietly left the workroom, stepped out of the shop, and went in search of cold drinks.

Delicious smells wafted down the sidewalk from the open door of a coffee house. I followed the scent and found myself standing in front of a large green menu board advertising too many kinds of beverages, hot and cold alike. I got Coco a big bottle of water, myself a soda, and both of us a brownie. The woman had already earned an entire pan of brownies and she wasn't even done yet.

A few minutes later, I was back in the brisk, morning air, walking across the street toward the water. I needed a minute before going back into that workroom or I'd nod off again. Taking a gulp of soda, I watched a boat motoring out of its slip and into the bay. The morning was glorious, with clear blue skies and steel green water. Boats bobbed and people wandered the docks. An iridescent dragonfly zipped through the long grass at the edge of the water.

Hackles rising, I realized what it was I was smelling. Wolf! I spun, trying to locate the scent. *Shit.* I'd had no contact with other wolves for seven years and now two in less than a day? What were the odds? When I needed to change every month, I used the Presidio or the redwood forests in the North Bay. I was always cautious, making sure never to tread near a pack's territory. A lone wolf, especially a female, was anybody's meat.

That necklace had been off my neck for less than ten hours and the hits just kept coming. I scanned the street, breathing in the scents of the Marina. Trying to locate the wolf, I eased back in the direction of the jewelry shop. A man walked out of the coffee shop I'd just left, tilting his head, scenting the wind. His eyes unerringly found mine, and I froze. Jogging across the street, he kept me in his sights. I itched to run but knew if I did, I'd become prey.

"Morning," he said, standing too close. "Didn't mean to startle you." He glanced around before stepping even closer, his voice low. "I'm visiting and having a hell of a time trying to locate your boss so I can get permission to be here. I can't scent the pack territory, and you're the first wolf I've run across." He scanned the street again. "Can you give me your alpha's name and number, or better yet, as I'm trespassing, can you call and ask him where he wants me to meet him?"

A lie. I felt it in my bones. Something he said wasn't true, but I didn't know which part. I didn't think he was an immediate physical threat, but he was a liar. The scent was wrong, though. This wasn't the wolf who'd chased me last night. Maybe, though, he was the one cutting up women and dumping them in the bay.

Tall, he had dark, curly hair, light brown eyes, and dimples. Too many years of reading Jane Austen had taught me to be suspicious of overly attractive men. He was a werewolf, after all. Savage was in the DNA.

"There's no pack in San Francisco." When he stared at me in confusion, I elaborated. "There's one in the North Bay, near Bodega Bay, and one in the South Bay, in the Santa Cruz Mountains." I inched away. "Not sure if the East Bay has one."

He put a hand on my arm, and something dark and predatory stalked toward me in my mind. "No pack? You're on your own?"

A deep growl rumbled through my chest. He did not get to put his hands on me.

Holding his hands up in surrender, he smiled, dimples flashing. "No offense intended."

I straightened my spine. "What I am or am not is none of your concern." I'd been warned, as a lone female wolf, males would look at me as fair game. He needed to know upfront that I wasn't a victim waiting for the next asshole to do his best.

He reached out again, gesturing toward the bench. "Sit with me."

"No." Hands fisted, I studied his body language, looking for the tell-tale tension in his muscles, letting me know he intended to strike. "I'm leaving now. Don't follow me."

Brown eyes scanned me leisurely from head to toe. "I like your city. I might stick around for a while. You wouldn't mind a little company, would you?" Sitting on the bench, he patted the seat next to him. "It's a beautiful day. Let's get to know each other."

I bared my teeth, a growl vibrating in the back of my throat.

He considered me. "Afraid? I won't hurt you," he said, with a gleam in his eye.

Ignoring the comment, I moved away, not willing to turn my back on another predator.

He stood, following me. "Don't leave. It's Sam, isn't it?" He scratched the stubble on his jaw, watching me. "I've been looking for you." His gaze snagged on the scar I couldn't cover with t-shirts, the one that crawled up the side of my neck. He reached out a finger, as though intending to trace it. "I've heard all about you." Predatory eyes found mine as his lips curled into a satisfied smile.

Rage consumed me. My body—my scars—were none of his business. He had no right to me. I'd said no and been ignored. "Back the fuck off," I growled.

Fear flashed in his eyes, there and gone, but he retreated. He sat back down on the bench, his affable smile back in place.

I turned and walked across the street.

"Oh, and Sam?" he called after me. "We're not done."

FIVE

Middle-earth, California

Not wanting to lead the wolf to Coco and my necklace, I decided I was safer at home and turned a corner. Once out of sight of the wolf, I started jogging. I made it back to the Presidio in no time, but then the path changed. Almost between one step and the next, the bright, sunny day dimmed. Huge trees crowded out the light, leaving me in an unnatural gloom. Turning around, looking for the Presidio I'd just been walking through, I found nothing but towering, ivy-covered trunks and vine-laden underbrush blocking my way. It was as though I had taken a wrong turn into Middle-earth.

Chittering and movement in nearby bushes had me moving again, quickening my pace. Yellow eyes glowed, little pinpricks of light in the dark branches. I ran, trying to outpace my surroundings. Was this like the Kraken?

Fearsome, not fearful. I had to find a way out.

A vine coiled around my ankle, yanking my foot out from under me and sending me crashing to the forest floor. Damp, fecund earth covered in branches and leaves made for a softer than expected landing. A vine twitched under my cheek. I reared back and then movement had me kicking at another as it slithered toward me. The sharp-thorned vine around my left ankle tightened. Fingers slick with blood, I yanked at it again and again, but it wouldn't release its hold.

Noses twitching, elongated teeth glinting in the low light, rats began to emerge from behind branches and leaves. There had to be dozens of them. The scent of my blood was bringing them out, making them swarm. *This isn't real. This isn't real.*

Wrenching desperately at the vine holding me, I brought my ankle to my mouth and bit down, tearing at it. Viscous liquid oozed between my lips, but I couldn't stop. Dozens of rats had turned into a hundred or more.

They circled, their chittering an unbearable squeal in my brain. One dropped from the trees above onto my head. In a mindless panic, I whipped my head around, trying to dislodge it but it clung, nails scrabbling, tearing at my scalp.

Grunting, I tore viciously at the razor-sharp vine, finally breaking through. I jumped to my feet, trying to locate the path that had just been there. The rats, sensing their prey was escaping, moved in. They ran up my jeans. Sharp teeth bit through the fleshy part of my hand, between and thumb and forefinger. I shook my hand, trying to fling it off, but it gnashed its teeth and wouldn't let go. More dropped from the branches overhead, clawing my face, neck, shoulders.

Batting them off, unable to stifle the scream that tore at my throat, I ran blindly through the trees, bouncing off trunks, tripping on roots. The rats clung, nails and teeth ripping at my skin. I was lost and being eaten alive. *This isn't real. This isn't real.* The pain and terror dissipated momentarily and then a vine slithered around my neck like a noose and squeezed.

I forced myself to close my eyes and calm my breathing. Rats tore at me, but I focused all my attention on the vine cutting off my air. *You're not real.* Doing my best to ignore the rat gnawing on my ear, I thought again, *none of this is real.* The vine sputtered out of existence. A moment later, though, it was back and squeezing so tight, I thought my head would pop off. I couldn't explain why, but the vine felt angry.

"Sam!"

Strong hands held my shoulders and shook. Chest pounding, I tasted blood in my mouth again. I opened my eyes and found myself staring straight into hazel green. Cringing, trying to shake off the phantom rats, I wrapped my arms around myself. I could still feel their sharp little nails crawling all over my body, but I was okay. I was out. Coco had been the one to pull me out this time. I breathed in her scent. Smoke and safety.

"Are you with me now?" Her voice was quiet and unsure.

Nodding, I touched my throat. "I was trying to get myself out, but it wasn't working." I coughed and looked down. The bottles and brownie bag I'd been holding were on the grass by my feet. I handed Coco the brownies and unscrewed the water bottle, drinking it down in one.

"It was the strangest thing, almost like the vision was pissed off I was even trying. Instead of freaking me out, it was trying to kill me. If you hadn't pulled me out…" I faltered. The memory was too strong.

Watching a man sunbathing and two girls playing frisbee, I took slow deep breaths. This was reality, not the squealing, biting vision I'd been in. Coco and I stood under a tree, shaded from the mild San Francisco sun. On a nearby path, joggers rounded a corner, coming into view as bicyclists peddled the opposite way. It was a gorgeous day in the Presidio, but I couldn't shake the feeling of phantom rats crawling up my legs.

"How did you end up out here? You were in my workroom with me." She laid a hand on my arm, offering comfort.

Heartbeat erratic, I let her hand stay there. "I only stepped out for a minute. I was falling asleep and then…" I'd always had a horrible fear of rats. I'd had nightmares for years as a child after watching *Lady and the Tramp*. Those red-eyed rats slinking through the nursery, climbing the crib, and trying to eat the baby. They scared me to death. I guess that was the point, wasn't it? Scaring me to death.

"I'm okay now," I mumbled.

"No. You're really not." She wrapped her hand around my shoulder, seeming to understand I couldn't handle more touch than that at the moment.

"How did you find me?" Shivering, I tried to relax into the heat and calm of her presence, trusting she'd keep me safe. At least for a little while.

"I heard you screaming in my head."

A dog barked, making me flinch. Coco moved closer to me as a fluffy, white mop ran by, on the heels of his boy.

"It's never happened before, but I think I was dialed into you as I cleaned and strengthened the spells on the pendant. I heard you scream and tore out of the shop." An owl hooted nearby. "And found you here, standing stock still. Eyes open and mouth closed. I could hear the screaming in my head, but I couldn't wake you. Your heart was beating so fast, I thought it would explode."

She looked around, sniffing at the wind. "Wolf."

"What?"

Shaking her head, she continued. "I called everyone I could think of and finally ended up on the line with Clive. He told me what to do, but we didn't know if it would work with my blood."

"Clive?" I looked up at the midday sun.

A buzzing sounded. Coco patted my shoulder and answered her phone. "She's okay. It worked…Yeah, sure." She put the phone to my ear.

"It happened again?" Anger threaded through Clive's voice.

"It would seem so," I said.

Coco gave us the impression of privacy by turning toward the small boy and his dog, watching them play.

"What was it this time?" Concern made its way through the anger.

"Rats."

Coco made a comforting sound in the back of her throat, still looking away from me.

"They were everywhere. Eating me alive." Fighting off a full-body cringe, I continued. "I was out in the open. Anyone could have walked up and killed me while I was trapped in the vision." I stared down at my feet a moment, considering. "Why didn't they?"

"Interesting question."

Coco turned back to me and took my hand, lifting it so I could see the slice on the fleshy part between my thumb and forefinger, right where that rat in the vision had bitten me.

"Damn." It was like when I yelled 'Open!' in the Kraken vision and actually opened my wards. The rat bit me in a vision and my hand was bloodied in real life.

"What is it, Sam?"

"Her hand was cut," Coco said when I remained silent. "Small. Almost like she was sliced while shaking a hand." She looked thoughtful for a moment. "Is there anything special about her blood? Someone went to an awful lot of trouble for a small cut."

"Excellent question. Do they want her dead or do they want her blood?"

"Well, neither sounds great to me." I'd had no control. I'd been standing here unable to defend myself. A shiver ran through me. Coco and Clive talked about me as though I were an interesting puzzle. I couldn't be that objective.

"Have you completed the repairs?" Clive asked.

"Not yet. I was interrupted," Coco said. Supernatural hearing meant neither was hindered by the fact that the phone was at *my* ear.

"I'm sorry. Do you have to start all over again?" I wasn't leaving her side, not until the necklace was back around my neck.

"Unfortunately. It's exhausting. I'll add it to your bill." Coco winked and then eased the phone out of my hand. "We're heading back now," she said to Clive.

"Good." *Click.* I guess Clive wasn't big on goodbyes. And how was he awake at this hour?

We were a few blocks away when I finally asked the question that had been flitting in and out of my brain. "You said 'wolf' earlier. Did you mean me, or did you smell a different wolf?"

"Different. Male. The scent was faint. He'd been in that location earlier, but I couldn't tell if it had been ten minutes or two hours." We'd made it back to the city streets, leaving the park behind.

I held up my left arm, the one that wolf had touched. "Was this the scent?"

Coco leaned down and sniffed my sleeve. She stopped walking, pausing to think. "Yes. That's the scent. But now I don't know if I was smelling your sleeve and assuming a wolf had been nearby or if he really had been standing next to you while you were trapped in that vision."

We were two blocks away when Coco's head shot up. She took off at a run, racing down the sidewalk and through the door of her shop. Following in her wake, I stepped in a moment later and my stomach dropped. It had been ransacked while she was out. Swearing, she jumped the counter and went straight to the workroom. Two of the cases had been smashed, jewelry scattered, valuable pieces no doubt stolen. Broken glass glittered on the worn carpet.

This was my fault. "I'm sorry. I'll pay for the missing jewelry." Somehow. I sank into a high-backed chair in the corner of the shop. I'd be paying off the bar for the next hundred years, assuming I lived that long. What was a little more debt?

Coco walked out of the backroom, her dark skin unnaturally pale. "The necklace is gone."

I stood, my breath caught in my chest. "Gone?"

"Destroyed. The glass breaking out here was probably just for show. The necklace was the goal. Every stone has been smashed to powder, settings broken, chain torn apart. Trust me.

This," she gestured at the display cases. "was window dressing. What they wanted was to strip away a defense."

Legs giving out, I dropped back into the chair. "It was the only thing I had of my mom."

"I'm so sorry." She paused a moment. "The only thing?" Coco crouched in front of me, a hand on my knee.

Dazed, I couldn't think straight. "It burned down. Our home. After she died and I was—I tried to go home, but the apartment building was a scorched ruin." Looking up, I found Coco's sympathetic gaze. "It must have happened during the funeral. I tried to get out of the car, talk to the firemen, but Uncle Marcus pulled me back and turned the car around. Drove us away." The glass dust glinted in the sunlight slanting through the window.

"I had nothing when I was sent here after the attack. Nothing but the clothes on my back and the pendant around my neck. Marcus sent me to live with Helena, a wicche friend of my mom's." Clutching Coco's hand on my knee, I asked what I needed to know. "Was my mom a wicche?"

"I didn't know her, but the magic shares harmonies with you." She shook her head. "I'm not sure how to explain it. I can see magic, but mostly I hear it. The spells in the necklace sound feminine. When you told me your mother had given it to you, I thought, of course. You share the same magical harmonies. A great deal of love and fear went into making that pendant. Your mother was worried about protecting you." She looked down at the carpet a moment, lost in thought. "How did she die?"

"She..." I paused, trying to remember. I forced the memory to surface but got nothing. "I don't remember." How could I not remember?

"Were you very young? Was it right after she gave you the necklace?"

"No. I was seventeen. I came home from school and there were women in the apartment, cleaning and talking in hushed tones. They said my mother was dead, but they wouldn't let me see her. I remember tearing through the tiny apartment, calling her name. It was empty except for the women. They said they were relatives, but I'd never seen any of them before."

Tears slipped down my face. "There was a funeral. I remember that. And a storm. My Uncle approached me as the cemetery cleared. I was standing in front of Mom's grave. The women were gone. Everyone was gone except for Marcus. He introduced himself and invited me to live with him.

"My mother had always told me to stay away from dad's side of the family, but I was so scared and alone. So lost. I followed him out of the cemetery." I found Coco's eyes again. "I used to remember more. It feels like it's right there, behind a curtain I need to open but can't reach."

Touching my forehead, she said, "The memory might have been stolen or buried so deep it amounts to the same thing. If they're hiding her death, though, it must be important." She stood, hands at her waist, staring out the window. "Have you ever tried hypnosis?"

"No. I've never done any kind of therapy."

Her gaze snapped back to me. "Not even after the attack?"

"How did you—does everyone know what he—what happened to me?" Long-buried fears and humiliations came racing back. I tasted bile in the back of my throat. Had I spent seven years hiding scars they all saw?

Coco dropped back down into a crouch. "I meant a turning, especially against one's wishes, can be traumatic."

I chuffed a short, derisive laugh. "Yeah, that's one way of putting it."

SIX

In the Tiki Tiki Tiki Tiki Tiki Room

I returned home with an antique hammered copper cuff that Coco had given me. She wouldn't let me leave without it. She said it wouldn't give me the protection my necklace had, but it should keep whoever was screwing with me out of my head. One could hope.

"Anyone need anything?" I asked the bar in general, as I stepped behind the counter, hip checking Owen out of my way.

"Could I have an oolong tea?" Hepsiba, an old crone, was in her usual spot near the window.

"Sure. Coming right up." I extracted leaves from a glass container and began preparing the tea. I offered almost as many tea varieties as I did alcohol. Wicches loved their teas. Waiting for it to steep, I realized my hand was resting below my collar bone, right where my mother's pendant used to lay. Copper cuff or not, I worried I might not live long enough to pay off this bar. Or Coco. Or, you know, see next week.

After delivering the tea, I carried a tray of empty glasses and mugs into the kitchen. Owen followed me in, carrying more. "So, what's been happening with you?" His piercings glittered in the bright overhead lights.

"Owen, do you get a lot of people trying to pick you up, people who are drawn to shiny objects?"

He smirked, raising one dark, glittering eyebrow and waiting for me to answer the question.

What was the question again? Oh, right. I counted off on fingers the weird shit that had been going on in the last twelve hours. "A wolf tried to kill me. An eel wrapped itself around my neck and tried to drown me. I was trapped in a vision with the Kraken. A different wolf threatened me. Or not. Not sure if I overreacted to that one. I was trapped in another vision. This one of rats eating me alive. And someone stole the only thing I had from my mother."

Owen stood with his mouth open, a tray of glasses forgotten in his hands. "All of that happened since I saw you yesterday?" Shaking his head, he said, "I don't even know which one to ask about first."

I took the tray from him and placed it on the counter by the dishwasher. "Do I seem different to you?"

After a moment, his eyes took on a faraway gleam and then he flinched. "Uh…that's weird."

"What?" I took off the cuff and placed it on the center island, in case it was causing any interference.

"Wait. What is that and why did taking it off just throw you into focus?" Owen leaned away from me, as though I was no longer trustworthy or safe.

How to explain? "I used to have something. From my Mom. It protected me, I guess."

"The necklace," he said.

"Sam?" a voice called from the bar.

"Be right there," I shouted back, before focusing on Owen again. "How did you know about that?"

Shrugging, he said, "I've never seen it, but you touch it all the time. Through your t-shirt, I mean."

"I do?"

Nodding, he stepped closer. "Yeah. It's just how you stand,

left arm across your chest, holding your right elbow. Right hand on the bump under the collar of your t-shirt. But," his voice softened. "I don't see that bump anymore."

My throat tightened with tears I wouldn't cry. The loss hollowed me out, but I refused to break down.

"That's what was stolen?"

Nodding my head, I swallowed. "My mother gave it to me. Made it for me." Tears threatened, so I turned, dashing them away. Picking up the cuff and returning it to my wrist helped me feel less exposed.

"Why didn't you ever tell us your Mom was a wicche?" Owen said it so matter-of-factly, my heart skipped a beat.

"Why do you say that?"

"I felt the protective spells when I first hugged you. Is that why you don't like being touched? Or is it the…" His voice drifted off as a finger pointed vaguely to his own neck, no doubt referring to the scars he'd seen trailing out of my collar and cuffs.

"I just don't like it."

"Gotcha," he said, clearing his throat. "Anyway, I'd assumed Helena or one of the other wicches who come in here made it for you." He leaned a hip against the counter and stared at me a moment. "That's what's different. I'm not only picking up the earth magic of the wolf, like usual. There's a deeper resonance today. You have your own inherent magic. How has that never manifested?"

It was my turn to shrug. "The necklace?"

"Damn. That'd have to be one powerful charm to hide your magic not only from us but from yourself."

"Owen," I asked, biting my lip. "Do I really seem different to you? Dave and Clive said my scent was off." I don't know why that bothered me so much, but it was like I couldn't trust who I was anymore.

"Well, my sense of smell is nowhere near as good as theirs, so I can only go by feel." He took one of my hands and held it, as though evaluating me. Dropping it, he gave me a quick kiss on the cheek and turned to leave. "I need to think on this."

The phone rang and someone from the bar called my name again. I pushed through the kitchen door and found the receiver laying at the end of the bar. Owen helped people waiting for service, while I picked up the phone.

"Slaughtered Lamb, this is Sam."

"Tara's working tonight, and she's willing to talk with us." As usual, Dave ignored niceties.

"Anything special I should do or bring?" Should I make sure to keep crosses away from her?

"She's a bartender in an island-themed bar that caters to tourists. The fuck? Order a fruity drink and bring money." *Click.* Such a charmer.

THERE WAS ONLY A FAINT GRUMBLING WHEN I KICKED EVERYONE OUT early. Even though Owen had agreed to stay, I shoved him out the door at the end of his work day. I didn't want to be responsible for messing up his love life. Pulling on my pea coat, I checked to make sure I had cash in my pocket, and then waited for Dave at the stairs. My first succubus. I was weirdly giddy, considering.

Dave walked out of the kitchen with a paper towel in his hand. "Here. Eat them while they're hot." The scent of brown sugar and vanilla had my mouth watering. He pounded up the stairs while I stared wistfully down at the six, fresh-from-the-oven cookies he'd dropped in my hands.

Taking a bite of the rich ambrosia of the gods, I paused, eyes closed, savoring the deep, rich chocolate encased in warm, buttery cookie. "I love you."

"Yeah, yeah," he mumbled.

"I was talking to the cookie." Damn, the man could bake.

"Are we leaving or what?"

"Yeah, yeah." I stuffed the rest of the cookie in my mouth, folding the paper towel carefully around the rest and putting them in my pocket for later. We had a date, those cookies and me.

The Tonga Room was a tiki lounge in the basement of the Fairmont Hotel. A narrow pool dominated the center of the dim room. Colored lights hidden behind fake palm trees illuminated the surreal scene. Floating on a grass-roofed raft in the center of the pool was a three-piece band. Around the pool were bamboo tables for two, four, and eight people, all with their own thatched roofs. It was ridiculous, and I loved it.

Dave walked straight to the bar, tucked into the corner of the island paradise. Ignoring him, I leaned against the bamboo rail surrounding the pool and watched a petite woman on the twinkle-lit raft sing *The Girl from Ipanema* while her bored-looking bandmates accompanied her on the keyboard and drums.

Lightning flashed across the ceiling. A moment later thunder rumbled through the room and rain began to fall in the pool. The band kept dry under the thatched roof of their raft. Reaching out, warm pseudo-rain spattered across my hand.

"Sam."

Yeah, yeah.

The woman behind the bar was a fantasy island girl, with long, dark curly hair, luminous, deep brown eyes, and the curves of a goddess. She was all doe-eyed innocence. Damn, I bet her victims never saw her coming.

"Hurricane, please." I took the stool next to Dave.

Her sweet smile lit up the room and made me feel content and understood. "A woman after my own heart."

"Sam, this is Tara. Tara, Sam." Dave grabbed a handful of nuts out of a bamboo bowl. When Dave was out in public, he wore a glamour that altered his natural dark red skin and full-black eyes. His skin was currently a warm brown and his eyes a deep whiskey color. I was so used to his normal shark-like gaze, the glamour was throwing me off.

Tara slid a drink in front of me, crossed her arms on the bar, and leaned forward. Her impressive breasts were on display, but in a way that made it seem completely unconscious. She wasn't highlighting her lady bits. She was just taking a break and leaning. This woman was a master.

"Put 'em away, Tara. No one here is interested," Dave grumbled.

One perfectly manicured nail ran along Dave's hand. "I remember a time when you were very interested."

A lecherous grin slid across Dave's face. "You were the star of all my adolescent fantasies. Pre-adolescent, too, come to think of it."

Her laugh was deep and throaty, a sexy joke between sweaty lovers in the middle of the night, in the quiet of their rumpled bed. "Not anymore? Ouch."

Smirking, Dave said, "You've met Maggie, right?"

Tara stood straight and adjusted her dress to better cover her soft, fleshy parts. "I have. Now, what do you two need?"

A waitress interrupted. Tara quickly made four fruity, umbrella drinks before the server rushed off.

"Someone's fucking with Sam." He tipped his head toward me. "She's getting caught in visions she can't get out of on her own."

Tara actually looked at me for the first time.

"Someone's trying to kill her." He watched Tara study me. "Can you tell? Is this coming from our neck of the woods?" A demon, he meant.

Tara took my hand and leaned forward, resting her nose on my neck and breathing me in. A shiver went down my spine at the contact. "You're a unique one, aren't you?" She turned to Dave. "I'm not sensing anyone we know." She gave me her full attention. "But I am sensing cookies."

Grinning, I took out my pack of cookies and passed her one. She ate while returning her attention to Dave.

"Someone new in town?" He grabbed more nuts off the bar,

glancing at the couple who walked in, heading for a table close to the pool. Lightning flashed and thunder rumbled in the room before it began raining in the pool again.

"Not that I've heard, but you know they consider my kind riff-raff."

"Okay. If you can keep an ear to the ground, I'd appreciate it." He turned to me. "Finish up. Tara's working, and we're in the way."

As if on cue, a woman sat down at the bar and eyed Tara with interest.

I took a long, last draw, fished two twenties from my pocket and left them next to my empty coconut.

Tara placed her hand over the money, tapped the bar with her finger, and winked. "You come on back and see me again, Sam." When she turned to the end of the bar, directing her smile at the lone woman waiting, I felt cold. She'd taken her light and warmth away, and I already missed her. I also realized that she'd slipped a scrap of paper under my hand. Damn, she was good.

Dave pulled my jacket to get me moving. "Stop staring."

Stumbling off my stool and pocketing the note, I followed him out. As we climbed the dark, narrow staircase to the street entrance, I pulled out the note and read. '2 a.m. Come back alone.' I actually had a confusing moment wondering if Tara was asking me back to put the moves on me before I realized she just didn't want to talk demon business in front of Dave.

When the cold, San Francisco wind hit me, my lust-clouded mind cleared. "Now what?"

Dave turned, brow furrowed. "'Now what' what?"

"I mean, where are we going now? Who are we questioning?" I clapped my hands. "Who's next on our list?"

A bell rang out in the dark as the Powell Street cable car made it to the bottom of one hill, across the intersection, and started down the next steep drop. The cable car held a quiet smattering of people. It was too late for the tourists. These looked like locals heading home. The acrid scent of burning wood brake was pungent in the air but there was something under it. Something familiar. Something that raised my hackles.

I scanned the darkened streets. Pale yellow streetlights reflected off wet asphalt. We were being watched. I could feel it. My eyes went straight to a narrow gap between buildings more than a hundred yards away. A figure stood, dressed in dark clothes, hoodie pulled up, barely silhouetted against the gloom. He stepped out and walked quickly, silently, to the corner and turned down Mason Street. It was the wolf from the Marina. The entire encounter had lasted only a second, but I knew it was him. I could feel his curiosity from here.

"No list. I'm taking you home. I've got other shit to do."

I shook it off. "Come on. There's gotta be other dem—"

Dave cleared his throat and gave me a dirty look.

"Relatives. I was going to say relatives."

"Sure you were." He pulled his keys out of his pocket and hit the fob. His car chirped as the doors unlocked.

Pouting, I dropped into the passenger seat and tried again. "I'm sure there are other people you know we could talk to tonight."

"Probably." He started the growling engine and gunned it up the steep hill. "But I'm taking you home. I've got a date and after spending time with Tara, I need that date right now. So, Nancy Drew, I'm dumping your ass as quickly as possible so I can get laid."

"Rude." I crossed my arms, staring out of the windows as the city went to sleep.

"Am I making you walk? No. I'm a fucking gentleman."

Pulling a cookie out of my pocket, I grumbled, "Yeah, yeah," as I ate.

SEVEN

Let It Go...

After Dave dropped me off in search of his girlfriend, I paced the empty bar, unsure of my next step. Tara wanted to talk with me alone. Why? What did she have to say that Dave couldn't hear? It was stupid to go out alone. I'd been attacked multiple times in the last twenty-four hours. Of course, I now had a cool copper cuff from Coco that was supposed to protect me, but it had yet to be test driven. I couldn't take another night of pacing, wondering, and waiting. I needed to do something, even if that something was talking to a succubus. As long as I didn't have sex with her, I was pretty sure I'd be safe. Dave seemed to trust her. And the reality was, I'd been attacked in my home last night. Nowhere was safe.

Growling, I stalked to the phone and dialed.

"Russell."

"Oh, um sorry. I guess I dialed that wrong." That's what I got for angry dialing.

"Miss Quinn? Clive is in a meeting right now. May I help you?"

"No. No problem. I just—" What? Just wondering if he'd be interested in babysitting? "Nothing. Sorry to interrupt. I'll handle it. Good night." I hung up and grabbed my coat. The reality was that nowhere was safe, so I might as well go chat up a demon.

It was a six-mile walk back downtown. If I detoured up through Pacific Heights and the Fillmore districts, I could add a few miles and visit the Painted Ladies, the row of ornate Victorian houses near Alamo Square. With the detour, I should arrive right on time.

Grabbing a scarf and a watch cap, I locked down the bookstore and bar again and headed out. Pulling the cap low over my ears and winding the scarf around my neck before stuffing the ends in my coat, I jogged up the steps at Land's End and mentally mapped my route. Would it be better to keep to green areas and back streets or busier, well-lit roads? It was an almost straight shot down California Street, but I decided to meander and kill time instead.

The wooded park was dark but no problem for a woman with a wolf's night vision. Animals scurried away from silent footfalls as I stuffed my freezing hands into my coat pockets. Wind off the ocean tore at my clothes and chilled me to the bone. Thinking longingly of my warm bed, I walked past the Legion of Honor, lit up and casting a gloriously columned mirror image in the reflecting pool before it.

When I emerged from the park, through a golf course, I wended my way through the palatial homes in Sea Cliff. Only in San Francisco were multi-million-dollar mansions snugged up against their neighbors. San Francisco was, comparatively, a small town and land was at a premium.

Streetlamps blazed yellow in the quiet dark. I decided to stick to the deserted streets rather than travel through the Presidio. Houses were buttoned up for the night, and yet I felt a prickle of awareness. Moving the scarf over my mouth to heat my face, I turned casually, as though checking the road before I crossed. Nothing. It may have been someone looking out their window, but just in case, I crossed the street and turned at the corner.

Zigzagging my way through the Lake Street area, the feeling

of being watched waned. The neighborhoods changed, houses shrank, apartment buildings crowded out single-family homes, and homeless people began to appear in doorways. If I was freezing, I could only imagine how desperate it was for those who had no warm bed waiting for them at home.

As I began to cross over an eerily quiet Geary Boulevard, a pile of blankets in a doorway stirred, a balding head emerging and tracking my movements. I almost kept going but couldn't. Backtracking, I pulled the knit cap off my head and slid it snugly over his. Before he could comment, I headed back toward the deserted four-lane street. Jogging across, ignoring the lights, I pulled my scarf up around my head before I lost heat.

San Francisco was a city filled with steep hills. About the time I crested one hill, crossed the flat intersection, and headed up another, I realized that the itch I had felt between my shoulder blades was back.

Touching the cuff Coco had given me, I assured myself that my mind was safe. Looking for menace in the deep shadows between buildings, I stepped up my pace, unable to shake the feeling I was being followed.

A light went on in a window to my right, helping me feel not quite so alone. When I passed a park, I saw someone sleeping on a bench. Deciding to cut through, I drew closer to the figure. It appeared to be an emaciated woman huddled under a thin, threadbare blanket. Pulling the thick scarf from around my neck, I laid it over her head and shoulders, hoping to block out the cold night air.

As I neared the edge of the park, a shadow separated from the silhouette of a tree. Caught short, I stumbled to a standstill. Muscles tensed, I prepared for a fight. The shadow moved silently toward me, details becoming clear in the dark. Clive.

"Will you give your coat away next?" The exasperation in his voice helped me shake off the sudden adrenaline spike and continue walking.

"What's it to you?"

"I wonder," Clive turned as I passed him and kept pace. "Why it is I bother to keep you safe, when left to your own devices, you choose to wander the streets alone in the middle of the night?" His shoes made barely a whisper on the pavement.

"Hey, I keep myself safe, thank you very much." One vision. He pulled me out of *one* vision—okay, two—and suddenly he's my guardian angel. Vampire. Whatever.

"Yes, of course. You're doing an excellent job." A broad shoulder brushed against mine before he moved a few inches away. His long, black overcoat seemed to absorb the faint light. It looked soft, although I doubted he'd appreciate my petting it.

We walked silently, side by side, for almost a mile. I ignored the rich, subtle scent of his cologne. Mostly.

"Is there a destination you have in mind?" Was there anything sexier than a deep British accent?

"I have no idea where you're going. I'm swinging by the Painted Ladies before I head downtown." Although I felt far more at ease with him by my side, I needed him to beat it. Tara clearly wanted to talk with me alone.

"Odd. Any reason you're sightseeing in the middle of the night?" Clive never stopped scanning our surroundings. I didn't know what he was looking for, but his being on alert allowed me to settle.

"Yes. Don't you have important vampire things to do? Necks to bite, women to seduce?"

He turned to me, eyes intent, a small smile tugging at his lips. "Are you offering?"

Flipping up the collar on my coat, I sped up, his soft chuckle trailing.

When I crested the next hill, Alamo Square and the Painted Ladies loomed. Glancing over my shoulder, I saw the fog rolling in, blanketing the city behind me. Mist hung in the air. Gloom and weak streetlights had leeched the color from the ladies, but they were still beautiful.

"Buy a postcard." His deep voice was barely a whisper in my ear.

"Oh. You're still here." Stupid sexy vampire.

"Why aren't you tucked up in your hobbit hole, where you belong?"

"You say that like it's a bad thing. I'd love to live in the Shire." I'd have a big, round door, a fireplace in every room. Second breakfasts! Let's not forget the second breakfasts. And elevenses.

"No doubt you would. Back to this evening, why are you wandering around the city alone?"

"Is it the wandering or the alone part that's tied your knickers in a twist?" I turned to head downtown, Clive settling at my side again.

"My knickers are twist-free. Thank you for your concern. I'm trying to understand, though, why I have multiple people trying to keep one bookish wolf safe when she has no interest in self-preservation." His coat brushed the back of my hand. It was every bit as soft as it looked.

"What are you talking about, multiple—wait. Is that why I haven't been able to shake the feeling of being watched?" Shoving my hands back into my pockets, I stopped and stared at him. "I'm nobody. I don't understand why you care."

His gaze took a leisurely stroll down my body before he shook his head. "That makes two of us." He started walking again. "Come on. Keep up."

"You don't even know where I'm going." Tucking my head down, I breathed into the upturned collar of my coat, trying to stave off the chill. Of course, Clive's nearness was helping, too. Good Lord, that man was potent.

"I'll figure it out." After a few steps, he guessed, "Strip club?"

"I moonlight." Snickering, I started jogging in place, knees high, trying to warm up. Jeez, it wasn't that cold. I didn't know what my problem was.

"Should have known." He watched me a moment. "Is there a reason you're doing that?"

"Yes. Yes, there is."

A cat sauntered out from behind a car, saw us, hissed, and streaked away in the opposite direction.

"That was all about you. I've passed lots of cats tonight. None of them hissed at me."

"Perhaps you weren't upwind before." He turned his head to study me.

"Quit it. That's creepy. Look ahead when you walk, like a normal person." His gaze was unnerving, not that I'd tell him that.

"I have excellent peripheral vision. Where are you going?"

When I tugged my collar up straight again to block the wind, he caught my hand, holding it between his two.

"You're freezing. It's chilly tonight, but not this cold." Tilting his head, he watched me. "You're trying to keep your teeth from chattering. I can see it." He stopped and as he was still holding my hand, I was forced to stop, as well.

"I'm fine." He was right, though. I was freezing.

"This means nothing." He stepped closer, enfolding me in his big, warm coat. "Where are you going?"

"Docks. I have a very lucrative smuggling career. I'd appreciate it if you'd back off. I've got cargo containers to unload."

He held me close. Seduced by the heat, I gave in, tucking myself up against him, my icy fists at his chest, my forehead against his neck.

"Don't get any funny ideas. I'm just using you for your body temp." Inhaling his scent, sinking into the comparative heat, I shivered uncontrollably.

"I run a quite few degrees below living but have at it. This isn't a vision, so what is it?" He adjusted, pulling me closer so none of me was outside the protection of his overcoat.

"Don't know. Coco gave me a bracelet. She said it would

keep my mind safe from attack. I guess it doesn't work as well on my body."

"I was surprised by her call. I didn't realize you and Coco were acquainted."

"Met today," I said through chattering teeth. Every icy breath I took felt like inhaling glass. My fingers had gone numb.

"Perhaps my blood again—"

"Nope." I shook my head against his neck, rubbing my frozen nose against his collar. "I've already got too much brewing in this body as it is." I did *not* need more vampire blood mixing with the dragon, werewolf, and wicche already in here, assuming Owen and Coco were right about my mom's lineage.

"Well, we have to do something," he said, exasperation clear. "I don't enjoy snuggling an ice sculpture."

"I can suck it up." I started to pull away, but he didn't budge. As he was stronger and warmer, I didn't fight too hard.

"Sam, why are you alone, wandering around the city? Are you meeting someone? If you'd been home, tucked up in bed *like you're supposed to be*, this wouldn't be happening."

"'Supposed to be'? There is no supposed to be." I pushed, and his grip loosened. "I hate to break it to you, but you're not the boss of me. I can wander around anywhere I want, anytime I want. I can—"

He put his hand over my mouth. "Shh. I'm thinking."

Narrowing my eyes, I crushed his foot under my boot. He didn't even flinch. When I tried to knee him, he spun me before I was able to graze his 'nads, my back pressed to his chest, still trapped inside his coat. Sneaky and fast. I had to respect that.

A dark, expensive-looking car slid up beside us and stopped.

"Are you kidnapping me?" My outrage at the thought was muted by my desire to keep warm in his coat.

"Exact opposite, actually. I'm trying to get rid of you."

"Nice." I rolled my eyes as the driver got out and walked around the car, opening the rear passenger door.

"Heat on high in the back." Clive shoved me in the car, pushing my frozen body over to make room for himself.

The driver resumed his seat behind the wheel, raising the dark glass divider between the front and back seats. When the heat kicked on, I almost cried. Eyes closed, I leaned forward and put my face up against the vents. My eyeballs were turning into novelty ice cubes. The pain was excruciating. It was hard to think. Everything hurt.

I heard a curse next to me and then I was in Clive's lap, his hot mouth fused to mine. I had a moment to wonder if I was hallucinating before I tasted blood in my mouth. That and Clive's tongue. I assumed it was Clive's, but as my eyelids were frozen shut, I couldn't exactly check.

"Come on, Sam. Swallow."

So many dirty jokes came to mind. Unfortunately, my larynx was frozen solid. And then he was kissing me again, and blood filled my mouth. I tried to swallow but couldn't get my throat to cooperate. I felt a quick, sharp nick on the top of my tongue and then the great thaw began. I was able to swallow, breathe, blink.

Almost immediately, I tapped Clive's shoulder to let him know he could stop. Almost. I think I might have tipped my cards when I started kissing him back. A moment later, I found myself on the other side of the backseat, Clive studying me, assessing.

"Are you all right now?"

I cleared my throat. "Mostly. Um, thanks for that."

Leaning back, he shook his head. "You're welcome." In a rare show of emotion, Clive dragged a hand through his hair. "Now, cut the shit. Why are you wandering the streets?"

It seemed churlish not to answer as he'd just saved my life. Again. "I was on my way to meet Tara downtown."

"Tara?" He paused, thoughtful. "Succubus Tara?" Confusion clear, he opened his mouth to ask something more when his driver spoke to him through the intercom.

"Shall I drive, Liege?"

"Yes. Tonga Room." Clive turned, facing me. "Why in the world were you meeting Tara in the middle of the night?"

"Well," I hesitated. "You see, when a woman really likes another woman, sometimes—"

"Did I not tell you to cut the shit?" His growly, angry voice should not have been so sexy, but I gotta say, it totally was.

"Fine. Fine. Dave took me to meet with Tara tonight. To see if it was a demon who was screwing with me. Before we left, she slipped me a note telling me to meet her at two." I checked my watch. "Which is in seven minutes. Good. I hate keeping demons waiting."

"Why didn't you ask Dave to go back with you?"

"Jeez, she didn't give us any info when we went together. She slipped me the note so he wouldn't see it. I figured I had a better chance of learning something on my own."

He opened his mouth, but I plowed on ahead.

"No place is safe for me, Clive. If I'd stayed home tonight, I'd have frozen in my bed alone. The only reason I'm not a chunk of ice is because I went out and ran into you. And for the record, I *did* call."

"Why do you think I was out looking for you?"

No idea.

EIGHT

Pole Dancing Is Harder Than It Looks

Clive's ride glided up to the California Street entrance of the Tonga Room. I assumed he'd drop me off, but instead, he slid out of the car, grabbed my hand, and pulled me along. The car drove away as he tried the handle of the Tonga Room's back door. Past closing time, but the door remained unlocked.

We found Tara sitting on a barstool, a cup of coffee in front of her. Her eyes widened at seeing Clive with me.

"Clive, it's lovely to see you again. Sam." She walked behind the bar. "Can I get either of you anything?"

"Nothing." Clive picked up her cup and motioned her to a nearby table. "Let's sit and talk."

Fear jumped into Tara's eyes. She appeared at ease, but I sensed a reluctance to abandon even that small protection of the bar. She played it off by lazily swirling a towel over the bar top as she rounded the side. I couldn't read the look she gave me as she breezed past. There was something, though.

I followed her to the table. The bar was empty, but it felt off. Was it a scent? No. I didn't think so. It was more a feeling, a raising of my hackles. Someone had just been in here. Someone or something left as soon as we'd opened the door.

Clive sat with his back to the wall, Tara across from him. I took the empty seat to his left. I had the bar at my back, but I trusted Clive to keep an eye out. The dark reaches of the long room drew my attention.

"Tara, I accompanied Sam because I, too, am very interested in what you have to tell her." He sat, legs crossed, the very image of a bored British aristocrat. Beneath the exterior, though, he was pulled taut.

"This is embarrassing." Tara's smile warmed the shadowy room. A rosy flush suffused her cheek. "I meant what I told her before. I don't know anything about anyone wanting to hurt her." She fingered the end of a curly lock of hair. "I—well, I just liked her. I was inviting her back for a drink."

She reached for me across the table. "I'm sorry if you misunderstood." Shrugging, she added, "I was attracted, and I thought maybe you might be, too."

"A succubus in love," Clive said. "What a charming lie."

Tara's body language changed. She crossed her arms over her impressive assets. "Not a lie. I thought she might be interested in more than the drink we'd had." Her eyes flicked toward me before going back to Clive. "She's lived here a lot of years. No man on record." A hand waved in my direction. "Thought maybe whatever caused the scars had put her off men, so I tried. No harm, no foul."

"Impressive. You have an almost fae-like ability to make truthful statements that are, in fact, lies." Clive studied her a moment. "Tara, what do you know?"

"Nothing." A sheen of perspiration appeared on her brow.

"Let me rephrase. Tell me everything you suspect." Clive hadn't moved, but his stillness felt like a snake preparing to strike.

"Clive, I'm low-level. You know that. The brass don't include me in their plans."

"And yet, here we sit." When Tara remained silent, Clive added, "You need to ask yourself, who do you fear more? Your kind or me?" The smile on his face caused sweat to pool at the base of my spine, and he wasn't even directing it at me.

It was my turn to try. "Tara, who was here? Right before Clive and I walked in, someone was here. Who was it?" Their gazes snapped to me, Tara's in fear, Clive's in speculation.

"Now, that is an interesting question." Clive turned from me and focused once more on Tara, who flinched, her fingers trembling.

"I've got no way out here." She flicked her hair back in frustration rather than seduction. "Either he'll kill me, or you will. He'll torture me first, though."

"You're underestimating me." Clive's voice was almost a purr.

Her eyes fluttered, and blood began to drip from her nose.

"Okay," I said. "I think we need to throttle back. No one needs to be tortured—or whatever the hell it is you're doing to yourself right now. Just give us something." When she opened her mouth, I held a finger up. "Something that is actually helpful. Someone higher up the food chain to talk to."

The look she gave me was one of pure loathing, as a tear of blood slid down her face. "And I will die because Dave decided to bring you to my doorstep."

I lost my breath.

"No. If you die, it will be because you lured her out tonight when you knew she'd be attacked." Clive leaned forward, and Tara jolted, her eyes rolling back in her head. "What do you know?"

"Sitri," she breathed, before falling to the floor unconscious.

"ARE YOU SURE SHE WASN'T DEAD?" I FELT GUILTY, SITTING IN THE passenger seat of Clive's sleek roadster, for leaving Tara lying on the floor. I mean, yes, she conspired to kill me, but other than that she seemed nice.

"Demons are not easy to kill." Clive changed gears, a low growl as it powered up California Street before turning right. "Unfortunately."

"So," I said, checking out the interior of his ridiculously posh ride. I was driving with Bond, Clive Bond. "Are we just stealing cars off the street, now? What happened to the sleek Mercedes with the silent driver?"

He barely spared me a look.

"Not that I have a problem with the thug life. I'm totally down with grand theft auto. Unless we get stopped. If that happens, I was kidnapped and am completely innocent." There were remarkably few people wandering the streets after two in the morning. Go figure.

"Good to know I have your support."

"I take a tase for no man. That shit stings."

"Been tased a lot, have you?" Clive swung to the curb, parking in front of the Demon's Lair. "Looks like we'll be hitting a strip club tonight, after all."

"Demon's Lair? Seriously? They don't believe in subtlety, do they?"

Clive got out and waited on the curb for me. "Regardless of how much of a stone-cold gangster you believe yourself to be, I'd appreciate it if you'd keep your mouth closed. I have no desire to buy your soul back after you've offered it up to a starving demon."

"Hey! I'm a hardass and super wily." Who the hell put him in charge?

"Remind me where are your cap and scarf are." Clive straightened his topcoat, checked his watch, and then grabbed my hand, pulling me along behind him. "I mean it, Sam. Don't speak."

When I flipped him off behind his back, he spun so quickly I had trouble tracking his movement. Between one blink and the next, he was in front of me, my hand caught in his, the incriminating middle finger standing between us. My sad little finger withered under his glare.

"What is it about you?" he said, almost to himself.

"My charm? My effervescent personality? My almost encyclopedic knowledge of Tolkien?" I kept my voice steady, but it was difficult in the face of...his face. *Damn.* He was all smoldering good looks, and I was a silly, scarred pain in his ass.

"No. That's not it." Shaking his head, he pulled me toward the door. "I mean it, Sam. Keep your lips zipped."

I mimed zipping them, not that he noticed.

Large, padded double doors were the only piece of ornamentation on the front of the Demon's Lair building. It was flanked by a liquor store on one side and a pawnbroker on the other. Both storefronts were still open. Anemic, yellow lights flickered in the liquor store. A sidewalk sleeper had wedged his curled form into the narrow walkway between the strip club and the pawnshop.

Clive swung open one of the enormous doors. Loud music throbbed in the still air. The shadowy entrance made me hitch a step. I'd seen nothing to explain it, but I wanted to run the other way and keep running until I was safely under my covers at home. Clive must have felt the sudden tension in my grip because he slowed as the door closed, rubbing his thumb over my fingers in comfort.

We followed the narrow hall to the source of the dark, pulsing music and murky light. The cavernous main room was filled with small tables, their chairs flipped over and hanging off the sides. A thin, hunched woman slowly shoved a dirty mop haphazardly around the floor. I *did not* want to think about what her half-hearted cleaning was leaving behind. Really didn't.

A topless woman in a g-string swayed to the music in the bright spotlight on the stage. She appeared dead on her feet. Swinging herself around the pole, she tried to hoist herself up, wrapping a leg around it. The awkward maneuver failed when her hand slipped, sending her sprawling to the floor. Low chuckles sounded in the dark, smoke-filled room. Four men sat at a table to the side of center stage, playing cards.

"If you can't work the pole, you don't dance here, Christine. Simple as that."

"Mr. Sitri." A man slid out of the gloom to tower over us. "You have guests."

All four men turned to us. On stage behind them, the woman pulled off the move she'd tried a moment earlier, but no one was watching. The men were an arresting array of terrifying. One was short and squat, built like a fire hydrant, with angry lesions on his face and hands. The man to his right was his opposite, rail-thin, sallow skin stretched over a skeletal face, his lips trapped in a rictus of pain. The man across from the fireplug could have been a model, golden brown skin, a face that made angels weep, with a predator's eyes. It was the one closest to us, the one who had turned to us last, that drew all the attention, though. Dark hair hung almost to his shoulders. Deep eyes burned black in his chiseled face. He radiated power. This was who we had come to meet.

"Clive. What an unusual surprise." He stood, walking toward us. "And you brought me someone." He reached out a hand to me. Clive's fingers twitched, but he made no other move to stop the demon from touching me, so I shook the offered hand. Sitri did more than shake my hand. He pulled it up to his lips and inhaled deeply as he kissed my knuckles.

Heat rolled up my arm and through my body. Painfully aware that I was surrounded by men, my breath shortened, nipples hardened, and an ache throbbed between my legs. I imagined in detail what each of these men, naked and ready, might do with me. I could think of nothing else.

"Was that necessary?" Clive's bored, oh-so-British voice momentarily cut through the morass of lust crushing me.

"One must have some fun in life." Deep chuckles echoed in the dark room, brushing against my overly-sensitized body. "You can thank me later."

Sitri was tall and broad shouldered. His hands were beautiful. They looked like something Michelangelo would have painted. His eyes slid from Clive back to me, a knowing grin tugging at his full, sensual lips. Lips like that…

"I was going to ask you if we could speak privately, but as I can no longer allow her out of my sight, I suppose we'll talk here." Clive's voice was like a cool wind, blowing frenzied sweaty fumblings from my mind, and causing nausea to roll through me. Until Sitri spoke again.

"You don't trust my friends to look after your little wolfic-che?" He made a tutting sound, causing the men at the table to laugh. Flames licked up my body as demons stared at me, hunger naked in their eyes.

"I'm here about her." Clive's voice doused the flames. I closed my eyes, concentrating only on him. The need to shift, to protect myself with sharp teeth that could tear his vocal cords out, was overwhelming.

"She doesn't look like a dancer." The men laughed again, but this time the touch of their words felt like rough, pawing hands. I mentally twisted to get them off me.

"Not unless your establishment now employs women in baggy jeans and long-sleeved t-shirts, no." Clive's voice pushed the invisible hands away. "Someone has been mentally attacking her. Prior to you, that is."

"What is it to me, what happens to her?" Sitri's words stopped tormenting me. Either he'd lost interest, or he'd heeded the annoyance in Clive's voice.

"That depends, doesn't it?"

I took a deep breath and opened my eyes. Bile, hot and sour, hit the back of my throat. Having a man take control of my body brought back memories I'd worked hard to bury. I wanted to run and hide in The Slaughtered Lamb, but first I wanted to hunt and kill every demon in the room.

"If this has nothing to do with your kind, we'll have only interrupted a poker game. And for that intrusion, you've already taken your retribution, considering the games you've been playing with her. If, however, I find that the visions incapacitating her are demon-based...well, let's just say, it would be better for the health of all concerned if that is not the case." Clive's voice remained pleasant if not bored, but the skin around Sitri's eyes tightened.

"I won't say her scent—the promise of her—doesn't intrigue me, but I will say I know of no plot against her." Sitri studied me with more interest than before. "In the name of professional cooperation, I can look into this for you. If I hear anything, I'll be in touch."

Clive nodded. "Thank you for your time." He turned to the table and inclined his head a fraction. "Gentlemen, sorry to interrupt your game."

Clive got us out without appearing to hurry. Once on the sidewalk again, icy air rushed through me, blowing away the last of the manufactured lust. I stood immobile, wanting to rip their smug, laughing faces from their heads, wanting to taste their blood on my tongue.

Suddenly Clive was there, standing in front of me, carefully not touching me. "I know. Please believe me when I tell you he will not live long. Once he's served his purpose, he'll pay for his games."

His words, the truth behind them, allowed me to pull in a deep breath and unlock my body. Vengeance would come soon. That would need to be enough for now.

Once back in his car, I had a moment of quiet to think. "Why are you going to so much trouble to help me?"

He glanced over, then returned his attention to the road. "You remind me of someone I knew a long time ago."

"Was she awesome, too?"

A grin tried to tug at his lips, but it gave up quickly. "I thought so." He turned down a dark, narrow street, slowing as a cat sauntered across the road.

I turned in my seat, angling myself toward him. "So, who was she?"

He was silent so long, I didn't think he'd answer. "My sister." He paused, as though gathering himself for the tale. "It happened when I was still human. My younger sister was a daydreamer. Our mother would get so angry, but Elswyth had no intention of ignoring her chores. She'd begin them and then get lost in the stories running through her mind. She'd wander unheeded through the woods for hours at a time. It wasn't her fault. She had a head for whimsy and fairytale."

He glanced over again, a soft smile on his face. "She'd tell such wonderful stories in the evenings, as we sat by the fire, tales of dragons and warriors, fair maidens and battles. I didn't mind doing her chores, especially when her daydreaming meant an evening's entertainment."

He parked at the top of the stairs leading down to The Slaughtered Lamb. The silence was charged as he turned off the ignition. "One afternoon, she didn't return. Our mother slammed pots, enraged that Elswyth had wandered off again. I, however, was concerned. It was close to dusk. Elswyth loved the woods but would never have been caught there alone in the dark. She believed her own stories too much. She worried over monsters and fairies. When I'd finished both our chores, I went out in search of her. By that time, our mother was beside herself, anger had given way to worry."

I reached out and placed my hand on his. This story wasn't going to end well.

"I found her about a mile from home." He shook his head, misery in his eyes. "I should have gone to look for her when I'd realized she'd been gone too long."

"You couldn't have known."

"Regardless, I was too late. She'd been brutalized. I found three sets of horse tracks, three sets of footprints. They'd beaten and raped Elswyth, left her dead body in the woods she'd loved, a mere quarter of an hour from safety."

"I'm sorry, Clive."

Nodding, he squeezed my hand. "Me, too." He looked me in the eye. "Those were the first men I ever killed."

I met his gaze, conviction ringing in my voice as I said, "Good."

NINE

Who Invited the Wolves?

I awoke abruptly the next morning from another nightmare. I'd been clinging to a pole while shadowy men watched and hooted. Staring into the darkness, I tried to see who they were, but the floor opened up and swallowed me down. I dropped into a dark, dank basement. Skittering sounds moved relentlessly closer. I opened my mouth to scream and then clear gray eyes filled my vision, startling me awake.

Clicking on the lamp, banishing the shadows, I went to the kitchen to make toast and coffee. A strange noise sounded out in the bar. *Not again.* I eased the door open to look into what should have been an empty bar and saw movement out of the corner of my eye. A squeak escaped before I realized it was Dave, stretching and yawning, walking out of the bathroom.

"What the hell are you doing here?"

Dave rubbed his eyes and rotated his shoulders. "That couch is shit for sleeping."

"How did you even get in? I haven't opened up my wards yet." It wasn't so much that I was afraid of Dave, but that a protection I relied on had failed. Helena and Nathaniel, the wicches who had created them, were out of the country. If my wards were failing, I had no way of fixing them.

"Maggie kicked me out, and I needed a place to crash." His jeans were unbuttoned, his shirt rumpled. He reached behind the bar for a glass and drew himself a beer from the tap. He continued to rotate one arm, trying to loosen it up.

"Was she upset about you visiting Tara?" Clearly not the most important part of this conversation, but he'd never mentioned a girlfriend before last night. I found it hard to imagine Dave living with someone.

"Because I talked to a woman? No." He rolled his eyes at me. At least, I think he did. When there were no whites it was hard to tell. "She might have an impulse control issue—"

"Her, too, huh?"

"Hardy har. Do you want to hear this or what?" He finished his beer while giving me the stink eye. It was impressive.

I mimed ticking a lock on my lips.

He poured himself another pint and downed it in one gulp. "We went out dancing, instead of staying in, which is what I wanted. This smokin' waitress kept leaning over, showing me her rack, and yeah, okay, I was still revving from spending time with Tara. So, I looked her up and down. I didn't touch her. Maggie got all huffy. By the time we got home, there was no talking to her. Banshees are pretty unforgiving, so I decided to leave. Give her some space to cool off."

He rolled his shoulders. "That's why I came here. I didn't want to wake anybody up to ask if I could crash, and I knew you had a couch sitting here. If I'd known how fucking uncomfortable it was, I would have slept in my car."

"But how did you get in?" Not that the Banshee revelation wasn't fascinating.

"Your wards don't work on demons. I thought you knew that." He ran a hand over his bald head.

"My wards will keep out hostile, lesser fae, but allow demons in?" I thought of the men last night, and a chill ran down my spine. Sitri could walk in here anytime he wanted and enslave me with a touch, a word.

"Your problem is relying on white wicches. They can't keep out demons. Don't have the juice. You need a black wicche or a demon to perform the rite. There has to be a blood sacrifice, and white wicches refuse to do that shit." He looked at his watch. "Maggie should be at work by now. I'm going to go home and catch a few. See you tonight." Dave took off and left me wondering if there was anywhere I was truly safe.

Later, wiping down the bar, I contemplated demons and wicches and wolves, oh my. Loud flapping sounded overhead. Much like the magical entrance I have for water fae, there was another one in the ceiling for our winged brethren. To the untrained eye, it appeared to be a skylight but there was no glass, only a warded magical membrane. I stepped out of the way as a woman with long, dark hair, gray, scaly skin, and massive, black wings descended into the bar.

"Hey, Meg. How's it hanging?" I pulled a bottle of scotch from under the bar and poured her a double as she regarded me with humorless, oil-slick black eyes.

Megaera was one of the three Furies, the goddesses of vengeance. She was terrifying, but strangely likable.

"Sam."

Meg's clothes were covered in blood. Her skin, while gray and scaly, was blood-free. Her skin absorbed the blood of those upon whom her vengeance was wrought. Her clothes didn't. Consequently, she often looked like she dressed in emergency room cast-offs. I think that was why she preferred to wear black. It forgave so much.

"Tell me, why do humans insist on having children they hate? I do not believe you can beat a child to within an inch of his life and then beg for your own. Tripping is an accident. Back-handing into a wall is not."

Reproduction was a touchy subject in the magical community. Many would give everything they have in order to bear young. Being long-lived alleviated the urgency to procreate, but not the desire. The fact that humans could have children so easily, relatively speaking, and then abuse or neglect them was unfathomable, and a source of rage.

I'd never have children. Wolves needed to change every month and fetuses didn't survive the shift. Hell, women have miscarried when they've fallen down stairs or had a big shock. Changing from a human to a wolf was a great deal more of shock to the system.

Male wolves have been known to get their human mates pregnant, but the percentage of miscarriages was higher than in the general public and the baby, if born, was almost always fully human. It was not unheard of, though, for a human mother to give birth to a werewolf child. Marcus's son Mick was a born wolf, but such cases were extremely rare.

"Sorry, Meg. I guess you've had a lousy morning." I refilled her Scotch when she'd drained the first.

She nodded, swirling the amber liquid in her glass. "Why do you smell of demon?"

"Still?" I sniffed myself. "I showered again this morning." Leaning over the bar, I whispered, "Should I be worried?" I hoped Meg would use some of that goddess power to protect me from the sulfurous bastards.

She shrugged, which for Meg could mean anything from 'I don't particularly give a shit' to 'No one is planning to gut you and steal your soul today.'

"How goes the dating?" I filled a bowl of nuts and slid them in front of her.

Taking a handful, she responded, "As expected."

"That bad, huh? I told you to let me write your profile for you. I could have—" How did I phrase this? "Softened the edges a little."

"I like my edges sharp. Nothing about me is soft, Sam. Stop trying to humanize me." She threw back her whiskey and slammed the glass back on the bar.

"You know what we need? A dating app for supernaturals!" I refilled her glass again. Alcohol didn't affect her as it did most.

She drank it like water. "You wouldn't need to waste your time with humans who are all wrong for you." This was all my fault. Meg had mentioned that without her sisters—who were currently living on the other side of the world—she was alone too much. I suggested a dating app and we had then spent an entire evening creating her profile, adding pics, and swiping left and right, while Dave plied us with cocktails.

"It's been tried. It was a dumpster fire." Meg ate another handful of nuts.

"Why? That sounds like the perfect solution."

"You are so very young and innocent. I have no idea why I like you." She took a sip. "Imagine, please, DMs asking if you'd like to get together and lay waste to a small village, maybe spread a little black plague. It became the go-to app for very powerful and bored supernaturals to find one another. Many miss the days when mortals would prostrate themselves in awe of our power. When human sacrifice was seen as our due. Remember that tsunami a couple of years ago? That was an IM couple having a little too much fun."

"IM?" I glanced around the bar, but no one needed me.

"Immortal Match. The death toll rose too high. They shut it down." Meg's gaze traveled over the other patrons, as well. "Where's your demon? I thought he was supposed to be here to guard you?"

"Dave? No. He's not my protection. He's my cook."

At a sudden sound, she turned her head to the stairway. "That's good, because as protection he sucks."

Footsteps thundered down the stairs, two sets, accompanied by the scent of wolf. I warded against wolves. Unless they were demon wolves—and wasn't that a charming thought—how did they get in?

The first down the stairs seemed vaguely familiar. There was something about his scent. I reached into the past, looking for a name. "Randy?" The last time I'd seen him, he'd been a teenager, maybe thirteen or fourteen, hanging around my uncle's campgrounds. Now, he had to be well over six feet, muscular—like all wolves—with sandy-colored hair and blue eyes. Three thin scars ran through an eyebrow and down the side of his face. I didn't know why, but the scars made me uneasy. Hypocritical, I know.

I hadn't seen Randy in seven years, since that week and a half I spent with my uncle in the Santa Cruz Mountains. I remembered him as a strangely intent kid. I often found him staring at me, but I hadn't been able to summon the energy to care. My mother had just died. I was reeling, lost in grief but trying to hide it in front of all those strangers. My uncle included.

Randy studied the bar before his gaze fell on me. "It's been a long time. I've gotta say, it was a shock hearing your voice in my messages. We'd thought you were dead until last week. We were going through the pack's paperwork and found records of wire transfers from this business with your name attached."

"But..." How had Marcus let this happen? The whole pack knew where I was. My mouth went dry. He'd done nothing to threaten me and yet the need to change clawed at me. I wanted sharp teeth to protect myself.

"You called about a dead wolf, sent a picture of Claire. It looked like someone really went to town on her, carved her up." He shook his head, but a predatory glint in his eyes belied the sorrow. "Why don't you show me the body, Sam, so I can take it off your hands."

Clenching, I stabbed my short nails into my palms, centering myself, trying to not feel vulnerable in a male wolf's presence. The Kraken and rats, now demons and wolves. The chances of my surviving this week kept get getting slimmer and slimmer.

Movement caught my eye, and I remembered there was another wolf. Two male wolves. "Marcus sent you?" Marcus knew what happened to me seven years ago. Why would he send male wolves into my den?

My dad had died when I was little, so it was just Mom and me when I was growing up. One evening—I was still really young—when I'd left my bed to use the bathroom, I heard Mom on the phone arguing with someone. Hiding in the dark, I'd listened. It sounded as though Uncle Marcus wanted to see me, but mom whisper-shouted that it'd be over her dead body. She'd said things that didn't make sense at the time, calling him jealous and inhuman. She'd said other things, but I hadn't recognized the words and therefore didn't retain them.

Marcus had spoken with me at my mom's funeral, said he'd promised my dad he'd look out for me. I'd wanted to believe and so agreed to go with him, to visit for a few weeks while I figured out what to do.

It was my fault, my mother's death. We'd stayed in one place too long. I'd begged my mom to let me finish the school year, to walk at graduation. Turned out, I never even went. The diploma was probably still filed in the secretary's desk. Instead of putting on a cap and gown, I'd been standing over a grave. Guilt and grief had warred. And then there was Marcus, a hand on my shoulder, saying he'd promised to look out for me. I'd stumbled after him in a daze, happy there was someone who knew what to do.

The sky had filled with a dark, roiling smoke as we neared the apartment I'd shared with mom. I wanted to pick up some clothes before I went with Uncle Marcus. Instead, I found the charred remains of our latest home. Marcus wouldn't let me out of the car. He scanned the parking lot, looking for something, and then spun the car and shot down the street in the opposite direction. He drove into the mountains to his home, a large, rustic house with a sprawling campsite of cabins in the woods. I'd met Mick, a cousin I'd never known I'd had, as well as other men I'd assumed were campers and hikers. Men, I was soon to discover, who were werewolves. A week and a half later, I'd been attacked by one of those men and sent here to recover or die.

Shaking off the memory, I glanced around the bar, my heart swelling. Everyone was staring down the wolves, some hands were already moving, readying a spell. I wasn't alone in the dark. Not this time.

"Marcus doesn't send anyone anywhere anymore. You called Claire's Alpha. That's me." Randy patted his chest.

My stomach dropped. "How can *you* be Alpha? Aren't you—what—twenty, twenty-one?"

"Take us to Claire." Tendrils of his Alpha power pushed at me. He was trying to rein me in, get me to fall in line with his pack. He was destined for disappointment.

I shook my head. I couldn't explain it, but I didn't want them to have her. They'd done nothing wrong, and yet I didn't trust them. To be fair, the fact that they were male wolves was probably enough to push them over into enemy territory.

"Sam," Randy lowered his voice. "It had to be done. I know he was your uncle, but he was weak. Our people were drifting off. A pack needs a strong leader in order to keep the wolves under control. Marcus couldn't do it anymore." He glanced at the other wolf and then continued. "There'd been a death. A hiker. The authorities put it down as death by misadventure, but we know a wolf kill. For the safety of both humans and shifters, Marcus had to be put down."

He was dead. I hadn't seen him in seven years, but we'd spoken on the phone occasionally. I sent money every month to repay the loan for my bar. He wasn't my father, but he'd been a connection to my dad. Another connection lost.

"What about Mick?" Marcus's son was older than me. He should have taken over as Alpha.

"Mick died years ago. About the time you disappeared. We found his body in the woods. Animals had gotten to him." Randy didn't sound too concerned. There had to be at least fifteen years difference in their ages. Maybe they hadn't been close.

As uncomfortable as they both made me feel, Claire was a member of their pack. She had nothing to do with me. I had no right to keep her from them.

"I'll show you where she is." They followed me through the kitchen and to the storeroom. It took every ounce of self-control not to run with two male wolves at my back. I opened the door and gestured for them to go first. Her body lay under a blanket in the corner of the room. The other wolf hunkered down, tucked the ends around her, and picked her up. When he nodded at Randy, they both turned to leave.

"We'll take care of her now," Randy said.

When the wolf shifted her body to get through the door, an arm slipped out from under the blanket. Scars. She was covered in scars. Why hadn't I seen them for what they were before? My stomach dropped, head spinning. Above her wrist, carved into her flesh, was an infinity symbol. Hands fisting, I stared at the symbol, envisioning my own wrist. Mine was thicker, the scarring corded, but otherwise identical. The wolf, eyes intent on me, tucked the woman's arm back under the blanket and followed Randy out.

Locking my knees to keep from hitting the floor, I breathed deeply. It was no accident. She hadn't been cut up on rocks or bitten by sharks. She was like me. The past wouldn't stay buried. It kept coming back to knock me off my feet. I wasn't the only one.

I ran, barely making it to the bathroom before I was sick. Not again. I couldn't do this again. I needed more information, and I needed it now.

TEN

In Which Sam Is Forced to Question Who Her Allies Are

It took talking to most of the patrons in the bar and bookstore, but I finally found someone who had Ule's number. Ule—he of the unblinking stare—was an owl shifter and a special collections archivist at the San Francisco Public Library. I'd asked him about his work when he'd first started coming to the bar to drink and stare. As a folklore librarian, he had access to very specialized databases, the kind I needed to search.

When Dave came in, I asked him to watch the bar because I was going out.

"No, you're not." Dave leaned against the bar, arms crossed, exuding annoyance.

"Pretty sure I am. Hold down the fort," I said as I passed him behind the bar.

"Stop." He held out an arm, barring the way.

I did, but mostly to be polite. I could have ducked under it. He glared. I glared right back.

"What the fuck, Sam? How many times does someone have to try and kill you before you stop making their job easier?" The bar got quiet at his words. "And I'm still pissed at you for sneaking off to see Tara without me. What part of 'demon' is confusing for you?"

"I've learned my lesson on that one." My stomach twisted at the memory of Sitri. "No place is safe for me. Do you get that? They manipulated my mind and body against my will. I can't hide and hope for the best. I'm doing research in Ule's archive. Now, are you going to let me by or what?"

He shook his head, resignation slumping his shoulders as he dropped his arm. "Take my car."

I thought about it a moment. "As much as I would love to get behind the wheel of that super sexy muscle car of yours, I don't know how to drive and there's no place to park downtown."

He studied me, as though checking to see if I was making a joke. "How the hell do you not know how to drive?"

"I understand how it's done. I've watched people do it. I've just never done it myself." I shrugged. "I was seventeen when I started all this. Remember?"

"Yeah, I remember." His face softened for just a moment, before the scowl returned. "Fine, but once we get rid of whoever's trying to kill you, I'm teaching you to drive. It's embarrassing."

"Fine by me. Don't worry—"

"I'll act as Sam's bodyguard today." Dave and I both turned to find Meg back on a barstool.

"I thought you left," I said.

"I did. Now I'm back. Keep up, Sam." Meg and Dave assessed one another, neither giving an inch.

"Fine," Dave grumbled.

Meg held out her hand, waiting.

"What?" Dave didn't dislike Meg exactly. It was more like two bulls in adjacent paddocks snorting and pawing the ground. They were both powerful dominants in their own right and didn't enjoy sharing space with the other.

"Keys," Meg said. Most patrons were pretending to read or chat, but all eyes were on Dave and Meg. Each, in their own way, scared the shit out of everyone in the room. The bulls had been moved to the same paddock and people were braced for blood.

"She can't drive," he said.

"No, but I can." Hand steady, she waited. "I'll watch her, but I won't walk her six miles out in the open. Don't be a stubborn ass. Give me the keys."

More grumbling, but he fished them out of his pocket again and dropped them into her hand.

The bar breathed a sigh of relief as Meg led the way out. I nodded to Dave and followed her up the stairs.

The day was bright and clear, the wind whipping stray hairs from my braid. Meg strode to the matte black muscle car, chirped the alarm, and slid inside. I joined her a moment later.

"I'm not trying to stir up trouble or anything, but I thought you had your own car."

Meg grinned, her eyes fierce. "I do, but I wanted to drive his. Now if we get attacked, it's his car that gets trashed, not mine."

"Nice," I said, shaking my head. It was, thankfully, a quiet ride downtown. Meg pulled into a private garage two blocks from the library and right into a reserved spot.

"Do you live near here?" I hadn't really pictured her as a downtown gal, but it *was* centrally located.

"No. The man who reserved this space has paid through the end of the year. As he's no longer among the living, it seemed like a waste not to use it."

Huh. "Good point, I guess."

She made an annoyed clicking sound. "He was a very bad man, Sam. We're all—especially his wife—better off without him. Okay?"

"Sure. I know it's what you do. I wasn't questioning you." She was a Fury, a goddess of vengeance. Her job was to punish the evil.

Wait.

"Meg, do you know who's trying to kill me, trapping me in these visions?"

"Yes."

I stopped walking, feeling like I'd been sucker-punched.

"You know and you didn't tell me? You're not wreaking your vengeance on them?"

She strode back to me, anger lining her face. "I have been *forbidden* to interfere."

"Forbidden? By who?" Someone higher up the food chain than a goddess wanted me dead? I'm surprised I'd made it this long.

"Whom, and I can't tell you. Suffice to say, all of this is your destiny and I have been forbidden to alter it." She turned and started back toward the library. "Come on. Let's get you off the street."

It wasn't that Meg and I were best friends, but she'd sat on my barstool a couple of times a week for years. We talked, shared bits of our lives. And if someone stepped out of a doorway right now and put a gun to my head, she wouldn't stop them. I walked numbly behind her, unsure if I could still count her among my allies.

The main library was a massive Beaux Arts style building of white granite that stood six stories high and took up a city block. It was located in the downtown area that held City Hall, the Supreme Court of California, the War Memorial Opera House, the Civic Auditorium, and Davies Symphony Hall. In these few blocks of downtown, giants lorded over the neighborhood.

The library, though designed as though it were from a bygone age, was actually a recent addition. The old library had been damaged during the 1989 Loma Prieta earthquake. That building had been renovated and later became the Asian Art Museum. So, while the exterior of the library was austere and in keeping with her far older sisters surrounding her, the interior of the library was quite modern.

Meg opened the tall glass door and held it for me, avoiding my gaze. I stepped past her, into the atrium. It soared over a hundred feet, topped with a huge glass dome. Each floor opened on the atrium, with large banners hanging from railings. It was Hispanic Heritage month, so literary luminaries were highlighted. Gabriel García Márquez, Sandra Cisneros, Julia Alvarez, Elizabeth Acevedo, Junot Díaz, Benjamin Alire Sáenz, Cristina Henríquez and more stared down like gods watching mere mortals scurry beneath them.

Pale stone walls and a glass ceiling, the architectural design gave the impression of airy openness. It was a temple to ideas, an equalizer, a repository of knowledge, free and available to all. I crossed the atrium, looking for a map. The café, an auditorium, and meeting rooms were on the lower level. Ule had asked me to meet him near the café so he could take me through an employee-only door that led down another flight of stairs.

When Meg and I found the cafe, we discovered Ule sitting at a small table, sipping a bottle of water and people watching. As soon as he saw us, he leaped to his feet and hurried over.

"Follow me." He hustled across the floor and scanned the ID card that hung at his hip in front of a black panel by a door that read, 'No Admittance.' We shadowed him down a dark passage to a large cement room, Meg bringing up the rear. The walls were lined with glass-fronted cases filled with ancient tomes. In the center of the room was a small table and chair, facing the passage we'd just come through. A large, hardwired computer took up most of the table space.

Ule gestured to the chair. "Sit. Already logged in. You may search." He opened a corner cabinet, pulled out a step stool, stood on it, and then crouched down to perch and stare at me. Cool. This wouldn't be at all awkward.

"Well, as much fun as it sounds to stare at you, Sam, I think I'll wait in the café. Where I can sit. And not stare at you." Meg saluted no one in particular and headed back up the dark passage.

As much as it hurt me to think it, I felt better once Meg had left. She knew. She knew who was trying to kill me and she'd said nothing. Yes, she'd been forbidden. But what if that person ordered her to kill me herself? Didn't she have a say in all of this? She was thousands of years old, a goddess, for goodness' sake.

I dropped onto the wooden chair and tried to push Meg out of my thoughts. I had work to do. The screen was completely white with only a search bar at the top. That was it. No logo. No title. Zip. I thought a moment. What did I want to know first? I typed, 'dead woman scars infinity.'

A moment later articles popped up with some of my key words, but not all of them. To be on the safe side, I scanned dozens of entries, newspaper articles, police reports, folk tales, urban legends, academic journals. None of them fit. I changed the search terms to 'wolf scar infinity,' as that was the bare bones of what we had in common. The results were almost identical, except for a few police reports of wolves being found mauled in the northern U.S. and Canada. Again, nothing fit.

I tried multiple combinations before I accepted that neither the police nor a journalist had ever found or heard about one of his victims. The supernatural community kept its own secrets. It wouldn't do for human doctors and scientists to test our remains, so I supposed it made sense.

Next, I researched wards. I may have inadvertently opened them during the Kraken vision, thereby allowing Clive and Dr. Underfoot in, but I had *not* altered my wards to admit wolves. I found quite a few articles on the theory of wards, on the types of spells necessary to create them, but little on the repair of them.

Helena, my mother's childhood friend who'd taken me in when I'd arrived bloody and broken seven years ago, had created all my wards for me. She'd tied them specifically to me, wanting them to respond only to me. Unfortunately, Helena was in Wales visiting her great aunt. She wasn't due back for weeks. I needed to figure out what I could do now. Dave had said that demons could create wards, but only if a blood sacrifice was involved. As I wasn't planning to kill anyone to protect myself, I went on to the next article.

This one appeared to be scanned pages from an ancient spell

book or journal. The handwriting was cramped and hard to read. I was going to skip it, but I'd seen the words 'blood' and 'ward' next to 'fail.'

I turned to an ever-staring Ule. "Can I print this out?"

Quick nod.

I hit print and heard the sheets sliding out of a printer somewhere behind me. Ule stepped off his stool, retrieved the sheets for me, and then returned to his perch.

I borrowed Ule's pen and started translating any words I could make out. Once I had those done, I used context clues to translate the words I was pretty sure of. Thirty minutes and a huge headache later, I'd pieced together a narrative written two hundred and forty years ago, although the incidents in the story appeared to have taken place long before this account was written. The story concerned a wicche worried for her newborn. Children had gone missing in the village and she feared for her daughter. Wards had been erected, sealing her tiny house in the woods.

When the mother woke one morning, she found the crib empty and the wards destroyed. She searched everywhere for her child, but never found her. What she did find was a streak of dried blood on the windowsill.

I looked down at the healing wound on my hand. Someone had expended an immense amount of psychic energy to plunge me into a vision, incapacitating me for an attack, and yet all they had done was cut my hand. Was this why?

"My supervisor will be checking on me in approximately seventeen minutes. You need to go soon," Ule said.

I checked the time on my phone and nodded. "One more thing and then I'm out of here, okay?"

He nodded eagerly.

While I carried an extensive collection of books by and about supernaturals in the bookstore, I had next to none on werewolves. As I didn't allow werewolves in my shop, it seemed pointless. That was what I told myself. The real reason was that I'd been denying a part of myself because it scared me.

I dove back in, searching for the history of werewolves. There were too many results. I could read all night and not scratch the surface. Scanning the titles, I looked for something to jump out at me. And then it did. The name 'Quinn' scrolled by. I stopped and clicked on an article. I skimmed as quickly as possible, hitting the print button so I could read it in full later. It seemed to be a creation myth, detailing the birth of the first werewolf. A small village was being menaced by a pack of wolves. Sheep were stolen. Chickens were eaten. Even a horse had been attacked and eaten by the pack.

When a baby had been carried away, the villagers were terrified enough to put aside one fear in order to slay a different one. They consulted a local Wise Woman. She told them to send a farmer named Alex Quinn out along the main road, east of town. She made a blessing—a spell, no doubt—and placed it in a leather pouch. She told the villagers that Quinn needed to wear it around his neck when he went out to confront the wolves. She told them that if Quinn did as she directed, the villagers would be safe.

Quinn's wife begged him not to go. His son begged to be allowed to fight with him. Quinn kissed his wife and son goodbye and strode down that dark, eastern road to meet his fate, hoping his sacrifice would, in fact, save his family and friends.

When Quinn hit a fork in the road, he found the pack waiting. Pitchfork in hand, he planned to kill as many as he could before the breath left his body.

"Now."

He turned to see the Wise Woman standing in the shadows watching. As one, the wolves descended on Quinn, tearing him apart.

"Stop!" The Wise Woman's voice rang out over the snarls of the wolves.

Quinn cried out, his pain-wracked body bowing off the ground.

"Wait, my children."

Quinn screamed in agony as bones broke and reformed, joints twisted, and his jaw elongated. Soon, though not soon for Quinn, a wolf stood where a man had fallen, intelligent eyes filled with hatred waited for the wicche's command.

ELEVEN

Never Piss Off a Banshee

When I got home, I read the articles I'd printed. They were fascinating and almost seemed linked. Was the baby stolen from his crib linked to the wolves menacing a village? I couldn't find enough details to tell.

Later, I stepped behind the bar to get myself a mug of tea. "Thanks for keeping an eye on things for me this afternoon."

"Yeah," Dave grumbled.

"How's it going out here?"

"How's what going?" He put his book down on the bar, his expression blank.

I gestured at the dozen or so patrons scattered around the bar, moonlight sparkling off the dark waves behind them.

He shrugged, seemingly baffled by the question.

I looked at all the empty glasses on the small, round tables. "You know you're supposed to be checking on people, getting orders, delivering drinks. Tell me if any of this sounds familiar."

"No," he scoffed. "That's how *you* tend bar. I sit here and read. If they want something, they can walk up here and ask for it."

"Dave—"

"Stop. You hired me to cook. Tending is bonus, so quit giving me shit about it." He raised his voice to the bar in general. "You people are fine, right?"

A small voice piped up from the corner. "Well, actually, I could use—"

"See? They're fine." He picked up his book again.

"Give me a minute. I'll be back for orders," I said to the room at large, holding up a finger.

Dave yelped as I walked toward the bookstore. "Fuck! What was that for?"

When I turned around, Clive was still sitting in his seat, watching Dave. Dave, however, was now on his feet, walking around the bar and collecting empties.

Clive stood, his expression unreadable. "Sam, if I might have a word." He walked toward the far end of the bar, and I changed direction to follow.

He held the kitchen door open for me, looking gorgeous in a charcoal gray sweater that accentuated his broad shoulders. Waiting for me to pass, he followed me in. He pulled at his sleeve before looking at me. He did it thoughtlessly, stylishly, but Clive didn't fidget. He was rarely, if ever, anything other than confident, controlled, and a little bored.

He checked his watch. "I have an appointment. I need to get going, but I wanted to make sure you were all right. Any lasting effects from last night?"

Oh. "No, I'm fine." It was silly to feel disappointed. We weren't friends. He'd just been forced to spend time with me lately because I seemed to have hit my expiration date.

Nodding, he checked his watch again. "Good." When he finally met my gaze, there was something there I couldn't interpret.

"Not to worry, no dates with demons tonight." I smiled, but as he was no longer looking, I let it drop.

"Probably for the best." He nodded absently. "Dave informed me you'd been doing research today. Did you learn anything new?"

"Some, yeah. I couldn't find any reports on women—anyone —being painstakingly carved up, their bodies being dumped."

"The bodies may not have been discovered or left where they could be discovered."

"Exactly," I sighed. "I also looked up wards. They're tied to blood and my blood could have been taken when I was trapped in the rat vision. That might account for how wolves waltzed in today."

Clive took my hand and studied the healing wound, little more than a red line at this point.

"And I rounded out my study session with the history of werewolves. I found a creation story naming a Quinn as the first wolf." Shaking my head, I said, "I have no idea what to make of that. It was the only specific name used in the account. The wicche who'd cursed him was referred to as a Wise Woman."

Clive looked up from my hand, gave it a quick squeeze, and dropped it. "A wicche? The legend you read said a wicche was responsible for creating the first werewolf?"

I nodded. "Right."

"But she wasn't named… Interesting."

"It was just a folktale, Clive. It probably doesn't signify anything." His question about the wicche did have my thoughts swirling, though, imagining connections that probably didn't exist.

"And what are folktales but stories that have been passed down, generation to generation, while sitting by the fire? Embell-ishments here and there don't change the core of the story. I'll ask Russell to research the topic, as well."

"I appreciate it."

"Of course. Now, about the wolves this afternoon…" He let the comment hang. He was letting me decide how much I would tell him, how much further I would pull him into my problems. After a lifetime of holding others at bay, it was hard to open up.

"She has my scar." I needed someone to know.

"Your scar?" His voice had softened, but I could read the

confusion in his expression. My body was covered in scars. Which one?

I pulled up my sleeve, just far enough for him to see the infinity symbol above my wrist.

He took my hand gently in his, his thumb tracing over the scar. "Exactly like this?"

I nodded. "Hers was in the same place. I saw it as they were carrying her out." Reluctantly, I pulled my arm away. His touch was comforting, but baring my scars always left me feeling sick to my stomach.

"I think I know why there are so many wolves in the city all of a sudden. Randy said they found out I was alive and living here last week."

"Ah. One mystery solved."

"Marcus is dead," I said, stuffing my hands in my pockets.

"I'm sorry."

Shrugging, I glanced back at Clive to find him watching me. "It's not like I really knew him. It's just—I don't know—another link to family gone."

"Someone does seem to be trying very hard to isolate you."

I chuffed a derisive breath. "I do that just fine on my own. No help needed."

Clive sighed and then checked his watch once again. "I need to leave, but I wanted to make sure you stopped sending checks to the pack."

"If I owe—"

"You don't owe Marcus or the pack anything." He leaned back, his hands gripping the countertop on either side of himself. "I'm the one who paid for the bar. Your checks have been coming to me through Marcus." He took in my confusion and almost smiled. "What would you have said if I'd offered to loan you the money for your bar when we'd met?"

"I...I would have..." What would I have done? I'd have said no. I never would have indebted myself to a man I barely knew. I wouldn't have had the last seven years in my home. I should have been angry for being lied to, but there was no anger, only gratitude for my beautiful bookstore and bar, my sanctuary.

Clive continued to argue a case he'd already won. "You would have refused. You were still dealing with the death of your mother, the attack in the woods. Marcus couldn't be bothered to take you to a hospital or see to your wounds. He shipped you off to a new city to live with a woman you didn't know."

"He said I couldn't go to a normal hospital, that they'd do blood tests and know what had attacked me, know the kind of monster I'd become." I'd arrived at Helena's doorstep in the middle of the night, barely able to walk, blood seeping through hastily-wrapped bandages.

"Yes, they would have done a rape kit. We'd have had evidence of who had attacked you." Clive's jaw flexed in anger before he could shake it off. "You were dealing with enough. When Helena told me you were talking about wanting to stand on your own, to move out of her apartment and start your own business, I wanted to help. You seemed to trust Marcus. He was family, at any rate. If I told you it came from him, I was fairly certain you'd accept."

I nodded. I think I surprised both of us when I leaned in to kiss him on the cheek. He tilted his face, wary interest in his eyes. I don't know what possessed me. Perhaps the understanding that life was short, that Marcus was dead, and that Clive—as much as he tried to hide it—was a hero, not a villain. Maybe—mostly—it was because I was sick of being isolated. Whatever the reason, I changed my mind at the last minute and kissed him full on the mouth.

I had a fleeting thought to pull back, but I couldn't. After years of daydreaming about Clive and this perfect kiss, I couldn't break it. After a moment's hesitation, he crushed me in his arms. I clutched his shoulders, becoming lightheaded.

A gruff "sorry" from the doorway shattered the moment.

I stepped back, glancing at the swinging kitchen door, unable to believe I'd finally kissed him. No life-saving blood exchange involved. "Thank you, Clive."

Shaking his head, a grin pulling at his lips, he said, "Perhaps I should say the same." He studied me for a moment, as though he couldn't quite figure me out.

He reached out and brushed his fingers over my cheek, pushing a stray curl behind my ear. "Regardless of what you think or what Marcus may have said to you, you are not a monster. You are a survivor." He gave me another soft, quick kiss. "I really must be going. Please don't leave The Slaughtered Lamb tonight. Stay safe in your hobbit hole." He grinned, and I felt a weight lift.

After he left, I escaped to the solitude of my rooms, needing a moment. Once my blood cooled, I returned to the bar to refill drinks and take up residence on my favorite stool. Clive was gone. Just as well. I was embarrassed about the kiss. I took a sip of spicy orange tea, and watched the dark ocean, trying not to brood.

Dave came out of the kitchen, bringing me cookies. "Sorry I was a dick before."

Clearly uncomfortable with the apology, I put him out of his misery. "Demon," I reminded him.

Grimace covering his grin, he said, "Yeah. There's that."

When I heard stomping down the stairs, I flinched. Dave gave a low curse before an absolutely stunning woman stepped off the stairs and into the bar. She was dressed in a filmy black dress with Doc Martens. She had long black hair and porcelain-like skin with ice blue eyes, surrounded by a fringe of thick, dark lashes. Her cheeks were reddened, but that seemed to have more to do with anger than anything else.

My first banshee. This was pretty exciting. Banshees were Irish fae, female harbingers of death. It was said that if you heard the banshee wail, either you or a family member was already dead. I'd also heard that like some other fae, they could look into a man's heart and read his soul. Creepy, but so cool.

"Damn it, Maggie. What are you doing here?" Dave's shoulders were slumped. He knew what was coming and that he couldn't stop it.

"Ach, there you are, you cheating bastard!" Her eyes sparked with fury.

I looked around the room. Everyone was glued to the unfolding drama. I should have charged admission.

Dave started around the bar, putting his hands up, trying to stave off the inevitable. "Maggie, you know that's not true. I never cheated on you." He was using the voice one does with rabid dogs, all soft tones.

"Bollocks!" she spat out. "You didn't come home last night. Where were you, then? I'll tell you where you were; you spent the night here with *that one*." She pointed in my direction.

I glanced around to see who was behind me. No one. I moved to the far end of the bar, assessing escape routes.

The rest of the people in the bar gave a loud, "Oooooooo."

"You're not helping," I reprimanded our audience.

"Oh, we're not trying to," a tiny wicche informed me. Their avid faces were ping-ponging back and forth, eating up the drama. Customers who had been browsing in the bookstore wandered over and were watching from the doorway.

"What do you have to say for yourself, you harlot?" Maggie screeched at me.

Shit. Didn't banshees have bone-chilling wails that could break windows? I looked over all those eager faces at the glass behind them. "Um, I don't think those windows were guaranteed against banshees."

Glancing nervously over their shoulders at the tons of seawater that would crush and drown them if Maggie lost control, the bar patrons were decidedly less enthusiastic about the drama.

"Oh, now you care. Real nice." I pointed two fingers at my eyes before turning my hand back to each of them. "You're on my list, all of you. No snacks for any of the bar-brawl-encouraging lot of you!"

Maggie started to run toward me, her hands resembling outstretched claws. Apparently, I wasn't showing her the proper amount of attention. Dave darted forward, snatching her out of the air as she launched herself at me.

One of Dave's arms had her body pinned to his; the other held her arms down tight against her own body. She struggled to get free while Dave whispered soothing words in her ear.

The loathing in her glare caused me to take an involuntary step back.

"Maggie, nothing happened. I slept on the couch in the bookstore. Sam didn't even know I was here until she saw me this morning. I scared the hell out of her...Maggie, come on. Look at her."

Hey, was that necessary? I may not be pretty anymore, but he didn't have to be an asshole about it.

"Maggie, stop. I didn't have sex with her. *Look at her*."

Hepsiba jumped to my defense. "Now, that's uncalled for."

I was kind of unnerved by the whole scene, but I appreciated Hepsiba's support, assuming it wasn't a ploy to get off the no-snack list.

Maggie got a strange far-away look in her eye and stared right through me. I'd noticed some of the wicches and fae do this when introduced to someone new. I had no idea what she could see, what she was discovering about me, but I doubted it was good.

She went limp in Dave's arms, and he released his hold. Fury gone, her voice was soft, but in the silent bar, it carried. "She's an innocent." She turned to Dave. "Why did you not tell me?" Then she turned back around to stare at me again. "All these years...only pain." She smacked Dave in the arm. "Why did you let me attack the poor thing?"

I was horrified at what she must have seen, what she seemed to know about my past. I looked around the bar and saw many confused faces, but more than a few pitying ones, as well. I backed further away before they all realized what Maggie meant and I was suffocated by their pity.

I left, walking through the kitchen on my way to my apartment. It was times like these that I wished I didn't have wolf-sensitive hearing.

Maggie was crying, "I made it worse. Tell me how to fix it."

"Some things can't be fixed," Dave said.

TWELVE

Wherein Sam is Shot. On the Bright Side, Mermaids Are Real. So, There's That

When I locked up at two, I wandered through the bookstore and bar three times, checking behind every bookshelf and counter, in the bathrooms and storerooms... I couldn't turn it off, couldn't relax and go to bed. I wasn't being dramatic when I told Dave that nowhere was safe for me. How could I possibly rest knowing someone could use my own blood to walk through my wards to find me asleep and alone?

By the time I finally stopped moving, I was sitting on the counter behind the bar, my back against the etched glass. The bay glowed in the foggy moonlight. White foam caps sloshed into the window, the dark water swirling out and down. It was hypnotic and helped to settle my nerves.

Something dropped, splashing into the ocean outside the window. I sat forward, staring at the place where the water had been displaced. What was that? There was a flash of something shiny, and then it was gone.

I approached the window and crouched, trying to find discernable shapes in the dark water. Another big wave crashed into the window and a few seconds later, the body it was carrying slammed into it, as well. I fell on my butt, my breath catching. Long hair swirled in the tide before she was dragged under.

Acid rose in my throat as I watched another woman being treated like so much trash. I couldn't leave her out there, but I wasn't a strong enough swimmer to go get her, either. My near drowning a couple of nights ago had proven that. Her body hit the window again, and I could see the signs of her torture.

When her body hit the window a third time, I saw myself as I had looked afterward, my face swollen with purpling bruises, lips split, burst capillaries making my eyes bright red. I remembered lifting my shirt, seeing the extensive gashes and bites. And then dropping to my knees and vomiting.

I couldn't do it. I couldn't leave another woman, who had been through what I had, out there alone in the dark.

I located an old wetsuit I'd found in a secondhand store years ago. It was too thin for the cold bay waters, but it was better than nothing. Sitting on the edge of the ocean entrance, my legs dangling down in the water, I took deep breaths before sliding into the ocean. The instant cold shocked my system. I forced my muscles to flex and move before I sunk like a frozen stone.

Swimming in black water was disorienting. Without light cues, I didn't know which way was up and floundered a moment before I was able to right myself. I swam out from under the bar, looking for the body. Diving, I followed the rock line as far as I could before I felt like my lungs would burst. I broke the surface, desperate for breath, before diving again. She had been here a few minutes ago, the waves forcing her into the window over and over. Where had she gone?

As I came up again, a wave hit, driving me into the bar window. My head cracked against the glass. I was seeing stars and swallowing salt water. Sputtering, I tried not to drown on my rescue mission. I needed to get away from the window before the next wave came. I kicked off the glass and swam straight out, scanning underwater for the body. I saw shapes moving below me and at the edge of my vision.

The tide tossed me around and pulled me under. My muscles burned, trying to fight against a force of nature. I fought for the surface, gasping for air when something brushed the side of my body. I pivoted, terrified, and then the tide dragged me back under. I kicked as hard as I could, pushing toward the surface.

Gasping air, I tried not to choke as waves capsized over me. I felt a bite in my arm and heard an echoing crack. What—was I was shot? Diving down, I tried to stay out of sight, struggling not to drown. Blood billowed from the wound. Perfect. Sharks were not unheard of in this part of California.

I needed air. If I surfaced, I'd be shot. If I stayed down here, I'd drown or be eaten. Excellent. Great options. I was so glad I'd decided to leave my nice, warm, safe home so I could die rescuing a dead body. Way to think it through.

My chest burned. I needed air, but my body was being tossed like a rag doll. I heard a crack, and the water a few inches from my head splashed up. I dove down as fast as I could, trying to avoid the bullet's path.

A large shape came straight at me. It wasn't the woman's body. It moved with intention, swimming, not floating. I panicked and started to surface. Another bullet tore at my leg, as strong arms went around my waist, propelling me toward the cliff. I choked, inhaling seawater as I was dragged deeper.

And then I was pushed up into the air. I rolled over on to my stomach, coughing up water, desperate for breath. After a minute of blinding panic, I lifted my head and looked around. I was in the bar. Dragging myself away from the water entrance, I pulled my legs out of the water. When I looked back, I saw a woman nod before she flipped, and a tail shot out of sight. I may have been shot twice, but it wasn't every day you got rescued by a mermaid. It almost made it worth it. No, never mind. It didn't.

Sitting up and sliding against the wall, I tried to assess the severity of the wounds. Even with my accelerated healing, I had a three-inch gouge in my thigh. The first shot, though, was worse. My arm felt like fire and knives. I twisted it, trying to see if I had a matching hole on the opposite side. That small movement caused unbelievable pain, black dots obscuring my vision. No. I was *not* passing out.

My fingers twitched. Hopefully, that meant nothing was broken. I was losing a lot of blood, the puddle of seawater around me steadily turning crimson. The wounds needed to be treated, but I didn't know how without losing consciousness. I couldn't make it to the emergency room on my own. Where was Clive when I needed him? Stupid, non-telepathic vampire.

I jumped when something smacked up again the ocean entrance. The dead woman floated near the surface with a familiar seal holding her up. "Come in," I breathed.

Liam, a selkie and one of my regulars, pushed the body through. He stripped out of his sealskin and grabbed a robe to check on me. "Are you all right? Kimberly said you'd been hurt, that she'd had to drag you back here." He looked at my arm and leg, confused. "What kind of bite is that?"

Sniffing at the wound, he exploded, "You were shot? What the hell? Why would anyone shoot you? And why were you in the water in the first place?" I knew he was worried, so I ignored the fact that he was shouting at the victim.

"It was after closing. Everyone was gone and..." What was I saying? Shit, the puddle I was sitting in was more blood than water now. "I didn't know I'd have to deal with guns, too." White noise roared in my ears.

"We need to get you to a hospital. You're—"

I brushed a finger near the thigh wound. It hurt like a mofo, but the pain jarred me awake. "The shooter could still be up there."

Gritting my teeth, I pulled at the hole in my wetsuit, so I could see the extent of the damage. If I did end up passing out from blood loss, at least someone would be here to call for help. "Could you get me a bar towel? I need to stop the bleeding. Wrap it. I don't know, something."

He jumped up to get me what I needed.

While he scavenged behind the bar, I looked over at our latest victim. Wolf—I could smell that. Like Claire, she had been torn to hell before she'd been killed.

"Sam, this is no good. Don't you have a first aid kit with real bandages and antiseptic?"

"Check the kitchen, under the sink." At least, I think that's where I put it.

"We need to call someone. Maybe Doc Underfoot would make a house call?" Liam asked, as he raced back from the kitchen, sliding to my side.

"Don't know his number." Doc Underfoot was kind enough to come when I was trapped in the Kraken vision, but Clive was the one who had contacted him.

I heard another knock. I'd had so many frights tonight, I didn't even flinch. I looked back over to the water entrance but didn't see anything. Liam pointed up. I followed his motion and saw Clive looking down from the roof entrance. What was he doing up there?

"Come in," I said again.

He dropped and was walking toward me as soon as he hit the floor. "Every time I turn around, you're in trouble again." Shaking his head, he took in the scene, me, another dead body, Liam. He shrugged out of his topcoat, laid it on the bar, and returned to me, kneeling in bloody water, studying my wounds.

"You're going to ruin your pants."

He spared me one annoyed look and then asked, "Are you hurt anywhere I can't see?"

"My heart was broken by Charlie Connor in the seventh grade. He had a huge crush on my friend Sheila and never even knew I was alive."

"Lucky man." He turned to the side, considered the dead woman, and then focused on me again. And just like that, the pain faded.

"Better?" Clive asked.

Nodding, I said, "Yeah, thanks. It's kind of a low-grade, background numbness now." With the sharp pain dulled, I couldn't help but notice that an alarming amount of blood continued to run down my arm and leg. That couldn't be good. "Totally not happy about almost drowning twice in one week." I lost my train of thought for a moment, saw Liam, and then remembered. "Can you thank Kimberly for me?"

He nodded.

"I can't close wounds this size, but I can slow the bleeding, if you'll allow me."

I scrunched my eyes closed and turned my face away.

"I'll take that as a yes." His tongue swirled around the bullet hole in my arm. I could feel my face flushing. It wasn't like the manufactured lust Sitri had caged me with. This was honestly earned and completely embarrassing. When he moved away from my arm, I steeled myself. At least I thought I had, but as soon as his mouth touched my leg, my lady bits throbbed.

When I dared a look, I found Clive crouched in front of me, his eyes vampy black.

I glared. He smoldered.

"Twice?" he questioned.

"Twice what?"

"You almost drowned twice," he said, as he straightened.

"Oh. Right." Breathing deeply, I tried to shake off the Clive effect. "I went running the night we found the first woman. A wolf chased me down. I couldn't outrun him. He was about to take me down, so I did the only thing I could think of. I jumped off the cliff."

"You could have died from a fall like that," Liam said from across the room. Smart man, getting the hell away from the blood-licking vampire.

"Better that way than at the hands of a wolf," I mumbled.

Rage threatened Clive's composure. I followed his line of sight and then we were both staring at the infinity symbol cut into her wrist. My stomach roiled. Clive pulled out his cell phone and walked toward the other end of the bar.

A moment later he returned. "Dr. Underfoot will be here soon. He'll call when he's near. Can I let him in, or will your wards keep him out?" He paused. "I also have two of my people checking for your gunman. If he's still out there, we'll have him."

I projected my voice. "When Dr. Underfoot arrives, let him in." I looked at Clive. "That ought to do it."

He nodded and began to pace again. "I take it this was another victim dropped at your doorstep?" He stopped pacing in front of the woman, looking at the wounds.

I explained what had happened after the bar closed. Clive looked murderous as he listened. I was pretty upset, too, but I didn't understand why he seemed to be taking this so personally.

"Do you know her? Is she another wolf from your uncle's pack?" Clive asked.

"I've never seen her, but it's been years and I was only staying with him for a couple weeks. Less. There's a pack in the North Bay. She could be one of theirs."

Clive answered the discreet buzzing of his phone. He listened for a few minutes and then snapped it shut again. "We're clear above. They scented a wolf, possibly two. There's a faint scent trail underlying a stronger one. As there were two wolves here today, it's possible that the weaker trail is from then. It is also possible that one wolf dumped the body and left while the other stayed to wait for you, shooting when he saw you in the water."

Any way you looked at it, the wolf who was torturing women was trying very hard to get my attention.

THIRTEEN

Wherein Clive Freaks Out Shakespeare

"Don't leave the bar unless necessary. And then, only with a trusted escort. No wolves. I can have one of my men stay here at night—"

"Stop." I held up my good hand. "In case you hadn't noticed, I'm a wolf, not a vampire."

He stopped pacing to stare at me, surprised that I would question him. "Yes, I'm aware and quite grateful. Unfortunately, I'm the one who keeps being called to fix your messes. Why do you suppose that is?"

I shrugged and then winced. "Just lucky, I guess."

"My luck has taken a turn of late." His phone sounded, and he pulled it to his ear. "Yes, I'll meet you at the stairs." He replaced it in his pocket and strode up the staircase.

Liam, who had moved back to my side, leaned in whispering, "He's claimed you as one of his own. To hurt or threaten you is a direct challenge to him. That's why he's so pissed off. Someone doesn't respect Clive's threat. Vamps don't take offense well."

"What do you mean he's claimed me as his?" I started to sweat in my wetsuit. Did the magical community see me as Clive's property? As his to do with as he chose? The sudden loss of independence and control made me lightheaded.

"Relax, Sam. It's nothing bad. It means that he's named himself as your protector. We all know you don't have a pack. Clive didn't want anyone to see that as a signal that you were fair game. He wanted it known that anyone who threatened you, would be taking on him and his nocturne. Trust me, okay? It's a good thing."

We stopped talking when footsteps sounded on the stairs. I wasn't sure how to feel about this news. On the one hand, it was wonderful that I had a nocturne of vampires ready to do battle for me. On the other, what kind of payment was expected?

Clive returned with Dr. Underfoot in tow, a doctor's bag at his side.

"Miss Quinn, it's nice to see you again. Although, I'm sorry this is the reason." His eyes went to the dead woman before returning to me. "Is there a better place for me to work?"

I thought about it a second. "There's a couch in the bookstore. Would that work?"

"Yes, I think that would put you at a good height." He smiled kindly. At least I think he did. I couldn't see much of his face behind the beard. The skin around his eyes crinkled, though. "Can we lose the wetsuit?"

I tried to get up, but slipped, my legs too weak to stand. Clive was there, his hand out, but I pushed it away. I could freaking stand by myself. I didn't need his protection or his hand. I bit back a whimper as I got my good leg under me and stood. My injuries flared to life, before a wave of sweet pain relief flowed through me again.

My hands shook as I tried to unzip the wetsuit. I was only wearing bike shorts and a sports bra underneath. I paused, looking at the men around me. I didn't want anyone to see my scars, but I needed a doctor to treat my wounds.

"Shall I?" Clive stood nearby, ready to help.

Shaking my head, ignoring the whine rising in my throat, I grabbed the zipper with a shaking hand and dragged it down. Without the use of both arms, though, I couldn't get out of it.

Swallowing my pride, I nodded to Clive. He gently peeled the snug neoprene down my arms, over my hips, and down my legs, helping me to pull my feet out. The struggle started the gunshots bleeding anew.

Liam disappeared behind the bar and came back with a blanket. Once the wetsuit was off, their gazes were directed anywhere but on my body, on the thick, corded scars, bisected by thin traceries. Clive took the blanket from Liam and wrapped it around me before picking me up and carrying me into the bookstore. It was embarrassing to be carried like a baby, but also warm and comforting. Both wounds were on the same side of my body so at least once I had been placed on the couch, I could keep the blanket over most of my body and not move.

Dr. Underfoot examined the bullet holes while trying to distract me with conversation. "Do you surf or scuba dive?" he asked, no doubt referring to the wetsuit. His very hairy hands were gentle, and I relaxed by degrees.

"Neither, really. The fish scattered when I tried scuba. I guess even underwater I smell like a predator. And surfing wasn't for me. It was fun when I caught a good-sized wave, but it's a time suck and I have a business to run. Mostly, I prefer to watch the water from in here."

Dr. Underfoot gave me a couple of injections. "The thigh wound is the easier of the two. Let me get that one bandaged up so I can concentrate on your arm. I'll need to do more work there."

I looked everywhere but at my leg as he treated the wound. "Doctor, can I ask you about your name?"

"Of course. What would you like to know?" When he'd finished with the gouge in my leg, he pulled sharp, shiny things out of his bag. I stared at the blanket, pretending I hadn't seen them. He gave Liam a light to point at the wound in my arm.

"I'm not sure. Anything you're willing to tell me." I tried to gather my thoughts, avoiding the sight of him digging into my biceps with a long, pointy instrument that I was pretending didn't exist. "I wanted you to talk...but I'm also trying to wheedle a story out of you, I suppose. I'm surrounded by people who live for centuries or more, and they never want to talk about it."

He chuckled. "Yes, I suppose you're right. We aren't always the most forthcoming about our personal experiences. You must understand, though, for many of us, trying to reconcile who we were with who we are now can be..." He stopped to dig deeper into my arm. "Ah, there we go—sorry, what was I saying? Oh, yes, it can be a bit off-putting."

Clive made a quiet sound of assent.

Doc Underfoot continued. "Think of who you were and what plans you had when you were turned. You appear much the same, but are you the same person?"

Not even close. I thought of the teenager I'd been, always on the run, wondering if college might ever be possible. I'd never envisioned a life as a bookish bartender. I'm content with the life I lead, but it is worlds away from where I started.

"That was a few years ago, wasn't it? Consider the changes if it had been one hundred years ago, five hundred, one thousand. There is a certain malaise some of us old ones experience. The weight of so many years can crush. Please don't be too hard on us when, for sanity's sake, we try to live in the present." He paused to let me consider that. "Now, to your question—"

"Sorry," I interrupted. "Forget I asked. I'll sit quietly and try not to bug you." I'd only been a supernatural for seven years, a blink of an eye to these two men. Sometimes that knowledge smacked me in the face.

"No, no, I didn't intend to chastise you, only to explain the reticence you often encounter when you ask for our stories. Underfoot is a common dwarf name. Dwarfs used to live underground; some still do. So, Underfoot is a surname that indicates residence. It is similar to the human names Carpenter or Weaver, names that indicated the occupation of a man. That's all."

Oh, I guess that wasn't too personal. "Why did you decide to become a doctor?"

"The reason behind that is a bit more complicated. You see, the dwarfs used to be a very warlike, vicious people. Again, some still are. The patience and restraint required for medicine do not come naturally to us. When your people are given to waging bloody battles, there must be someone to deal with the carnage, one way or another. I have perpetrated many atrocities in my long years, but the last was enough to change me. And that, my child, is a story I will *not* tell," he said, his voice hollow.

Biting the inside of my lip, I stared out the moonlit window. When the silence began to stretch, Clive came to my rescue.

"I once met Shakespeare."

And at other times, their long lives and their infinite well of stories made me positively giddy. I silently begged to be told the story. He rolled his eyes and sat down on the arm of the sofa, near my feet.

"I was living in London during Elizabeth's reign. Before you ask, no, I never met her. I'm a vampire, not royalty. Theaters were good places to find a meal, lots of warm bodies, pressed close together, everyone's attention elsewhere. I was attending a performance of *Richard III*. Shakespeare hadn't been a playwright for long, so there wasn't a great deal of importance attached to the man or his name at the time.

"I'd intended to eat and run, but I was drawn in by his portrait of a physically and psychologically deformed man. I forgot why I was there, and instead was lost in the play. Shakespeare played Richard. Burbage must have been ill, a last-minute substitute needed."

He shrugged. "I have no idea why Shakespeare had taken to the stage that night, as he normally didn't perform the lead in his own works. I've seen the play performed many times since. The actors often use humpbacks, slings, wheelchairs, but none have ever conveyed the twisted body and soul with the brilliance that Shakespeare did, using only his voice and a subtle adjustment of his stance." Clive made a gesture, an echo of what he'd seen, before his hand dropped to my foot. He squeezed and continued his story, his thumb rubbing my instep.

"After the performance, I hunted and then caught up with the players at a nearby tavern. Most were spending their wages on women and drink, but Shakespeare was sitting in the back, in the shadows, watching. A few women approached him, offering themselves, but he declined and sent them away. I watched him watching the others. As I'm sure you are aware, I can make myself unnoticeable if I choose."

I nodded, pretending I'd known that.

"He studied the boisterous crowd. There was one man in particular, an overly large, loud, uproarious fellow that I noted some years later depicted in one of his plays. He became Falstaff."

If only I'd known Clive earlier in life, studying Shakespeare in school would have been a breeze. Of course, if I'd met Clive earlier, I probably would have been a snack. The thought didn't creep me out as much as it should have.

"I approached Shakespeare that night. His eyes took in every detail in seconds. I explained how compelling I found the characterization as well as his performance, how well I understood the dark soul he brought to life. After a lengthy pause, he leaned forward and asked me if I were one of the fair folk."

Clive smirked and shook his head. "Well, he knew I wasn't human, and was trying to puzzle me out. He gave the barest of shudders and then sat back. He may have guessed my true nature, though, for after he thanked me for my comments, he left. He had a strange look in his eye. I've often wondered if it was genius or fear."

I stared at him, absorbing every detail. "Wow, I should get shot more often," I couldn't believe that Clive had told me a story.

He pressed more firmly on my foot. "I'd prefer you didn't."

Yeah, I'd prefer that, too.

FOURTEEN

The Strange Case of the Wolf Puppet

Once Dr. Underfoot had me bandaged, he bid us good night. Liam departed soon afterward. Clive, however, didn't move from his seat on the couch arm. When I tried to stand, he was there, gently picking me up. The blanket slid, but I snatched it back, covering myself with my good arm. Clive held me a little away from his body, so my bandaged parts didn't get banged. When he'd carried me earlier, with Dr. Underfoot and Liam watching, I'd been embarrassed. Now, however, I felt something different.

My head settled back against his shoulder so I could watch him. I didn't know what to make of my vampire protector. He'd claimed me as his own and yet I seemed to annoy the holy bejeezus out of him. "Clive?"

"Hmm."

"Thank you." Watching the play of moonlight on his face, I experienced the strangest desire to reach up and touch his perfect face. I couldn't bring myself to do it. My heart beat faster at just the thought, though.

Clive glanced over, caught me staring, and adjusted his hold, pulling me closer. He strode across the bar, through the kitchen, and waited at the door to my apartment where I had more wards.

"Clive may enter," I said.

He carried me past the living room and into my bedroom. "You need to take a shower before bed, to warm up and wash off the seawater and blood."

"Do you ever stop bossing people around?"

"Rarely. If I could rely on others to make sound, rational decisions, I'd be freed of the burden. Unfortunately for me, people will insist on being idiots."

"Hey!"

He carried me into the bathroom and set me down, holding me steady until my legs worked properly. "Remind me, who was it that was wandering the city alone in the middle of the night after multiple attempts on her life? Who jumped in the ocean to retrieve a dead body?" He tapped his chin in mock contemplation. "Let. Me. Think."

He waited as I stood motionless in the bathroom, door open. "What now? Do you need help undressing?"

I snorted, pushing the door closed. Knowing I needed help, but unwilling to ask for it, I dropped the blanket and tried to figure out how to get out of bike shorts and a sports bra without bleeding all over the place. I knew Clive and the medication were keeping most of the pain away, but I still suffered sudden jolts when I moved the wrong way.

I was finally able to get my shorts and panties past my injury, letting them fall to the floor and stepping out. The sports bra was another story, though. I tried repeatedly and unsuccessfully to get it off, sweat breaking out with the effort and jabs of pain. Maybe I should just shower in it.

"Why haven't you turned on the water?" Clive's voice through the door startled me, yipping in pain when I flinched and pulled at my stitches.

"Getting undressed is proving more difficult than I thought."

He mumbled something I didn't catch. Louder he said, "I can

help."

"Hard pass."

"I won't look."

"Yeah, right," I said, staring at the scars reflected in the mirror. And what the hell happened to my hair? "You can't help me with your eyes closed."

"We're able to see a kind of infrared image of warm bodies, even with our eyes closed."

I thought about that for a minute. "Handy."

"It is, yes. May I come in?"

I looked at my reflection in the mirror over the sink. This damn bra wasn't coming off. I could use my scissors to cut it off, but I liked this one. Sighing, I mumbled, "I guess."

Clive opened the door and stepped in, his eyes closed. "Put your arms up."

I turned back to the sink and raised one arm above my head, the injured one halfway. He pulled the edges of the sports bra from my skin and gently eased it over my head.

"You can get cleaned up now," he said, as he dropped the bra on the floor. "Oh, and Sam?"

"Yeah?" I caught his reflection as he shut the door.

"No more late-night swims, yes?"

I WAS CLEAN AND MODERATELY AWAKE WHEN I OPENED AT NOON.

First down the stairs was Owen. "Hey, beautiful. Ask me how my evening went." The wiggling eyebrows and leering smile told me all I needed to know.

"Okay, who is he and will he be around long enough for me to meet him?"

"Yes, he will. He's sweet and smart and adorable. You'll love him." Owen was glowing even more than usual.

The tightness in my chest eased. Giddy, romantic love was a much better topic for reflection than gunshots and dead bodies.

"So, what does Mr. Wonderful do?"

"He's a veterinarian. I met him when I took my niece to the zoo a few weeks ago. He works with the large exotics." He winked at me. "I'm not going to tell you what he looks like. See if you can figure it out when he visits."

Normally, I'd be okay with this game, but not today. "Owen, I've had a rough couple of days. Could we do this without the mystery?"

He stopped smiling at my words. "Did something else happen?"

"Yeah. A few things. Another cut-up woman was dumped in the water outside the bar. When I went to fish her out, someone shot me."

Owen's eyes got big as he scanned my body looking for injuries. "Shot you? Why would anyone shoot you? Wait." He paused, shocked. "Does that mean these women are being dumped here *on purpose*?"

"I wish I knew." Although, I was afraid I did know. "I'm okay. A gouge in my thigh. A through-shot in my arm. Doc Underfoot was here to check me out and bandage me up."

"I'm sorry. Here I am, gushing about my beau, and I completely missed the limp. Sit down. Sit down. What can I do?" To know Owen is to love him.

"What do you know about wards?"

"Hmm?" Owen took my arm and led me to a chair. "Sit. Now, what about wards?"

"Mine don't seem to be stable. Mostly they work, but people I ward against—werewolves—walked in yesterday. I did some research, but I wanted the plain English opinion from someone I trust."

"I know wards are Helena's specialty. If yours aren't holding, I'm not even sure who could shore them up. I can ask my dad. He can build them well, but his magic isn't as nuanced as Helena's. What she did here is almost unheard of. She not only tied the wards to you, she taught them to respond to your thoughts.

It's—oh! I just realized. If Helena was your mom's friend, she would have known that your mom was a wicche, that you carry wicche blood. Maybe that's why your wards were so elastic and intuitive." Owen pulled out his phone and started texting. "Mom'll know."

"Listen, I know you were scheduled for the bookstore, but would you mind taking the bar? I'm not up to running around. I'd like to just sit behind the counter and read."

"No problem. Can I get you some tea to take with you?"

"Thanks, I'd love some tea. Whatever you recommend is fine with me." Wicches knew the restorative properties of herbals much better than I did. I deferred to their expertise.

As I was walking through the doorway to the bookstore, unfamiliar footsteps sounded on the stairs above. It wasn't as though I knew the sound of each of my customers, but these sounded strangely hesitant.

And then I smelled it. Wolf. A growl built in my chest. It was the wolf from the Marina who said he'd been looking for me.

"Finally found you." He nodded at Owen and then studied me. His bespectacled gaze intent. Holding out his hand, he said, "Ethan. I didn't get to introduce myself before."

I left his hand hanging. "You can turn around and leave now."

Owen stepped out from behind the bar and stood next to me.

Hand dropping to his side, he ducked his head. "I'm really sorry about before. When you're a lone wolf, new in town, you've got to project strength, maybe some homicidal urges, otherwise, you're seen as weak and attacked. I didn't stop to think I was talking to another lone. I shouldn't have come on like that. I'm sorry." He cleared his throat. "I wanted to talk to you about something. Is that okay?"

Ethan watched me through his dark-rimmed glasses. There was something different about him. Not just his smell, although he did smell like melting plastic or burned paper. It was something else. The glasses were new. Wait, why was he wearing glasses? Wolves had perfect eyesight. Was this an attempt to appear less aggressive? Whatever the reason, I decided I wasn't ready to kick him out yet. He knew something about those dead women. I could feel it.

"It's okay, Owen. You can finish restocking."

He moved away reluctantly as I led Ethan to a nearby table.

"Actually, would you mind if we talked in the bookstore? I'd love to look around." Ethan ducked through the doorway, scanning bookshelves as he made his way toward the window wall and the view of the bay.

"Okay." Following at a distance, I breathed deeply, trying to place that strange scent that seemed to ooze from his skin.

Head moving back and forth as he took in everything, Ethan dropped into a chair. "So, I've been looking for you for quite some time."

"Why?" I was almost positive I'd never met him before. Sitting in the chair opposite, I tried hard to remember everyone I'd met at my uncle's compound.

"I've missed you." His eyes scanned me avidly, from head to toe. "I haven't seen you since you were a baby. So much like your mother, but with your father's coloring."

Stupid. I knew that wolves could live centuries or more without aging but had forgotten. Stupid and potentially lethal.

"Your mother disappeared with you, and I've been looking ever since." He threw his hands out, gesturing all around. "And look where I finally find you. So strange, really. Nothing for the longest time and then—pop—you're back on the plane and easy to find. I never knew your mother was so gifted."

If I hadn't already met Ethan, I wouldn't have found his behavior strange. Since I had, I began to wonder if someone else was pulling his strings. His voice wasn't as deep. His mannerisms were, well, more feminine, I suppose. When I'd met him in the Marina, he'd sat with his knees spread, an arm thrown over the back of the bench. He'd taken up space. Now, his legs were crossed, and one hand seemed to play with an ear, almost as if he were absently toying with an earring. I wasn't sure who I was talking to, but I doubted it was the wolf in front of me.

"How did you know my mother?"

"Oh," he laughed. "We go back." The humor fell away as he studied me once more. "I'm not sure why she felt the need to hide you. You don't seem particularly special to me."

"Who are you?"

With a quick grin, he replied, "Ethan. Remember?"

"I meant who's hiding behind the Ethan mask?"

He tapped his chin, a sneer pulling at his lips. "Hmm, that *is* the question, isn't it?" Shrugging, he stood. "Well, I suppose I know what I need to know. She hid you out of sentimentality, not because you could ever rival me." Walking toward me, he added, "Best to take care of little problems before they become big ones, though, right?"

The deranged glint in his eye had me rising out of my chair and moving back. Shaking his head, he tutted, a finger wagging back and forth. Then he leaped, knocking me to the floor, slamming my head against the hardwood. Light exploded in my brain a moment before I felt his large hands wrap around my neck.

I pulled at his hands, my body bucking underneath him. He was too strong. Gasping for breath, I knew I was one twist away from a broken neck. I tried to punch him, but he was too tall. The angle was all wrong. My blows glanced off his shoulders. He was crushing my windpipe.

Flattening my hands like planks, I stabbed at his eyes. Roaring, he reared back. I sat up and slammed my forehead into his nose. The bone snapped and blood poured out. I scrambled, trying to get away, and then his huge hands were wrapped around my neck again. He lifted me up and pounded my head against the floor with enough force, I heard my skull crack. Vision going dark, I caught a glimpse over Ethan's shoulder. Owen, gripping a full bottle of whiskey by its neck, swung for the bleachers.

FIFTEEN

Ow

When I awoke, I was lying on the couch in the bookstore. Dave was right. It was freaking uncomfortable. Tentatively but with growing concern, my fingers skated over my neck. I was pretty sure the wolf's meaty fists hadn't actually squeezed my neck to the spine, but it hurt so freaking much, I wouldn't have been surprised.

"Sam? Are you awake?"

Squinting one eye, I tried to focus on the concerned face of Owen. Why was there so much hurt? "Thanks for..." *saving me.* Knives stabbed with every whispered word.

"Shit, Sam." The couch jostled as Owen fell to knees next to me. "Healing magic isn't my thing. I've been trying, but I don't think I've done much good." He rested his forehead on my shoulder. "I don't think I've ever been so scared in my life. Not even when Jenny Lim tried to kiss me in first grade," he said with a shudder.

"Underfoot?"

"I called. It took a while to track down his number and then he didn't answer, but I left a message. I also called my sister. Healing magic is her gift."

"Clive?" If anyone could get Underfoot here in a hurry, it was Clive.

"Ah, no. I didn't try him. I mean, the sun is still..." His voice trailed off at the end. "And, well, he's kind of terrifying."

I started to nod, but my neck and head screamed in pain, so I tried instead to lay as still as possible. "Clive." Scary? Maybe to some but never to me. "Please."

I opened an eye again and felt horrible for putting that pained look on Owen's face. Over his shoulder, I saw Ethan lying on the floor. He was facedown, the whiskey bottle lying near him, with his arms, legs, and mouth secured.

"Duct tape?"

Owen glanced over. "Well, it's not like we have ropes or chains around here. I found the duct tape in your toolbox under the sink. I used the whole roll."

"See that." Every word felt like stabby fire in my throat.

Shrugging, Owen added, "I don't know how strong those guys are. Unless he's like Wolverine and blades pop out of him, he should be secure." His eyes flicked back to the bound wolf. "Probably."

Even breathing hurt.

"Here's hoping, anyway." He grinned and stood. "Okay, I'm getting rid of this guy." He picked up Ethan's feet and dragged the bound body across the floor. "In answer to your unspoken question, yes, I could have rolled him over, but I wanted his face to get scraped up on the long drag."

Smiling didn't hurt. "Ocean?"

"What?" Owen stopped and stared out the window at the teaming water. "No! I'm not killing him. I'm dumping him in the storeroom for people on a higher pay scale to deal with." He paused, thinking. "How many bodies are in there now?" Shaking his head, he continued dragging the wolf. "I swear, it's getting all *Sweeney Todd* up in here." Owen pulled the dead weight around the bookshelves and out of the room.

It was long past noon, but the bar was empty. The silence

complete. Where was everyone? Then I felt it. I'd chalked up the pressure in my head to having it slammed repeatedly against the floor, but that only accounted for most of it. Some of the pressure came from patrons being stopped as they tried to enter. I hadn't opened the wards for business. And yet a wolf walked right in. If it was the wolves who stole my blood in order to bypass my wards, were they the ones working with a demon? Ethan did reek of burning things. I needed answers.

"Open," I whispered, and people began tromping down the stairs.

"What the hell, Sam?" Pause. "Sam?"

"Where is she?"

"Owen?"

"Shit. Somebody call Clive."

Owen must have returned from the storeroom then. His low, reassuring voice calmed the patrons before he started getting drinks, all while avoiding the 'Where's Sam' questions.

I struggled up, not wanting anyone to find me like this. Once vertical, my head pounded like a drum being beaten by a deranged chimp on crack. Eyes closed against the bright light battering my brain, balance iffy, I swayed to the side and ended up clutching a shelf for support. Using it as a guide, I made my way to the back of the bookstore, to the panel with the hidden latch. Twisting an ornamental wolf's head carved into a decorative bookcase frame, I heard a click. The shelves swung out, revealing an entry to my apartment. Securing the door behind me, I stumbled to my bed and fell into blessed darkness.

I awoke to cool fingers brushing lightly against my throat. My apartment was warded against everyone but myself, so I should have been more panicked, but I recognized the scent and touch. Clive. I'd told my wards to let him enter the previous day and then forgot to revoke the access. Mostly forgot.

"You do insist on courting danger, don't you?" His deep British accent was comforting in the dark.

"Not my fault." Stabby but not *as* stabby as before. Swift werewolf healing at work.

"No, it never is." His fingers left my neck, but then glided across my forehead. "You have a concussion, a rather severe one. Owen's sister Lilah says your skull was cracked. Her magic and your own healing have repaired that. I spoke with Underfoot. He's out of town but is familiar with Lilah's magic. He says that she is the better choice for healing this type of injury than he is."

"'Kay" *Ow*. I knew it shouldn't, as this was silent, brooding Clive, but having him here allowed the fear forever knotted inside to relax, just a little. Clive may be annoyed more often than not by me, but I knew he'd protect me. I wasn't alone.

"Are you here to keep me awake?" I was shocked anew every time I heard the raspy croak that had become my voice.

"Hmm?" His voice came from my living room and then there was a scrape in the dark by the side of my bed. "No. You're healing. Staying awake with a concussion is just for humans. Feel free to go back to sleep." His voice had settled to my right.

"You're staying?"

"I've moved one of your chairs in and I'm quite comfortable for the moment. Since talking is difficult for you, I can wait to hear what happened. We have a strange wolf bound and struggling in your storeroom. I need to decide how long he lives, but that can wait until you're able to talk."

I didn't think I'd be able to sleep again, but there was something about Clive watching over me that allowed me to relax, secure in the knowledge that whatever came for me, Clive would battle it. Between one breath and the next, I dropped back under.

The scent of chocolate woke me. I reached out, only then realizing that my hand was being held. I had one brief moment to experience profound contentment before the hand slid away.

"Good. You're awake. I'm going to turn on a lamp in the other room, so we have some light. We'll see if your head can take it." A moment later the bedroom was bathed in dim, shadowy light.

"Okay?" He stood silhouetted in the doorway to the living room.

"Yes." And it was. My throat didn't hurt as much, either.

When I tried to sit up in bed, the movement set off fireworks of pain in my head. I had one horrifying moment when I feared I'd vomit in front of Clive, but then he was there, gently pulling me up to a seated position, tucking pillows behind my back. He froze, almost as if he, too, realized what he was doing. A second later, he was on the other side of the bed, sitting in my reading chair.

"Your alarm clock." He gestured to the mug on my nightstand. "I asked Dave to make you cocoa." A shadow of a smile touched his lips. "You should drink it before the whipped cream melts."

Cocoa and a hand to hold. Tears prickled. "Thank you."

Nodding, he asked, "Can you tell me now?"

I did. I explained the whole weird history with this wolf, the meeting in the Marina that was laced with menace, the glimpse I caught of him watching us outside the Tonga Room, and now this latest attack when he'd seemed to be little more than a puppet.

"And you're sure you don't recognize him? He wasn't one of your uncle's wolves?"

"I'm not sure of anything. I know I don't remember ever seeing him before a few days ago, but it's possible he just kept out of sight when I visited. I'd been there less than two weeks before I'd been attacked and sent away."

I reached for the mug. Before I had a chance to stretch my arm, the mug was in my hand and Clive was leaning back in his chair.

"Did anything unusual happen when you visited the Santa Cruz Mountains' pack that would have caused a member to stew and plot for seven years?" Clive's voice was low, nudging my conscience to remember a long-buried incident. It was a little like changing Siri's voice. My conscience now had a deep British accent. I liked it much better.

"I don't think so. I don't remember anything out of the ordinary before..."

"Before the attack?"

"No. I mean, yes, I remember things like hiking, playing poker, taking pictures, a campfire. I don't think I'm missing memories from that week."

Clive leaned forward, his elbows on his knees. "That's an odd way to phrase it."

"Coco thinks I've had memories stolen."

Clive stilled at my words, waiting for me to elaborate.

"When I said my necklace was all I had of my mother, she wondered why. In trying to explain, I realized I didn't remember how she'd died. I had the memory and then I didn't—that's what scares me. Someone poked around in my head, looking for the memories they wanted, and then stole them."

"It's a different kind of rape, isn't it?"

"Yes." Relief at being understood swamped me. "That's it exactly. Someone invaded my mind, searched for my mother, and plucked her out." Emotion tightened my throat as I blinked back tears. "She's been erased."

Clive's hand wrapped around mine again. "Let's see what we can do about finding her."

AFTER ANOTHER VISIT FROM OWEN'S SISTER LILAH, I WAS FEELING well enough to work. I checked my watch. Owen would be off soon. Dave could work the bar, while I sat behind the counter in the bookstore.

Once the schedule had been worked out with everyone, I was settling in when the phone rang. "Slaughtered Lamb Bookstore and Bar, this is Sam."

"Hi. Could I speak with Owen, please?"

I didn't recognize the voice. Pain and suspicion had been weighing me down all day. I was shaking them off right now. "It depends. Is this Mr. Wonderful?"

He laughed in a way that let me know he enjoyed that Owen had talked about him. "Well, that would depend on who you asked."

"Okay, is this Mr. Dreamy Veterinarian?"

"Hmm, I don't think I can wriggle out of that one. I doubt Owen knows any other vets."

"Good. The reason I haven't passed the call on yet is that I need some information. Owen said you might be stopping by soon, and I'd like to mess with him. Could you tell me your name and what you look like or what you're wearing so I can pretend that I already know you?"

He laughed. "Sure. I'm George. Mom says I look like a taller version of my sister Coco. Black, dark hair, lighter eyes. I'll be wearing my green, V-neck sweater over a white t-shirt with jeans. Does that help?"

"Perfect. Play along when you get here, okay? Listen, I've been talking with you too long to pretend we haven't been plotting. Would you mind hanging up, waiting a few minutes and calling back? Then either Owen will answer, or I'll forward right away, and he'll never know we've spoken."

"Sure thing. I'm looking forward to meeting you in person."

Ten minutes later the phone rang again. I ignored it and let Owen answer. We needed normalcy and teasing. We needed something other than threat and dread and dead bodies.

Later, when I heard Owen's voice warm in greeting, I stood slowly, not wanting to lose my balance and go down. Pleasantly surprised at feeling mostly fine, it was time for a long-overdue prank retaliation.

I looked around the bar and spotted a gorgeous guy in a green sweater that matched his light eyes sitting at a table close to the bar. Owen was mixing a drink, his gaze on Mr. Large Exotics. Perfect.

I walked in, leaned against the bar closest to the bookstore and pretended not to notice his beau. "Hey, Owen, aren't you off now?"

"Almost. Good timing. I just brewed you some tea." He placed the mug in front of me and tilted his head toward my apartment. "Go lie down. I can stay."

"Thanks, but I don't want to wreck your—" I pretended to spot George, glared at him, and spat, "You!"

He looked from Owen to me, swallowing nervously.

"Did you think you could just waltz back in here? Is that it? You've been 86'd! That status doesn't change."

George stood, holding up his arms in surrender. "I just thought maybe enough time had passed. Maybe you'd forgiven me."

"Forgiven? There's no coming back from, 'Hey, baby. You look like a hooker I knew in Fresno.'"

He goggled, his face reddening. "Um."

"'I only have a twenty,' you said. 'Do you have change?'"

I glanced over my shoulder at Owen, and saw his eyes bugging. I smiled and winked at him before turning back to George and offering my hand in introduction. "I'm Sam."

He laughed, pulling me into a hug. "A ten-dollar hooker, really? Did I have to be a sleaze in this scenario?"

"You didn't have to be, but it made it more fun for me." I didn't even mind the hug, which was odd. Owen's fella smelled nice. Familiar. Yep, this was Coco's brother, all right. I wondered if I could get him to shift for me.

Owen came around the bar and snapped the wet bar towel at my backside. I yipped and jumped, my leg starting to throb in earnest. He gave me a one-armed side hug that was tighter than necessary, saying, "That was not nice." But he had a big smile on his face, so I knew he wasn't too upset.

I whispered, "Dragon? Nice!"

He nodded smugly, releasing me in order to grab George's hand.

"How's Coco doing? No more break-ins, right?"

"No," George said. "She told me. I'm so sorry about what happened. Don't give up hope, though. Coco is seriously pissed that it was stolen right out of her shop." He shrugged. "I don't know what she's working on, but she's trying to make up for your loss."

"Please thank her for me but let her know I don't hold her responsible for any of it. It's my fault her store was vandalized, not hers."

Owen leaned closer, his voice low. "Are you sure you don't want me to stay? George can keep me company while I work, and you can rest." Owen turned to George. "Do you mind?"

Shaking his head, George said, "Not in the least."

"Nope. I'm much better since your sister visited. You two have fun. Oh, and George, it was lovely meeting you. Thanks for playing along. Owen lives to torment me, and I rarely get a chance to pay him back."

George kissed me on the cheek. "It was my pleasure." Then he and Owen walked out, hand in hand. Young love. It gave me hope.

The phone rang, and I limped behind the bar. "Slaughtered Lamb. This is Sam."

"I've been speaking with your wolf." Screaming in the background drowned out Clive's voice for a moment. "Quiet." Silence echoed. "I think it would be best if you came here so you can hear this for yourself."

"Where's here?"

"My home. I'll send a car to pick you up."

Apparently, the quiet portion of my evening was over.

SIXTEEN

How the Posh Vampires Roll

When I made it up the stairs and to the Land's End parking area, a car was already waiting. Clive's dark-suited driver stood by the open back door. "Ms. Quinn." His head tilted toward the car in invitation.

I slid onto the soft leather seats as the door closed. The man got behind the wheel and the engine purred to life. As he drove down the deserted road, he glanced in the rearview mirror. Lights from the dash illuminated dark skin and darker eyes.

"Ms. Quinn, I am Russell. If there is anything you require, please let me know."

"I'm fine." The last time I was in this back seat, I'd been trying desperately not to freeze. Now, though, I was able to take it all in—buttery, black leather upholstery, wood-grained side panels, what may or may not be a mini-fridge. I would have checked if I weren't sure Russell was watching my every move, ensuring I didn't steal anything.

"So, where are we going?"

"The Master's home is in Pacific Heights."

Of course it was. Pacific Heights was an enclave within San Francisco of the ridiculously wealthy. Every mansion was worth multiple millions, often in the tens of millions.

Russell eventually slowed before an edifice that glowed like white marble in the moonlight. We stopped before ornate, wrought iron gates. A man waited at the entrance for Russell to lower his window. Once he'd verified who was driving, he opened the gates. A circular courtyard of dark slate paved the way to the residence. A portico jutted above the carved double doors, while delicate, night-blooming trees encircled the urban palace.

Homes in San Francisco didn't have large yards. Pacific Heights was no different. The homes, albeit spectacular, took up most of the property, leaving only small side and backyards.

Clive's estate, however, was an exception to that rule. It was a three-story architectural gem that reminded me of the Spreckles Mansion a few blocks away. Tall stone walls encircled a property that boasted rolling lawns, leading down to the next street. His home encompassed a city block in a town where every inch of real estate came at a sky-high price.

The eight-foot, double doors were opened by what appeared to be a real-life butler. He nodded to Russell, before stiffening at me.

"Master is downstairs with the prisoner."

Russell thanked him and then led the way. The entry was marble, white with veins of black and gray, showcasing a large, round table with a massive floral arrangement. Sweeping up on either side were curved stairways to the second and then third floors. I knew Russell was moving quickly, but I was transfixed by the ceiling. A dome of stained glass rose forty feet above the marble floors. Lights must have been trained on it from the roof because the glass glowed in spite of the night sky.

I didn't want to fall too far behind, but my head swiveled this way and that, trying to see everything. Clive's home was extraordinary. Russell skirted around the large, round table and disappeared through a doorway, hidden by the flowers. When I stepped through a moment later, I found myself trailing him through a hall that led deep within the property, albeit by a circuitous route. It ended at a rounded doorway that opened on stone steps leading down. There were wall sconces that insufficiently lit the darkened passage. I could barely make out the glow of Russell's white shirt collar in the torchlight as I descended.

The dark stairs opened on a sitting room, the décor mirroring the opulence above ground. I wasn't expecting Persian rugs and Degas paintings in a basement. I guess this was how the posh vampires rolled.

I followed Russell down an adjoining hallway, passing closed doors before stopping at the final room. He opened the door. The room was empty of furniture but for a metal folding chair holding Ethan, bound by ropes, as Clive and two of his vampires ranged around him. All four turned at the sound of the door. I didn't scamper away, but it was close.

I recognized one of the vampires. He'd come into the bar once with Clive. I'd never seen the other. She was a woman, blonde, petite, and lethal-looking who seemed somehow familiar. The vampires remained stony-faced. It was only Ethan who appeared both desperate and contrite, his body language screaming submission.

"Sam," Clive said. "This is William and Leticia," He said, gesturing to the vampires. "Please join us. Ethan has been telling us some very interesting things."

Ethan made a gagging sound.

"Or, I should say, his inability to answer certain questions has been quite enlightening."

Ethan struggled with the ropes, his face sweaty and pained. "That wasn't me. I could see myself doing it, hear the words coming out of my mouth, but it wasn't me. You need to let me go before—" Choking sounds took the place of words.

"I've been trying to lead him through the tale, switching tack every time he begins to choke. He appears to have been forbidden from sharing information. It's fascinating." Clive motioned me closer. "What we've been able to glean so far is that he was sent to look for you. He says he doesn't know why. Given the pattern of his gagging, I don't believe him."

"An Alpha can do that to a pack member, forbid him from saying something," I offered. "At least, I've heard that's how it works."

Clive nodded. "The magic of wolf packs is unusual." He gestured toward Ethan. "Would you touch him, please? I'm testing a theory."

I didn't want to appear nervous in front of Clive's vamps, so I strode up to Ethan and placed my hand on his cheek. The change was instantaneous. He snarled and snapped. If my reflexes weren't as fast as his, I'd be missing fingers. Muscles bunching, he struggled violently against his bindings, a low, angry growl reverberating in the cold, stone room.

"Whatever is controlling him is still there, lurking, waiting for the opportunity to act." He touched my elbow, wanting me further away from the werewolf. "That's why I wanted you here. I needed to see how he'd react to his target. With us, he was contrite and confused, unable to explain beyond assuring us he didn't know what happened. I knew he was lying. I did not, however, know if *he knew* he was lying. Is he under orders or being possessed? The answer to that leads us in different directions."

"If he's possessed, isn't someone listening to us, through him, right now?" Please, don't let it be the demons. I did *not* want to wrangle with them again.

"Whoever is in there has been watching and listening for a while. I could kill the vessel, but that won't help us discover who's lurking behind his eyes. We'll give it some time. A starving wolf should be easier to break."

And this was why it was good to have Clive on your side. Instead of simply killing an enemy, he was trying to track the sorcerer through the connection that had been forged with Ethan. Very tricksy, this one.

He studied Ethan a moment and then said, "William, I'm

afraid you must continue on guard duty. Leticia, you may resume your usual duties."

Clive led me out of the room, where we found Russell leaning against a wall, waiting. On seeing Clive, Russell stood straight and bowed his head, murmuring a "Master." Russell followed us down the hall and up the stone steps to the main floor. Clive turned in the opposite direction of the front doors.

We ended up in a two-story library that put the Beast's to shame. I stopped walking, just stopped. I couldn't get past the sheer number of books. His library had to be four times the size of my bookstore. I wanted nothing so much as the time and freedom to climb the ladders and scan the shelves.

Clive turned. Taking in my expression, he shook his head, a grin tugging at the corner of his mouth. "Russell, I need to update you. Sam, you can explore but first I need to properly introduce you two."

"Oh, we've met." I glanced at the man who stood beside Clive. "He drove me here."

"Yes, I know." Clive moved to his dark, mahogany desk. "What I mean is that I'd like you two to become better acquainted. Sam, Russell is my second."

Russell flinched at the words.

"Russell is uncomfortable that I have informed someone outside the nocturne of his status. He prefers others believe him to be a kind of servant, because they never see him coming."

Russell cleared his throat.

"This is important, my friend." Clive turned back to me. "If you are in trouble, if you need me, but can't find me, seek out Russell. Most vampires wouldn't bother to throw water on a burning wolf, unless they were discomfited by the heat. Russell is unlike the others. I trust him to protect you, as I trust him with my life."

Russell bowed. "Liege."

"Good. Sam, you're welcome to join us, but if you'd prefer…" He inclined his head toward the shelves.

"The books are calling. I must make friends."

Clive grinned. "That's what I assumed."

I tried not to run, but I made haste to the shelves. He had everything here. And, oh, little brass tags screwed into the wood shelves gave browsers the subject headings. The first case I came to contained books on world religions, the next mythology and folktales. Some books were old and crumbling, others new and crisp. My head was spinning as my fingers brushed over spines. I heard the low murmur of voices across the room, but I didn't care. I was surrounded by every kind of book. The sheer volume of thought and imagination contained within this room was humbling.

I climbed a ladder to Brontë and pulled down a first edition *Jane Eyre*. I held the book like a fragile baby bird. Looking around, hoping against hope he'd have one, I spied a window seat. It even had curtains, pulled back with a sash. I strode past Clive and Russell, who were discussing a party of vampires visiting the city, and climbed into the window seat, releasing the curtains. The bench was the size of a twin bed, with cushions and pillows. The heavy drapes cut the men's voices to a lower rumble.

The view from the window was breathtaking. A large fountain dominated the portion of the patio I could see. Trees and flowering shrubs were dotted throughout the garden that stretched to the bottom of the property. Clive's estate was at the top of a hill, though, which meant I saw far beyond the walls to the rest of the city, lights sparkling in the dark, fog rolling across the bay, the bridge dwarfed in the distance.

There was a sconce on the wall opposite me. I looked above my head, and sure enough, there was another. Feeling around, I found a cleverly hidden button that turned it on. The window seat was bathed in warm light. I fluffed the pillow and got comfortable before turning the first page.

Ever since I was young and read *Jane Eyre* for the first time,

I'd wanted a window seat of my own, one like Jane's, a place to read and hide, far from the real world.

Jane had just arrived at Lowood when the drapes were pulled back and Clive sat down. My legs were curled to the side. When I started to straighten, Clive patted my knee, letting me know I was fine. He left his hand there, as he glanced around.

"So, you like it, then?"

"Like?" I put my finger in the book to save my place. "This is the most perfect room ever created. In fact, I was wondering if we could bring the builders back to create a tunnel from The Slaughtered Lamb to this window seat. I promise not to make noises and bother anyone. The other vampires won't even know I'm here. Just lock up the room at night—no, day—and I'll content myself to wander and read."

"Good." He squeezed my knee, before moving his hand. "Now, since I wouldn't want to ruin this space for you, we should probably move. I need to share with you what Russell has learned."

"Oh." That didn't sound good. I glanced around for something I could use as a bookmark.

Clive plucked the book from my hands and placed it open to my page, face down on the seat.

"No! It's a first edition. You'll weaken the binding."

"Then I guess you'll need to return soon to continue reading, won't you?"

SEVENTEEN

How Many Enemies Could One Book Nerd Have?

The drive home was less exciting, given the topic of discussion.

"You've been living a quiet life in the city for seven years. Now, it doesn't seem as though a day goes by without someone trying to kill you." Clive studied me. "It's not only the wolves. They can't trap you in visions. I'm not sure how many directions the attacks are coming from. What prompted all of this?"

Shrugging, I gave the only answer I had, "The necklace? I lost my mother's protection and all hell broke loose." I stuffed my hands in my hoodie pocket.

"Russell, turn up the heat, please."

I sat up from a slouch. "I'm okay. Just feeling like I have a huge neon sign pointing at me. 'Unprotected Idiot Ready to be Slaughtered: Apply Within.'"

"One thing you are not is unprotected," Clive said.

"Mr. Clive has been keeping an eye on you since you moved to San Francisco, Ms. Quinn."

Russell caught the squinty-eyed look I directed toward Clive and laughed. "Not like that. Mr. Clive is—" Russell sought Clive's okay in the rearview mirror before he continued.

"Please, Russell, drop the Mister. I feel like a primary school teacher when you call me that."

I snorted a laugh. "I was thinking the same thing!"

Clive rolled his eyes, settling back more comfortably to talk with me. "Russell was being respectful, albeit awkwardly. A lack of respect is tantamount to an open declaration of war among vampires. Russell, it is far less important with wolves. When Sam is with us, you may speak to me as you do when we are alone."

Russell's eyes shot to Clive's in the mirror. "I see."

"After speaking with you, I asked Russell to do some investigating of your past and lineage. On your birth records, your mother is listed as Bridget Corey Quinn."

"Yes." At least I remembered that.

"Your father is listed as Michael Quinn, brother of Marcus Quinn, son of Alexander Quinn, the original Alpha of the Santa Cruz Mountains' pack."

"Wait. Are we related to the Quinn in that story I researched about the first werewolf?" Why had my mother never told me?

Clive nodded. "Probable. The Quinn line of wolves goes back to the beginning. They came to the New World in the 1700s, when local farmers had had enough and began to hunt and kill everyone in the line. As far back as we've searched, they have all been born male wolves. We believe you're the first female, which may be due to having a wicche for a mother."

"Is that confirmed? She was definitely a wicche?" I hadn't had a chance to visit Ule again to research wicches.

"Yes," Russell said. "I've spoken with a number of sources and they all confirm that your mother was a Corey wicche."

"But why do you think I'm a born wolf? They're extraordinarily rare, and I'd never shown any symptoms until after the attack." None of this made sense.

"There are precious few female wolves, period. If we're talking born female wolves, you may be unique." Clive pulled the nearest fist from my hoodie and held it, his fingers gently tracing my hand until I unclenched. "From what we've read, most females don't survive the turning. There's much conjecture as to why, but even experts don't agree. The fact is, even though your turning was a sadist's fantasy, you survived. And aged."

Yes. I'd read that werewolves didn't age after their turning and yet I clearly had. I hadn't known what to make of it, and the books I'd found on the topic hadn't helped. I could have called my uncle to ask, but I'd barely known him. I'd been attacked while under his protection and then sent away to survive or not on my own. Sending him money every month was the extent of our relationship. Unfortunately, that meant I knew far too little about what I was.

"If you'd been turned at seventeen," Clive continued. "You should still appear that age. You've continued to mature. My understanding is that born wolves age until they hit their prime, and then physically remain there until death."

Russell pulled up to my stairs and turned off the engine.

"You've worn your mother's protective amulet since you were a child. The purpose may have been more than to keep you hidden. It may also have been to mute your inherited traits. That attack seven years ago seemed to have brought the werewolf strain to the fore. Now that the necklace is gone, it will be interesting to see if you manifest magic from your mother, as well."

I GOT VERY LITTLE SLEEP. I KEPT DREAMING ABOUT DARK PASSAGES and vicious werewolves who lurked around every corner. It was one of those horrible dreams where I did nothing but run from one menace after another. I awoke sweaty, the sheets twisted around my legs.

After showering and opening the wards, I left a message for Ule to see when I could get back in his archive. In the meantime, I pulled books on wicchecraft from my bookstore shelves, looking for any references to the Corey wicches.

When the sun went down, the phone rang. "Slaughtered Lamb, this is Sam."

"Ms. Quinn, this is Russell. Clive asked me to call you. Members of the Bodega Bay pack have asked for permission to visit the city. The Alpha should be with them. Clive thought you might like to speak with them."

"They're coming tonight?"

"Yes. Admittedly, the timing seems suspect, but it is not an unusual request. I checked our records. They were last in the city six weeks ago. We've directed them toward a vampire-run night club south of Market. You will be protected."

"He's right. I do want to talk with them. We don't know who the second woman we retrieved from the ocean is. She might be a member of their pack." I wanted her body returned to people who knew her.

"The Alpha has been in charge for a long time," Russell said. "He may have information for you, things we couldn't find in legal documents, about your father."

"Good point." I looked out the window at the pink afterglow of the setting sun reflecting off the water. "Hey, aren't you guys supposed to still be napping right now?"

"Clive will be by at ten this evening to pick you up."

"Gotcha. Still wondering about you being awake, though."

"There is much you don't know about us, Ms. Quinn." *Click.*

Aside from a drunken pixie who regularly broke out in song—preferring show tunes from the 1950s—the evening was thankfully uneventful. I was working up the nerve but waited until Owen was almost off before I pulled him into the kitchen where Dave was making shrimp pad thai.

"Out!" Dave bellowed.

"We'll be quiet and stay out of your way," I whispered, as I pulled Owen toward the door to my apartment. "I need your help."

He waited.

"Clive," I pointed vaguely toward the bar, not sure why.

"We're supposed to go to some South-of-Market nightclub tonight to interview wolves from the Bodega Bay Pack."

He nodded, "Okay, and..."

I spread my hands out, indicating my clothes. "I don't exactly own nightclub wear."

Dave snorted.

Owen moved, blocking Dave from my view. "I see. Use Owen for his unparalleled fashion sense but refuse to give him any sexy vamp details. Is that the kind of one-sided friendship we have, Sam?"

"What sexy vamp details? I have none of those."

"You've been spending a lot of time with Clive lately. The grapevine is all aflutter." He grabbed a cookie from the cooling rack and bit in. "All I'm saying is that if and when there are sexy vamp details to share, I expect to be informed."

He was right. I'd kept myself separate and alone for so long, the change so gradual, that I'd missed it. Owen was my friend. Actually, the more I thought of it, Dave was, too. Look at me! Two friends.

I smiled, "When he kissed me my brain turned off. Quite literally, I was kissed stupid."

"I knew it! I've heard rumors about their prowess between the sheets." He waved a hand. "C'est la vie, I have George, who is smoking hot, by the way. Don't let that mild-mannered, farm boy vibe fool you. Okay, let's find you some clothes."

"Wait. Let me check." I jogged across the kitchen floor and ducked out the door to the bar. "Anybody need anything?" At the murmurs of no, I led Owen into my apartment.

He wandered through the living room, checking things out. "Nice."

I'd never invited him in before. I hadn't invited anyone, actually. Except for Clive, that is. It was weird but nice, sharing a little of myself with him.

He flung open the door of my closet, turned to me, then back to the closet. "Is this a joke?"

"What?"

"Why do you have stacks of boxes labeled books in your closet? Where are your clothes?"

I pointed to a chest of drawers against the opposite wall.

"All of your clothes are kept in four drawers?"

I counted off on my fingers. "Socks and underwear, jeans and t-shirts—they take two drawers—sweaters and sweats. Done."

He looked me up and down. "I thought these were just the crap clothes you wore for work. I didn't realize these were *all* you had."

I shrugged, embarrassed.

He gave me a quick hug. "Sorry. Shock and too-little sleep have messed with my filters. This is totally fixable." He stared into space for a minute. "I have an idea." He took off for the apartment door again. "Make sure I can get back in!" He shouted as he left.

"Let Owen enter." I opened a drawer and stared at all my silly t-shirts. I was in trouble.

When I heard a strange noise, I wandered back to the living room. Owen's hand tentatively poked through the open doorway and waved around, before he stepped through.

"Thanks. I was afraid to just walk through in case the ward threw me across the kitchen." He had a scarf in his hand and a little flowered bag.

"I don't think that bag is going to fit me."

"Haha, ye of little faith." He clapped his hands. "Let's do this. First, go get cleaned up." He shoved me towards the bathroom while he went straight for my clothes drawers. He called over his shoulder, pulling out pairs of jeans, "Use that body wash I got you for your birthday. You'll smell so good no one will notice what you're wearing."

When I got out of the shower, he had clothes laid out for me on the bed and some makeup on the dresser. "Where the heck did you find makeup?"

Owen grinned. "You may not wear makeup, but many

women do. I just borrowed a few items from your patrons. They were happy to pitch in."

My shoulders slumped. Great, now they all knew I was a pathetic fixer-upper.

Owen gave me a sympathetic smile. "It's nothing like whatever you're thinking. I discretely asked a few women for some assistance. They were excited to help and promised not to say a word." I was still looking pouty, so Owen patted the top of my head. "They love you, Sam, and they want to help in any way you'll let them. Smile. Say thank you. Let them feel good. Okay?"

I was being a baby. "All right, so what am I wearing?"

"Well, let's face it. Your wardrobe is atrocious, even for a ten-year-old boy. I found a fabulously grungy pair of jeans. They aren't party wear, but it's not like I had much to work with."

I looked at the jeans. "No, those are too small and have holes in the knees. I just keep them to clean in."

"You seem to be confused on the topic of fit. The jeans you normally wear are at least two sizes too big. These," he held up my old battered pair, "will fit you perfectly and I've added a few more strategically placed holes." He turned them around and showed me that he'd broken through the threadbare seat, so I now had two ventilation holes right below my butt.

"That's obscene!"

"No, that's sexy." He gave me an exasperated look. "Trust me, Sam. You'll look hot, and they'll be lining up to dance with you."

I looked at the top on the bed. "Where did that come from? Did you borrow someone's shirt?" What the hell? Was he stripping my customers?

"No, silly. I bought you this top last year. Remember?"

I grimaced.

"Yeah, yeah, I know. You've never worn it. I found it at the bottom of your dresser. It will be perfect for tonight." He shoved the jeans and top, along with a thong into my arms and herded me back into the bathroom to dress.

"Where did the thong come from? And I need a bra." I was not wearing someone else's undies. I drew the line at borrowing unmentionables.

"Damn, you didn't even look through the box I gave you. The thong was under the top."

"I still need a bra."

"You don't need one with that top."

I wasn't exactly built, but I also wasn't one of those women who was sleek enough to go braless and not be uncomfortable.

"The top has built-in support. Trust me." He shoved me in the bathroom and closed the door. "Just put the clothes on, Sam."

I took off my robe and started dressing. The thong was creepy. I felt naked, but with a wedgie, which was wrong on so many levels. The jeans were now especially drafty with holes in the seat and no back to my panties. The top was black, long-sleeved, and skintight. Owen was right. There was a built-in support panel and wolves have perpetually perky boobs, but I thought it was obvious that I was braless. I looked at myself in the mirror, uncomfortable wearing such form-fitting clothing.

Owen knocked. "Come on, let's see." When I opened the door, Owen just stared. "Holy shit, you look hot." He grabbed the thin, colorful scarf off the bed and tied it around my waist, sarong style. He fiddled with the top, pulling it up, so there were a couple of inches of skin showing, meaning a few inches of scarring were on display.

I pulled the shirt back down and tucked it in. "No, no, no."

"If I had a stomach like yours, I'd go shirtless every day."

I gave him a look.

"Fine, be that way. Turn around so I can do your hair and makeup."

"How do you know how to do all this?"

"Sisters. Three of them. It was either learn or never get in the bathroom." He made my green eyes smoky, and my lips dark red. He blew my hair out straight and left it long. It had been many years since I'd done anything other than wash and ponytail it. It was now down to the small of my back. Luckily, I'd inherited my father's thick, wavy golden-brown hair, rather than my Mom's thin, black hair. Hey! I remembered something about my Mom. She used to complain about having thin hair when she brushed mine.

Five minutes later, Owen declared himself a genius and me ready to go. I pulled on my leather jacket and started for the door.

"Wait." Owen dropped a necklace over my head. It was a pendant of a howling wolf. Helena, the wicche who had taken me in when I first arrived in San Francisco, had given it to me years ago. It looked like silver but was white gold. "It's cheeky. You should wear it."

When I walked through the kitchen, Dave froze and then let out a long breath. "Fuck. Has Clive seen you?"

I looked down at myself, nervous. "Is it bad?"

He grinned and shook his head, "Ah, no." He went back to cooking. "Make sure those wolves keep their hands to themselves or they may lose them."

"Is what I'm wearing inappropriate?"

"For a south-of-Market club? Hell, no. I'm saying Clive's not above pulling off arms if someone gets grabby with you." He turned back to stirring the contents of his sauté pan. "Try not to start any species wars."

EIGHTEEN

At the Bottom of a Ravine, You Say?

Clive stood at the end of the bar, waiting. He showed no reaction to the new look, save for the raising of one eyebrow. He didn't appear displeased, so I hoped I passed for a normal human being who knew how to dress properly. Actually, that probably gave me more credit than I deserved.

We made it out of the bar with little fuss. Everyone was pretending not to stare at us. I felt self-conscious about the holes in the back of my jeans, so I tried to get Clive to go first. Stupid, ingrained politeness meant he insisted I go ahead. I'm sure he got an eyeful of my ass as we climbed the stairs. Thankfully, his good manners extended to staying silent about my overly drafty jeans. I hoped it was too dark to see anything.

A sleek, dark roadster was parked at the top of the stairs. I guess no driver tonight. The car chirped as we approached. Before I could touch the handle, Clive pulled the door open. I slid into a low, soft leather seat. It was the sports car he'd driven the night we'd visited the demon strip club. Clive got in, and the throaty engine growled to life.

"Have you learned anything from Ethan?"

Clive's hands fisted on the wheel. "Yes. I've learned there's something amiss in my nocturne." He sounded so angry I wasn't sure if I should ask, but I did anyway.

"Meaning?"

"Meaning I either have a traitor in my nocturne or a spell was able to make it past my protections." He glanced at me as he stopped at a light. "Ethan is dead. William stood guard outside the door. When I went back to deal with him after dropping you off, I found his body on the floor."

"A locked-door murder mystery. It doesn't sound too tricky, though. Have you considered William is your murderer?"

Clive shook his head as he turned the corner. "William. That never occurred to me."

I threw up my hands. "Fine. Who do you think it is?"

"If I knew, I'd be dealing with them right now." He made a sound of annoyance. "I questioned William. He is not able to lie to me. No one went in or out, but still the wolf is dead."

"Sounds like whoever was controlling him pulled the plug."

"Yes, it does."

I was sick of contemplating death. "Where to?"

"The Crypt. The wolves have just checked in."

Clive parked a block from a nightclub that had a line around the corner.

"Are you cold?" Clive held my door as I climbed out.

I shook my head.

"Good. Are you wearing the bracelet Coco gave you?"

Pulling up the sleeve of my jacket, I showed off the hammered copper cuff. "Never leave home without it."

Nodding, he led the way to the door of the nightclub. The bouncer moved the people waiting in line, so Clive and I could breeze past. Once in, Clive took an immediate right down a short hall ending in a door with a 'no admittance' sign. He knocked once. The door was opened immediately by a woman in black leather pants and a white silk collared shirt. It was the nightclub equivalent of the vampire uniform.

"Master." She gave Clive a quick bow, before moving out of our way.

"Eve. Are our guests still with us?" Clive moved to the wall of screens, each running the feed from a different in-house camera.

Eve pointed to the screen on the far right. "They're in the back booth, Sire. Just as you requested."

"Thank you. I know Hollis and his second Andre. Do we know anything about the others in his party?"

"We're investigating now, Sire."

Clive nodded. "Tell me when you know." He turned his attention to me. "You can leave your jacket in here, if you'd like."

"Sure." I unzipped and shrugged out of the leather bomber, handing it to Clive.

He hung it on a coat rack in the corner, and then led me out of the office and into the nightclub proper.

True to the club's name, the interior looked like a crypt. The walls appeared to be aged stone. There were booths along the outside of the room. Each booth was in its own crypt. The walls between the booths displayed row after row of bones and skulls, floor to ceiling, like the Capuchin Crypt in Italy. There were screens around the periphery with colorful images writhing in time with the music, like stained glass windows come to life. The center of the room was a teeming dance floor. The bar, to the right of the entrance, was crowded with black-clad patrons.

Dark, sensual music pounded through the sound system. Clive led the way through the crowd, before Russell stepped in front of us.

"Liege, Ms. Quinn, the Bodega Bay wolves are seated in the booth at the end of the room. If you will allow me, I'll make the introductions." He inclined his head in a show of respect to Clive and then led the way to the far corner of the nightclub.

I scented wolf as we got close. There were six of them lounging in the large booth in the back corner of the club. The last time I'd been around this many wolves, I'd been human—or at least I assumed I'd been—and unaware that werewolves were real. My skin was crawling.

"May I present Hollis Rawlins, Alpha of the Bodega Bay Pack and his second, Andre." Russell stepped back, so Clive could take over.

Shaking Hollis's hand, Clive said, "It's good to see you. This," he gestured to me, "is Samantha Quinn, a friend."

Two vampires appeared out of nowhere, each with ornate chairs in hand. They placed the chairs next to Clive and me.

"May we join you for a moment?"

"Your club," Hollis said, wariness in his eyes. He was big and imposing, even while seated. He looked like two hundred and fifty pounds of solid muscle. He had dark hair, light brown eyes, and a scar running down his darkly tanned face, from the side of his eye down his cheek and neck, disappearing under the collar of a black t-shirt. He sat in the back of the large booth, his presence commanding. Alpha.

"It is, yes. We were hoping you'd be able to share some information with us."

Hollis made a sound somewhere between a grumble and a sigh, which Clive seemed to take for assent.

"First, I should ask. Do you know Sam?"

Hollis's gaze traveled over me slowly before returning to Clive with a quick shake of his head.

"I didn't think so. Sam is our lone San Francisco wolf." Hollis's expression said he didn't much care. Clive continued, "She's the daughter of Michael Quinn, niece of Marcus, granddaughter of Alexander."

The eyes of every wolf at the table snapped to me. There were four men, all equally burly, and two women. The women, though, were interesting. One was wearing a tank top, arm muscles toned and flexed as she leaned in, ready to jump. The other woman was soft and bunnyish.

"I see that means something to you. Were you aware Michael had a daughter?"

Hollis shook his head, studying me, probably looking for signs to confirm or negate Clive's claims. "I never heard he had young."

"I found two women in the ocean in front of my bookstore, two female wolves who were tortured and killed. Their bodies were dumped. One woman was a member of the Santa Cruz Mountains Pack. I didn't recognize the other. I—we—wondered if one of your wolves had gone missing."

Hollis glanced at Clive and then back to me. "We lost Charla about a year ago. She washed up on the beach. They thought she'd been bashed against the rocks, but that didn't feel right to me. I believed then, and still believe, that she was killed." He took a gulp of beer. "I haven't heard about anyone missing now." He raised his eyebrows at Andre who gave a quick shake of his head. Andre did, however, pull out his phone and start texting.

"Do you have a suspect?" The Alpha seemed only mildly curious, but I knew if we gave him a name, someone would be dead by tomorrow. Which maybe wasn't such a bad thing.

Derailing that thought, I asked, "Did you notice anything out of the ordinary around the time Charla died? Or since?"

Hollis stared though me, deciding what to share. "Yeah. Someone's been doing black magic in our territory. We noticed…" Hollis's gaze swung back to Andre, who had put his phone away and was following our conversation closely. "Maybe six or eight months ago."

Andre nodded, confirming Hollis's guess.

"I didn't feel anything like that around Charla, but she'd been in the ocean a while." Shrugging, he added. "I don't have a wicche on retainer. Don't trust 'em." He glanced around the room and then focused on Clive. "That was actually part of the reason we came into the city tonight. I was hoping to talk to you. When we've gone running recently, we've found spelled areas. It's pack territory. No fucking wicches, black or white, should be using our land!" His fist slammed down on the table. In the noisy nightclub, no one noticed or cared.

"One of our young almost died last week. Do you—" He stopped, clearly uncomfortable having to ask for help, especially from a vampire. "Do you have anyone who can clean the spells out? It's pack land, has been for almost two hundred years." His gaze traveled between Clive and Russell. "I thought someone was working with a wicche to take me out, steal the pack...but no one's made a move against me."

"Had I been informed of any such plot against you or your pack, I would have contacted you." Clive's words settled the Alpha. The tension in his shoulders eased.

"Well, hell. If you and your people don't know anything about it, I'm not sure who would." Hollis downed the rest of his beer.

Watching the two other men Hollis brought with him was fascinating. They refused to look either Clive or Russell in the eye, but neither would they appear weak by *not* looking at them. Both seemed to have perfected the forehead stare.

"As for whether or not we can help with spelled pack lands..." Clive nodded to Russell. "We'll send out someone who may be able to track the spell to the source. At the least, they should be able to clear your land for you."

I turned sharply toward Clive. If he had people who could do that, why were we here? Why didn't he have that person track the spells against me? He didn't appear to acknowledged my unspoken rebuke, but his hand found my knee under the table. A quick pat to let me know we'd talk later.

"Appreciate it," Hollis said.

"If we might ask in return, you said you didn't know Michael Quinn had a child. Had you heard anything about Michael or his wife?" Clive sat back in his chair, relaxed, surveying the group of wolves. As we all had supernaturally sensitive hearing, our voices had remained low and unnoticed by the loud, dancing throng around us.

"I don't know much. Michael disappeared a long time ago—

twenty, twenty-five years ago. Marcus took over as the Santa Cruz Alpha when Alexander passed."

"Do you know what happened to either of them?"

Hollis shook his head. "Never heard for sure, just rumors."

I leaned forward. "What did you hear?"

He watched me for a minute and then seemed to decide. "Heard the son got married to someone daddy didn't like. Heard there was a big family blow up. Marcus backed Alexander and ended up with the pack after his father mysteriously fell to his death." Hollis's eyes found mine again. "I don't know if any of this is true. I heard his body was found at the bottom of a deep ravine. His neck snapped. He could have fallen and died. It's possible. Just really fucking unlikely."

"Was this before or after my father disappeared?"

Another shrug. "Can't be sure. It was all around the same time. Your grandpa found out your dad was married, they fought, your dad went missing, grandpa died, and your uncle took over the pack. All within maybe six months. I knew your dad a little. Liked him. Marcus, now, that's a different story."

"What do you mean?" Had my mother been right about Marcus all along?

"Only met Marcus once or twice. He was a weak sister. Your dad inherited all the power. He was the rightful heir to Alexander Quinn. I have no idea who Michael married or why she was so unfit. I assumed, though, after it all went down, that Marcus had bided his time, looking to collect the prize at the end. He never could have challenged either his father or his brother." He spun his empty beer bottle in his hand. "I wish I could give you more, but I just don't know."

I tapped the table near his hand. "Thank you for sharing what you know."

"What about the new Alpha, Randy. Have you heard anything about him?" Clive leaned to the side as Eve bent down to whisper in his ear. He nodded, as she placed a drink in front of him.

The female with the crazy eyes had snapped to attention when Clive mentioned Randy. Wasn't that interesting?

"That pack is a fucking mess. Marcus was too weak to lead. Wolves who should have been put down weren't. The pack's dominant wolves left in disgust, and Marcus just kept posturing like he had it all under control." Hollis waved down a passing waitress, holding up his empty beer bottle. "I told my people to steer clear of that pack."

I had a feeling at least one of his pack had ignored that order.

"I don't know anything about that Randy kid other than he's been with Marcus since he was young, younger than kids normally survive the turning. Maybe the kid's tough. Don't know. Marcus's son Mick was dead, so... Probably why Randy ended up as Alpha. The kid's like twenty." He shook his head. "Marcus must have driven off all the dominants who were left in the pack after Alexander died. Otherwise, I don't know how a kid like that could have taken over the pack." He glanced over at the dance floor. "So, we done with the questions?"

Clive and I exchanged a look and nodded.

Hollis grinned, pinning me with his eyes. "Wanna dance?"

NINETEEN

I Could Have Danced All Night

Hollis hopped on the bench, walked across the table, and dropped down next to me a second later. Springing up, I shoved the chair between us. Face impassive, his eyes glinted with suppressed humor. "Didn't mean to scare you." He offered me his hand. "Shall we?"

Reluctantly, I took his hand and let him lead me to the dance floor. I still hated being touched. Mostly. Okay, Clive holding my hand didn't bother me at all. In fact—not important. The point was, I could do this. Fearsome, not fearful.

The dark, atmospheric music had a driving bass that whipped up the horde. Bodies bounced and flung themselves around the dance floor. Hollis ignored the crowd around us, pulled me into a tight embrace, and then began to salsa. Mouth dry, I followed his lead, meeting him twist for turn.

How did I know how to dance? And there it was, a flash of memory. Mom teaching me to dance. A radio playing in a yellow kitchen. Laughter. Dancing was our exercise and our fun. Mom didn't like us to go out, so music and reading filled our days. I held the memory close as I danced with the Alpha.

He had me pulled in tight, before flinging me out and spinning me back. His hand rode low on my back while we swayed in rhythm to the music. The man had skills. When a guy almost barreled into me, Hollis growled deep and spun me out of the way, placing himself in the path. The hapless dancer bounced off Hollis's powerful back, ricocheting into a group that moved, letting him fall to the floor.

Pulling me in close again, he whispered in my ear, "I meant what I said. I liked Michael. I don't like talking with a leech listening in, but if you ever want to visit, call me. I'll give you safe passage through our territory."

"I appreciate that."

Grunting, he spun me out and then back. "Alexander hated wicches as much as I do. The only thing that would have set Alexander against his favorite son would have been a wicche." He shrugged. "My two cents."

Nodding, I wondered if all this pain, these deaths, could have been avoided if my grandfather had just accepted his son's wife.

Hollis paused, looking over my shoulder. Following his gaze, I found Clive, standing still, like a rock in a stream, as a hundred dark-clad dancers swayed and jerked around him.

"May I cut in?" Sometimes that deep British voice made me breathless. This was one of those times.

Hollis nodded before focusing his attention back on me. Grinning, he pulled my hand up to his mouth for a kiss. "It was brief but a pleasure. If you'd ever like to do it again, you know where to find me." He sauntered back to his table, the eyes of countless men and women following him.

"Shall we?" Clive held out his arms and I walked right in. He pulled me in close and we slow danced, ignoring the pounding throng around us.

Smiling at the ridiculousness of swaying to music only we could hear, I tucked my head into the crook of his neck. He always smelled so good, like linens warmed in the sun. I clung to one shoulder, my other hand resting on his chest, cradled in his hand. The arm around me flexed, pulling me in tighter. This was the Clive he seemed to keep well-hidden. The face he presented to the world was one of threat, power, and authority. Privately, though, he'd shown me great kindness, gentleness even. Had I not been targeted, had Clive not felt the responsibility to protect me, I'd have missed it, too. I'd have missed him entirely.

And then I heard it. He was humming, something lovely and slow. The music in his head shared a bass beat with the house music blasting through speakers, making the floor tremble. I could block it all out, though, and easily. Clive wove an enchanted circle around us, as we danced, out of time and place, alone, lost in the moment.

His thumb brushed back and forth, making lazy circles on my spine. The index finger of the hand holding mine moved almost imperceptibly, making me hyper-aware of every point of contact we shared. The music rumbled through his chest against my ear. It was as if the world had shrunk down to this small circle, ancient music filling my head as Clive moved his fingertips in time.

When the music changed, the humming was cut short with a soft sound of irritation. "The gnats in my ears won't leave me alone tonight. I suppose I should be happy they subsided long enough for one dance." Clive walked me through the dance floor, the crowd parting and then joining as we passed.

Russell, waiting off to the side, fell in step as we passed. "I apologize, Liege. They are restless, and I was unable to put them off."

"I don't owe them this. I refuse to sacrifice the possibility because of their bigotry," Clive spat. He stopped in the dark hall leading to the office before turning back to Russell. "Make sure Sam gets home safely. I'll deal with the outraged whisperers." Clive was seething. I'd never seen him this angry before and had no idea what had prompted it.

"They may never be able to understand and accept, Sire." Russell's voice had taken on the quiet apology of one not wishing to say what he must.

"My patience can only be stretched so far. I expect loyalty. If they can't give it—" Clive stalked down the hall and threw open the office door, slamming it behind him.

What was that about and who were the gnats?

"Ms. Quinn. If you could come with me, I'll drive you home now." Russell extended his arm toward the entrance. We'd only gone a few steps before Russell was stopped by another vampire. They spoke quietly for a few minutes. Russell appeared annoyed but listened to the vamp before sending him on his way.

I realized my jacket was still in the office, but there was no way in hell I was knocking on that door and asking for it, so I walked with Russell out the front of the club and into the cold San Francisco night. The line was just as long as it had been earlier. People, dressed for a sweaty club, not a cold night, stamped their feet to warm up.

"I'm sorry, Ms. Quinn. I know this isn't how Clive wished for the evening to end."

"It's okay." I needed to think anyway. Hollis's take on my grandfather and uncle had my head spinning as I considered every conversation with Marcus through this new lens, memory and interpretation realigning.

We were just crossing the street when I asked, "Russell, what was that back there? Why was Clive so—"

"Sam." We both turned to find Clive jogging toward us, my jacket in his hand.

When Clive tilted his head, Russell turned and walked back toward the club. "You forgot your coat," he said, as he held it open for me to slip on.

"You didn't have to deliver it." But I was glad he had.

"I don't want you to be cold." He spun me around so he could align the bottom and zip me in. "There." He grabbed my hand and led the way to his car. "I'm taking you home."

"But I thought—"

Clive opened the passenger door. Eyes still sparking with anger, he nevertheless gentled his voice and movements for me.

When he slid in and started the engine, I put my hand on his arm. Taut, he vibrated with rage. "I'm sorry. Whatever happened back there that made you so angry, I'm sorry it interrupted our dance."

Clive turned to me, his gray eyes glowing like fog in the moonlight. His expression softened, anger fading in the charged stillness. "Me, too."

His hand left the steering wheel and brushed lightly over my jaw. Fingertips holding me in place, he leaned forward, slowly, inexorably, giving me time to stop him. "So beautiful," he breathed.

I closed the distance. Clive's mouth melded to mine, as his fingers dove into my hair. Gentle, tentative, exploring kisses rained down on me. This couldn't be real. It was a lovely dream from which I would all too soon awake.

He nibbled along my jaw and then kissed a spot behind my ear that pulled a gasp out of me. I could feel him smile as he dragged his lips down my throat. Hot, open-mouthed kisses in the crook of my neck tickled and soothed, creating champagne bubbles in my blood.

"Clive?" I could barely hear my own voice over the hammering of my heart. This man, at once terrifying to the world and yet so gentle with me, was more than I thought I could ever have in this life.

He dropped kisses on my eyelids and cheekbones. "Hmm?" His hand slid around my waist, finding a strip of exposed skin to caress, sparks trailing from his fingertips.

"Could you…" Oh, my. His tongue skated over the shell of my ear before he nibbled at the lobe. Internal muscles clenched as he found a pulse point and sucked.

"Could I?" Twin needle points glided down my throat, and I lost my breath, lost my name. Internal tectonic plates converged, tremors overloading my system.

"Uh."

He leaned back, eyebrows raised, a soft smile playing on his lips as he waited. "Could I?"

"Kiss me again?" I knew my face was flaming, but he didn't laugh.

His mouth came down on mine with a ferocity and passion I hadn't expected. My whole body went up in flames. I wanted his hands on me. Everywhere. His tongue slid along my own, and my brain functions shorted out. Reaching, I gripped his arm, his biceps flexing as I pulled him closer. I never wanted this moment to end.

His hand slid up my thigh, clutching my hip, fingers finding the hole in the back of my jeans, as he deepened the kiss, a growl in his throat. It was perfect and endless and over too soon.

Something in the car buzzed in a relentless rhythm. Clive cursed and then pulled a phone from his pocket. He contemplated it for a moment and then squeezed. The tortured sounds of metal and circuits being crushed filled the car.

"Let's get out of here." He turned over the engine and took off. Something to the right caught his eye, and his expression darkened.

Exhaling slowly, I took advantage of the distraction to cool my blood. It was more than I'd ever dreamed. In private, unguarded moments, I'd fantasized about kissing Clive, something dark and yet chaste. He was gorgeous and thrilling and way out of my league. I'd never thought anything could happen. I mean, come on. A scarred book nerd in sagging clothes wasn't anyone's fantasy.

And I'd have been okay with that. I'd contented myself to a quiet life of books and booze, with the occasional vampire-fueled daydream, but now everything had changed. The safe, predictable life I thought I'd lead had been upended. I was terrified, and yet felt little sorrow over watching that old life fade away.

"I'm sorry, Sam. I have some business to take care of. If you hear I've wiped out the entire nocturne, it probably won't be true." Clive downshifted as he drove up a steep hill. He checked traffic in both directions, before gliding through the intersection and powering up the next hill.

"It's okay." It'd take a few hours for my breathing to return to normal anyway.

"It's really not. I apologize for stopping the way I did." He reached over and held my hand for a moment. "Some of my kind need to be beaten within an inch of true death."

"What's going on?"

"Too many people feel they have a say in how I live my life. I am Master, not— Sorry. I've wanted to kiss you for quite some time. I wanted it to be perfect."

"It was."

Grinning, he shook his head. "Before the cursing and phone crushing?" His gaze darted to me and then the road. "It was, wasn't it?"

"Clive, you said you have someone who could trace a spell for the wolves. Why aren't we using that person to trace the vision back to the source?"

"He tried. I was talking about Dave," he said, as he turned toward the Land's End parking area.

"My Dave? He can trace spells?"

"Dave can do many things. I'll send him out. If he has the same trouble with the pack lands that he does with you, they may be connected." He pulled to a stop at the top of the stairs leading down to The Slaughtered Lamb.

"I've been thinking about that. What if it's *all* connected? What if the women we found in the bay were being tortured to feed the demon working with the sorcerer who keeps trapping me in visions?" What I didn't understand, though, was why? I'm nobody, just a bookish bartender. Why would anyone put so much effort into killing me?

"We'll figure it out. Remember, no wandering off in the middle of the night. Lock your wards down tight. Don't go out into the bay, no matter what the lure. Call me if anyone or anything tries to hurt you."

"How? You just crushed your phone."

He paused for a moment, considering the crushed metal. "I'll have a replacement tonight." Leaning over, he kissed me soundly before opening my door. "Off you get. I've got vampires to discipline."

TWENTY

In Which Sam Learns the Fastest Way to Piss Off a Wicche

The following morning, Max, a crossword-challenged wicche, was sitting at a table in the bar and working on a new puzzle. He appeared to have cleared out the Philosophy section of the bookstore, looking for answers. Didn't that count as cheating? Horus, who I was told was *the* Horus, Egyptian sky god, was sitting near the bookstore, drinking a black and tan. Don't ask. I have no idea if he was the real Horus, or what he was doing in San Francisco. He kind of freaked me out, so I spoke with him as little as possible.

When Owen came in, I hit him up for information, considering myself polite for letting him stow his backpack before I jumped on him.

"What do you know about black wicches?" I asked.

"Huh?" He poured himself a soda, while he looked at me like I was a crazy person. He probably had a point.

"I spoke with the Alpha of the Bodega Bay Pack last night. He said they'd found spells in their territory. One of their young almost died. They think it's a black wicche. Clive is sending Dave to go check, maybe trace the spell." I dropped a cherry into his glass. "I wondered if maybe it was all connected, if whoever is spelling pack lands is also screwing with me."

"Really? I mean about a black wicche laying curses on pack land? And Dave tracking spells? Well, that's all mighty interesting." Brow furrowed, Owen stared out the window, lost in thought.

"They say so. The Alpha is anti-wicche, so maybe it's not them, but the threat seemed real enough."

"Us," he said.

"Us, what?"

"Wicches aren't 'them.' We're us. You're a part of us." Owen shook off the concern and lifted his glass in a salute.

"We don't know that yet for sure." Maybe my mother was a wicche. Probably she was. But that didn't mean that I was.

"Trust me, we know. I can feel your magic building. It's like a low hum in the air." He finished his drink and then started twisting the bottles, so their labels were all facing forward.

I didn't want to think about whether or not I was emitting a magical buzz, so I changed the subject. "Do you know any black wicches? Any you know and trust? I have some questions."

Owen stared at me, disgust playing across his features. "No. I do not associate with black wicches. And before you ask, I don't hang with sorcerers either."

I put up hands. "Sorry. Too ignorant to know that that was offensive."

He shrugged off my apology, but I could tell he was still annoyed with me.

"Owen, I'm sorry. I'm trying to figure out who wants me dead, who's dumping those poor women on my doorstep. Are they connected? It doesn't seem possible that they're not, and yet, what's the connection?"

"You."

Pretending I didn't hear that, I continued, "I was in no way intending to cast aspersions on your character." When he nodded a reluctant acceptance of my apology, I continued, "You said sorcerer like it was different from a wicche. I thought those terms were synonymous."

Owen looked around. "You better hope no one just heard you say that." When no one rushed the bar to punch me, Owen explained. "I'm a wicche. All the wicches who come here use white magic, earth magic. We do no harm in our casting.

"Black wicches use blood and death in their magic. Animal—even human—sacrifices are used to increase the power of their spells. It's done at a very high cost to their souls. Each time they do black magic, they sully their souls. That's why it's referred to as black magic; the practitioner's soul bears the mark of their work."

"You can see people's souls?"

"Their auras, yes. The aura's a manifestation of the soul. When you do evil, your soul becomes more sooty or black. We can see the evil surrounding black wicches. We stay away from them, and they stay away from us." Owen had switched to filling snack bowls and glancing around the room, uncomfortable with the topic.

I lowered my voice even more. "Can you see my aura?"

Owen smiled, the first since I brought up this topic. "Weres are almost impossible to read. We think the duality of your nature makes auras hard to perceive. Yours, however, is hard to miss. It's a bright, shiny gold." He gave me another grin. "It's also why so many wicches come here. One look and they know you can be trusted."

"Is it just a wicche thing or can everybody see auras?" That would be a cool trick and damned helpful.

"Wicches, some fae, not vampires or weres. Anyway, you never let me finish. Black wicches use blood and sacrifice in their craft. Sorcerers use demons." Owen must have noticed my confusion and continued to explain. "Sorcerers sell their souls for power and knowledge. A black wicche might slaughter a cow to power a spell. A sorcerer takes the farmer hostage, and calls up a demon to tear off the farmer's skin, one strip at a time. He uses the pain, terror, and blood to feed the demon who then helps the sorcerer do magic."

I was feeling sick to my stomach and wishing I hadn't asked. Clearing my throat, I said, "Okay, now I get why my question was offensive. Again, sorry. So, is that what happened to those women we found? You know, one strip of skin at a time. Were they being tortured to feed a demon and power a sorcerer?"

Owen looked a little sick himself.

"If I could find one, would a black wicche even talk to me?"

"Doubtful. They're secretive as hell. Maybe we can talk to Schuyler, though."

"Schuyler who owns the wicchey shop downtown?"

"Yeah. Most wicches come here now for grimoires, but we still go to her for spell ingredients. She sees just about all the wicches in the area so she might be able to help us. I'll call and check if she's working this evening. We can go when Dave gets here."

"Us? You'll go with me?" Thank goodness. I doubted she'd be willing to tell a werewolf anything.

Owen gave me an assessing look before smiling. "Yeah. You're benefiting from my being giddy in love. George makes me too happy to be annoyed by you for long."

"I'll take it!"

WHEN DAVE ARRIVED, I BROKE IT TO HIM THAT HE'D BE ON HIS OWN again tonight.

"How am I supposed to cook and serve drinks and sell books? This job was better before you decided to get a life." Dave shooed me out of his kitchen.

Trying to hold my own, I said, "Someone's trying to kill me!"

"At least you're not boring as fuck anymore." He gave me a shove that sent me sailing through the swinging kitchen doors. "And stay out," he muttered.

I ducked my head back through. "I mean it, Dave. You have

to come out here while Owen and I are gone. I'll be back as soon as I can."

"Go!" He roared.

Owen was leaning against the bar, smirking. "You really told him."

"Shaddup, you." I checked my pocket for cash, in case I found something cool at the wicchey shop.

"Come on. The bookstore's empty. I just refilled everyone's drinks, and Horus said he'd keep an eye on things when Dave is in the back." Owen grabbed his backpack and headed for the stairs.

"Uh, thanks, Horus." A chill ran down my spine, saying his name.

He looked up from his book, nodded imperiously, and went back to reading. Good enough.

On the drive downtown, Owen asked about the nightclub.

"We went to the Crypt. Apparently, the vampires own it."

"I didn't realize that, although it makes total sense. Who else would crave the ambiance of a skeleton-filled catacomb? Vampires, gawd. I don't know any other supernatural group that works so hard to stay on message. Just once, I'd like to see a sunny vampire named Petey who wears pastels and enjoys watching the *Great British Baking Show*."

Laughing, I tried picturing Clive in a pink shirt, sitting on my couch, and watching TV with me. It was remarkably easy. Maybe it was just thinking about Clive that was easy.

Owen battled through downtown traffic while I daydreamed. "Did you do any dancing?"

"Yeah. I danced with the Alpha and Clive."

"Reeeeally," Owen said, drawing out the word. "And how is Clive on the dance floor?"

"Good. Nice. It was—I liked it."

Owen turned to stare at me when he stopped at a light. "I see."

"No. I just—It was nice." *Stop talking now.*

Nodding slowly, he drove on. "Not touching that." He turned onto a one-way street. "George said he heard the vampires were all up in arms about something. Did everything seem okay last night?"

"There was definitely something going on. Clive cut our dance short and was pissed off, saying something about needing to discipline some of them."

"Hmm, I wonder if they're upset about him slumming with a werewolf."

Slumming? Oh. Was that it? I replayed the evening in my head. Clive had told Russel he wouldn't give something up because of bigotry, that gnats were buzzing in his ears. Was all that rage really about me? My stomach cramped.

Owen squeezed my knee. "I didn't mean that the way it sounded. The vampires look down on all of us. I can just imagine how some of them would react to Clive willingly touching a wolf." Owen snagged a street space a block down from the store.

He threw the car into park and turned to me. "I hear there's unrest among the vamps, so it may have absolutely nothing to do with you. I guess there are some high-ranking vamp and his entourage visiting right now. It could be a power play to wrestle San Francisco away from Clive, or it could be a visit to pay respects. From the little bit of vamp gossip I've heard over the years, Clive is scary powerful to other vamps, too."

I stared out the window, remembering. I used to think of Clive as scary, too. Then I spent time with him and realized I felt safer with him than with anyone else. I'd need to think about the reasons for that. Later.

Owen patted my leg. "You know, it may have nothing to do with you being a were. They could still be pissed off about him killing one of his own for you. Don't let it get to you, though. They're a snooty lot."

What? "Back up. What do you mean he's killed for me?"

"I thought everyone had heard the story." At my growl, he

continued. "Okay, don't get furry. I guess six or seven years ago you were attacked by a kelpie when the bar was being built."

"Yes, I'm aware. I was there."

"Right, so this vamp had been assigned bodyguard duty. I guess he resented being forced to watch a wolf, so he took off and wasn't there to protect you. The story goes, it was Clive himself who came tearing to the rescue. He later found the vamp —what was his name? It was something fancy and French— anyway, he tortured him to find out whether or not it had been done purposely to hurt you. I think if—Étienne?—had meant you harm, he'd still be hanging somewhere in pain. Since he hadn't, Clive killed him quickly."

Damn kelpie was nothing but trouble.

"Étienne's mate—no, wait. Vampires don't mate. Girlfriend? Lover? I don't know what term they use. Anyway, she went a little bonkers. I hear it was a close one as to whether or not Clive would have to kill her, too."

Vampires didn't mate? "Oh."

"Now let's see if we can find a black wicche."

TWENTY-ONE

Eye of Newt

The magic shop Owen brought me to was nothing like I was expecting. The walls were not dark purple with silver stars. There were no strings of beads serving as doors. There wasn't even any creepy music. It looked like a spa. It was clean and bright, with light walls and serene photos. It was a real letdown.

"Where's the bubbling cauldron, the eye of newt, the jars of dark scary things floating in liquid? You call this a magic shop?" I whispered to Owen.

He rolled his eyes and smirked. "No, I don't. A magic shop is where little boys buy trick cards and finger traps. This is a wicchecraft supply store. And the eye of newt is on the back shelf."

"Seriously? I am so getting some of that." I scampered off in search of other cool wicchey things. Ooh, wands. I totally needed one of those. I wondered where she kept—I'd only made it a few steps before I saw a display of grimoires, or spell books. I carried most of the ones here, but there were a couple that appeared ancient, with cracked leather covers and intricate metal bindings that locked the books closed. I reached for one and was repelled.

It was as though the book had its own force field, one that didn't want me to touch it. I reached out again and was pushed back almost immediately. "Owen, come look at this!" I whispered.

"Good evening. What can I do for you?"

I turned at the woman's voice. Like the shop, she defied the stereotype. Short ash blonde hair, pinched features, conservative clothes in neutral tones. She looked more like an accountant on casual Friday than a wicche.

"Schuyler, it's good to see you. Thanks for meeting us." He turned to me. "This is Sam."

Walking back, I smiled and shook her hand. Pain. Intense, unbelievable pain. Her handshake was like getting hit with a taser. Assuming there was something horribly incompatible with our magic, I tried to tug my hand free. She gripped my wrist with her other hand, a hard glint in her eye, her smile turning knife-sharp.

A growl vibrated in the back of my throat. No damn wicche was going to overpower a wolf. Yanking, I pulled her off-balance and sent her crashing into a display case, shattering glass and sending candles flying.

Eyes wide and swimming with unshed tears, she made a production out of getting up, reaching out for Owen's help.

"Sam! What are you doing?" He looked at me as though I'd turned rabid.

Cringing, she moved behind Owen, placing him between us, before she checked the shallow cuts on her palms. She looked to Owen, offering up her shaking hands.

Owen took them in his own, worrying over her injuries, mouth moving in silent spells. "Do you have a first aid kit? A couple of these cuts look deep and you know it's Lilah who has the gift of healing magic, not me."

Looking at me with shock and disappointment, Owen said, "You should wait outside. I need to take care of Schuyler, and she shouldn't be afraid in her own shop."

"Why are you petting her? She's the one who started it," I said, glaring at the wicche.

"She shook your hand, Sam. You're the one who threw her into the glass." He turned his back on me. "I need to stop the bleeding. Please leave."

"She tried to electrocute me!"

Owen's eyes darted to me and then back to Schuyler. His gaze turned strange and distant. Disbelief was etched in his features. He moved further away, eyes narrowing as he said, "What have you done, Schuyler?"

"Nothing. She's the crazy one who attacked. She's a werewolf. They're animals." Chin lifting in anticipation of his censure, she continued, "I think a better question, Owen, is why you'd side with her kind, rather than our own."

"Excuse me?" Owen was a step behind and seemed to be struggling to find an explanation that didn't cast either Schuyler or myself as the villain.

"What is so special about her?" Schuyler grabbed at Owen's arm, but he moved before she could latch on. "Wicches, demons, vampires, even the fae defend and protect her. Why? Because of her, good people have been lost. Why shouldn't she have to pay for that?"

"What the hell are you talking about? I haven't hurt anyone—"

"You have no idea the pain you've caused," she ground out.

And then I sensed it, just like at the Tonga Room, a barely-there scent lingering in the air. Wolf and vampire. And…demon? I'd never been here before, so I couldn't be sure, but an odd scent hung in the air. I was surrounded by a brew of candle fragrances battling for dominance, but what caused my pulse to jump was the sulfurous undertone. It was similar to the way Dave smelled after moving heavy boxes in the storage room.

Feeling we were in over our heads, I started to back toward the door, my shoulders tight, sweat forming on my brow. My wolf wanted to come out and deal with all possible threats. This close to the full moon, she was hard to rein in. The woman was unhinged, and she could do magic. We needed to get away from her before something very bad happened.

Owen, however, wasn't moving. "Since when do you do black magic, Schuyler? Your aura has black running all through it. Have you been working with a wolf, using the torture and death he inflicts in your magic? Is that where those black streaks are coming from?" Owen looked formidable, staring down the psycho wicche.

Schuyler blanched. "Of course not. How could you accuse me of such a thing?"

That didn't smell right. Was it a lie, an evasion? I didn't know if she was the one who was torturing women or the one who kept sending me horrible visions. Maybe neither, but she was dirty.

"Owen." The shop appeared empty except for us, but the lingering reminders that others had recently been here had me ready to go.

"Oh, yes, by all means. Run along home and tell your vampire and your demon. Who will die this time? Go home and cry so all your big protectors can tear the city apart looking for whatever scared you." Her voice dripped disdain.

"Listen, Glinda, I don't know what the munchkins have been telling you, but you don't know me. You have no idea what I have or haven't done, so back the fuck off! Owen, it's time to go now." I walked forward and grabbed his hand, pulling him towards the door. I would not let Owen get hurt because of me.

"Schuyler, you're being used. Look at her. There isn't a stain on her. She's never hurt anyone or encouraged anyone to hurt another. Think about what you've been doing. If you want to help us stop the murder of innocents, tell us what you know."

When Schuyler only glared, Owen reluctantly left with me. On the drive home he was so quiet, I was worried he was thinking about doing or saying something that would put him more firmly in the crosshairs.

He slammed his hand down on the steering wheel. "She knows something, Sam. She's involved in this. I can't believe it. How could she be involved in something so evil?"

I didn't know how to respond. Someone, maybe a few someones, had a hand in these deaths. At this point, I wasn't sure if the why of it was as important as stopping them.

OWEN DROPPED ME OFF IN THE LAND'S END PARKING LOT. "I'LL stop by my parent's house on the way home, talk to my Mom. She knows everyone and has an ear for gossip. If anyone knows what's going on with Schuyler, my Mom will find out." He grabbed my hand. "Hey, I'll ask about you, too. Maybe she knows something about your Mom or your family line, something."

I leaned over and kissed his cheek. "You're a good person, Owen. Thank you."

"Sam Quinn willingly kissing someone? The world has gone topsy-turvy." Shaking his head, he squeezed my hand. "Okay, go away. I've got to get my Scooby-Doo on, and Dave has probably scared all your customers away."

"True."

"I'll wait until I see you go down the stairs."

"Thanks, Mom!" I left Owen with a wave and a backward glance.

The night was cold and clear, the moon heavy in the sky, its reflection dancing on the water. Jogging down the stairs, I realized something was wrong, the night unnaturally still. No roar of the surf. No car engines revving. No dogs barking. No footsteps sounding, not even my own.

"Sssssaaaaammmmm," hissed a voice in the stillness.

Panicked, I scanned the bushes near the path, the murky

shadows at the base of the stairs. Face raised, I scented the air. Nothing. And yet I knew someone or something was watching me. I was close to home and wards that would hopefully keep me safe, if I could make it.

Before I'd taken more than a few steps, the ground swooped out from under me. Sliding, I was pitched into total darkness. I threw my arms out, scrabbling for something to hold on to, something to slow me down, but there was nothing. I screamed and yet the silence remained unbroken.

Tumbling around an unseen turn, I realized the darkness was taking form. My arms and legs were inky shadows silhouetted against the dark. Light. There had to be light source somewhere far ahead. Perhaps a way out. Whatever the reason, the tunnel I was racing through was gaining definition.

Throwing myself backward, I barely avoided an outcropping of rocks from taking my head off. Stomach turning inside out, I tried to think. I'd been falling too far for too long. It was impossible. If it was impossible, it was a spell.

A blast of heat from below took my breath. Sweat prickled my scalp as the light increased almost imperceptibly. I reached for my mother's necklace before I remembered. The cuff. Grabbing my wrist, I needed to dispel the vision, to grind the bracelet into my skin. I ripped up my sleeve. Nothing.

I hadn't taken it off, not even when—Schuyler. She'd grabbed my wrist when she sent an electrical current through me. She'd known I had it. Or one of those visitors I'd sensed in her shop had told her. It had all been a ploy to strip me of another layer of protection.

I was slowing. The light was growing, and the passage was beginning to level off. This vision wasn't as terrifying as the previous ones. Maybe Owen was right, and my natural powers were growing, my mental barriers getting stronger.

Sliding around another bend, the passage seemed to widen. Dull red light and another blast of heat hit me. And then I was plummeting through the air, into a deep cavern. Fires flickered in the oppressive dark as I dropped like a stone through the void.

Stalagmites rose from the rocky floor of the cavern. Certain death raced towards me, as I hoped against hope for a miracle. A shadowy figure emerged, watching as I dropped like a stone.

TWENTY-TWO

In Which All Hell Breaks Loose. Literally

I had no way to know if this is what it felt like to simultaneously break every single bone in my body, but I had a pretty good idea it was. Skull crushed, my head rested on the ground like a sack of wet cement mixed with shards of glass and gray matter. I wasn't sure if my body had exploded on contact. It felt as though it had. As my eyeballs were currently pressed against the back of my skull, I couldn't look.

Except…this wasn't real. It couldn't be. There had to be a glitch somewhere in the matrix. I needed to look for—Cacophonous sirens and drums battered my brain, making me weep. How? How could this much pain dwell in one body? There was something important I was just thinking about. What was I—

Wait. Oppressive heat, deep underground, shadowy figures, unending pain. How did I end up here? And was this really my eternity, splatted face down on the floor of a cave? Damn, whatever I'd done to deserve Hell, it must have been epic.

"Ms. Quinn?" Someone was tapping my eyeballs, via the back of my skull. I didn't know how to respond as I no longer had a working mouth. Or vocal cords and breath, for that matter.

"Why are you lying there? Get up, for evil's sake."

I tried to wiggle a finger. Shattered bones ground against one another, but the finger did wiggle. I tried with a foot. An avalanche of pain made me seize.

"Pathetic."

I was yanked off the floor and righted on broken legs. Swaying, I tried to remain standing and was mostly successful, though I did require the stalagmite I was leaning on to stabilize me. The darkness began to take shape, my vision returning. Everything was drenched in red, although that may have had more to do with the blood in my eyes than anything else.

Spine splintered, my head fell forward, chin resting on my chest. Two polished black shoes appeared within my limited view. "What do you want?" is what I intended to say. Unfortunately, the noises leaking through my crushed face sounded more like, "Mmuuhh."

"I want you to be more interesting than this. If I'd wanted a broken meat puppet, I'd have asked for one. Snap out of it." He slapped my face, causing my head to spin around backward.

"Now, you're just being grotesque. This is it. You're dead. Do you really want to spend your eternity flopping about like a carp?" He grabbed my hair and yanked my head around. "Now, listen. All this wet noodling about is ridiculous. That's your mind telling you how it thinks a broken body should behave. Look over there. That bloody heap of flesh is what remains of your mortal life. Now, stand up straight and speak properly. I have no desire to spend the next few millennia listening to garbled grunts and watching you slide down walls."

I couldn't tear my eyes from the carnage that was my life. It was really over. I'd never see my bookstore and bar again. Dave, Owen, Helena, Meg, Liam, all gone. Clive. Cool gray eyes and strong, safe arms. That elusive grin that felt like it was mine alone. And kisses. Kisses that made me forget every painful memory because there was no room for anything but Clive when his lips touched mine. It was all gone. But…he wasn't gone. He was waiting just on the other side of this vision. They all

—*BOOM!* A bomb detonated in my head, scattering my thoughts.

Heart shattering, I forced my gaze away from my own remains and turned back to my tormentor. Standing straight, cold numbness taking the place of pain, I realized I was talking to one of the demons who had been playing poker in that strip club. It was the male model with the golden-brown skin and the predator's eyes.

"I am Irdu. I'll be your orientation guide this evening." He threw out his arms, grandly taking in the whole fire-lit cavern. "Welcome to Hell."

"This is Hell?" God, how did I end up here? No. Seriously, God, I'm asking.

"Hell is vast. This is little more than a way station. We scoop up the souls and assign them to the circle of Hell they'll least enjoy." He winked. "We have a reputation to uphold."

Looking up, he pushed me to the side. "You're in the splash zone."

A strange whistling sound grew in intensity. Following the demon's gaze, I looked up and saw a man falling, heading right for where I was standing. I scrambled back ten feet right before the body hit. It was every bit as gruesome to watch as it had been to experience.

"The quiet ones have already accepted death. Come on. Lots to do."

He led me toward a tunnel cut into the side of the cavern. As I glanced around in the gloom, I noticed many similar tunnels, some larger, some smaller. Did they lead to different layers or circles of Hell?

"What did I do to deserve this place?"

"Hmm?" He looked over his shoulder at me and shrugged. "I'd have to check the paperwork and I don't actually care. Maybe because you're a werewolf. Aren't you guys soulless monsters? Like I said, though, don't care." He turned into a dark passage. Torches were scattered about the long tunnel, too few to light the way properly.

Soulless? Was I—it felt like I had a soul rattling around in there. Wait. Wasn't this my soul following the demon deeper into Hell? And why the frick was I doing that? Why had I accepted my death and damnation as though they were my due? This was not the time for quiet politeness. There were no perks for good behavior in Hell. At least, I didn't think so. He hadn't come to that part of the orientation yet.

Irdu was walking with his head down. When I glanced around his arm, I saw a phone in his hand. Huh. Phones apparently worked in Hell. Dave had mentioned that demons had ADD problems, never finishing one threat before wandering off to stir up other shit. Maybe, like Irdu, they were too busy tweeting to focus. Perhaps this was where the internet trolls lived.

I stopped walking to see if he'd notice. When he continued on without me, I began walking backward. If he turned around, I'd look as though I was still following him, while actually going in the opposite direction.

"Wrong way," he called, without breaking his stride. "Although, if you wander off, I won't have to finish this orientation. So, ta!"

He turned a corner ahead, and I was left standing in an endless, deserted tunnel. Confused, I assessed the situation. Shouldn't they be goose-stepping me to a demon with a whip fetish? Was the fact that I had been abandoned due to a short attention span or were they confident there was no way out, so I was free to wander until I stumbled into a random hellscape of my own choosing? Maybe the fact that I mattered so little, could be so easily forgotten, was part of my punishment.

But this wasn't real. This was a vision. I needed to find a way to fight my way ou—Screeching nails on a chalkboard tore through my head. The pressure behind my eyes was unbearable. *Oww.* Wasn't there someone with me a minute ago? Spinning in a circle, looking for a clue, I decided to walk in the direction of the way station. Maybe there was a way out of here.

When I passed a side tunnel on the right, I paused to look in. The smell that hit me was horrendous. I peeked my head around a pillar of rock and found a sea of people eating in a crazed frenzy. I watched the emaciated man closest to the entrance and realized he wasn't actually eating. He was trying to eat. Every time he opened his mouth to take a bite of the loaded burger in his hands, it disappeared and reappeared on his plate. Looking around, I realized it was true of everyone. The harried, unwashed people were different, the food varied, but the maddeningly frustrating inability to eat was the same. Hell, indeed.

Ducking out, I continued down the main passage, looking for the way back. I found the spot where it should have been but wasn't. I had an excellent sense of direction and spatial awareness. An entrance should have been carved into the rock on my left. I looked up and down the passage and saw no tunnels on the left side. There was no way back. Which explained why Irdu didn't give a shit if I wandered.

A murmur of shouts came from a tunnel on the right. As I got closer, I started to make out words. The question, 'How do *you* like it?' echoed over and over in the deafening din. Silently ghosting in, I saw men, mostly men, huddled on the ground while women with rage in their eyes used their shouts and overlarge fists to beat and berate the men whose impotent cries filled the cavern.

Stomach roiling, I backed out and found myself again in the main passage. At least I wasn't being trapped in these side caves. I needed to check each of them for a way out, but I worried that if I stumbled into a hell tailored to my sins, I might not escape.

I walked the passage for hours—maybe days—listening at cave entrances, becoming more and more depressed by all the ways in which we hurt ourselves and others. The more Hells I passed, the more a pattern began to form. Self-loathing. They hated themselves and that hatred was either directed inward in horribly self-destructive ways or it was directed outward in horrifically cruel ways. At the core, though, were people mired in pain and anger because they felt themselves worthless. They had been taught they were worthless by others afflicted with the same hopelessness.

Something dripped on my shirt. Glancing up at the dark rock above, I saw nothing. Belatedly, I realized it was coming from me. Face awash in tears, I shuffled down the endless passage to nowhere.

I'd wasted so much of my life hiding in fear. My mother had trained me early, moving from town to town, apartment to apartment. She was trying to protect me. I knew that. What I'd learned, though, was to disappear. Hide in my hobbit hole, hide in my books, hide from emotions that scared me. Look what happened when I'd reached out to my uncle. I'd been attacked and mutilated, and so I'd hid again.

And yet there had been wonderful people in my life, people who'd cared about me, even when I'd kept them at arm's length. Passing another cave entrance, the sound of sobbing trailing me, I wished I'd chosen differently. In life, I'd found some twisted comfort in isolation. And now here I was, cut off from the rest of the world, this endless, lonely passage my Hell.

Cold saltwater splashed against my legs and pooled at my feet. I spun, looking for the source and realized that the passage was thigh-deep in seawater. How had I missed the tunnel flooding? Where was it coming from? Gasping, as the water hit my waist, I looked for a side passage with higher ground. The side passages were all gone, the rock walls smooth and unbroken. Torches sputtered out as the water rose. *No! Damnit, this wasn't real!* Cymbals crashed in my head again. Alone in the dark, ears ringing, the freezing water hit my chin and splashed over my face.

A shout sounded nearby. I couldn't make out the words, but someone was with me in the black teeming water. Another wave capsized over me, knocking me off my feet. Disoriented, I couldn't determine up from down. Kicking and struggling, I was trapped beneath the water.

A strong arm wound around my body and yanked me into the air before slamming me against the ground. Around me, Hell was drowning, but I felt cut off from it, adrift. My eternal isolation was complete.

Blood filled my mouth. I blinked, and the stone passage receded, open air and moonlight taking its place. Clive leaned over me, concern etched on his beautiful face. Reaching up to touch his cheek, to brush my fingers over his perfect brow, I pulled him down, kissing him with all the hope and joy left in my battered heart.

TWENTY-THREE

"Merry Christmas, You Wonderful Old Building and Loan!"

Soaked and shivering, I had Clive's lips on mine. My stomach swooped as he picked me up and climbed the rocks with me snug in his arms. I was home! I'd been given another chance at my life. I felt like I should be running through Bedford Falls with George Bailey, wishing everyone a Merry Christmas.

We passed a couple of his vampires, who looked nauseated by their master kissing me. The old me would have struggled to be put down and then distanced myself as much as possible. Post-Hell Sam threw her arms around Clive's neck and kissed his cheek.

Studying me from the corner of his eye, as he made his way down the stairs to the bar, he muttered, "Holy Saint Francis, what a change is here."

"I totally had that, though. Just so you know. I was backing my ass out of that vision." I was so sick of relying on others to save me. I *had* to figure out how to tear through the visions on my own.

As we descended the final steps, Dave jogged around the bar to meet us. "Where did you find her?" Dripping water echoed in the deserted room. "And why are you both wet?"

"Is there still a blanket behind the bar?" Clive lowered me to my feet.

"Yeah." Dave retrieved the blanket and handed it to Clive, who shook it out and wrapped it around me. I sat at the closest table, Clive pulling up a chair to sit next to me. Dave dropped onto a barstool, waiting for answers.

"She was in the ocean, struggling against the tide, walking backward. It looked like she was trying to extricate herself, when I pulled her out." Clive rubbed my back as he spoke, as though needing to maintain contact.

"Another vision?" Dave asked.

Both men looked at me, and I nodded.

"What about that cuff thing the dragon gave you? I thought that was supposed to protect you." Dave was seriously pissed off. It was sweet.

Shoving my arm out from the warm cocoon of the blanket, I showed them my naked wrist. "Snatched. Schuyler, the woman who runs the wicchey shop downtown, has apparently gone to the dark side. She zapped me when I shook her hand. In the struggle to get her the heck off me, she snatched the cuff from my wrist. I didn't realize it was gone until I was already on my way to Hell."

"You went to Hell?" Dave asked. "In your vision?"

"I don't know. It felt real, but I suppose it wasn't." How would I know?

"What did it look like?" The intensity in Dave's voice made me wonder what he knew, or suspected.

"There was a huge, fire-lit cavern that he said—"

"Who said?" Dave leaned forward, his arms braced on his thighs.

"Irdu? I think that was his name." I turned to Clive. "He was the really good looking one who was playing poker at the demon strip club. Do you remember?"

Clive nodded, confusion and anger warring in his expression.

"He said it was the way station and that he was going to take me somewhere else."

"Describe the way station," Dave said.

"I just did. It was a massive cavern with stalagmites and corpses scattered about. My stairs," I gestured to the staircase, "they'd turned into a kind of slide. I sped down a chute for what seemed like forever and then I shot out and dropped a couple hundred feet, splatting on the rocky ground. Can I just say—if you get the chance—don't ever do that. It was more pain than one body should be able to live through. Which I was told I didn't.

"He said I was being pathetic, just lying there, that I was dead. I eventually did stand up and accept that I was gone. He led me through tunnels, but when I stopped following, he didn't care. Said he didn't want to give me the orientation anyway."

"The way station was a cavern lit by fire and you dropped into it?" Dave asked.

"Yeah."

He leaned back against the bar, lost in thought.

"What?" Clive asked, impatience clear.

"The way station she described, that *is* how it looks. Irdu *is* the name of a local demon. New top dog, actually, as Sitri's gone missing."

I turned to Clive, who met my gaze with grim satisfaction.

"Did he introduce himself at the Demon's Lair?" Dave was still talking, missing my reaction to the news that Sitri was no more, that Clive had gotten rid of him.

"No," Clive said. "We only spoke with Sitri. We saw the other demons sitting at a card table."

"Irdu is an incubus. He's been in San Francisco for a while now, but he still goes back to do the Welcome-to-Hell duty. It's a crap job, but everyone has to take a turn."

"Wait." My heart started racing, trying to push Sitri from my thoughts. "Are you saying I really died and went to Hell?"

Dave looked at me like I was nuts. "Of course not. You were in the ocean, not Hell."

"But for those details to be right," Clive said quietly. "The person trapping Sam in these visions knows who Irdu is and what Hell looks like."

Dave nodded, pointing at Clive. "Give the vampire a prize."

"So, it is a demon after me?" Pulling the blanket tight and tucking my hands under my arms, I tried to hide the tremors racking my body. I was just cold. That's all it was.

"Maybe, but it's more likely a sorcerer. Demons don't have the focus needed to put this much effort into a kill. A sorcerer, though, they'd use a demon's knowledge and power to juice up their spells. I could be wrong, but I think we're looking for a black wicche who's tipped over into sorcerer territory," Dave said.

"Which, as Sam guessed, is probably where the tortured wolves come in. What do we know about Schuyler?" Clive asked.

Dave shrugged.

"Owen said he was going to ask his Mom about her, said he's known her for a while and the black streaks in her aura were new." My teeth started to chatter.

"Dave, can you make Sam some cocoa?" Clive leaned closer, wrapping his arm around me.

"Thanks. I don't know if it means anything, but I think I smelled a vampire, a wolf, and possibly a demon in her shop. There were a ton of scents in there, so I could be wrong, but it was like the Tonga Room. The scents were faint, but lingering, like the people had been there earlier in the day. If my nose is right, I have no idea if they were all there at once, or in different combinations."

"You're sure you smelled a vampire?" Clive asked quietly. His voice was at odds with the anger tightening his jaw.

"It was faint, but I think so." I took the mug filled with hot chocolate and whipped cream from Dave. "You're the best." I took a sip and almost choked. It had to be half Bailey's. When I looked at him, he grinned and winked.

"I can stay here tonight," Dave said. "Keep an eye on things. I ain't sleeping on that bookstore couch, though. If you want a guard, I'm sleeping on your living room couch." He warmed my heart with his gruff offer.

"That won't be necessary. Sam is coming home with me. A nocturne of vampires should be able to deal with a sorcerer." He turned to me. "Your wards are not as strong as they once were. It's not safe for you here. Will you come?"

The old, pre-Hell me would have begged off, assuring everyone I'd be perfectly fine staying by myself in The Slaughtered Lamb. The new, post-Hell me didn't want to be alone right now. I nodded and took another gulp of spiked cocoa.

After throwing stuff in a backpack, I joined Clive in the bar. "Did Dave leave?"

"Yes. He's going to ask around—quietly—and see what he can find out. We know part of the equation now. If it's not Irdu himself, and Dave thinks that's unlikely, then it is someone he knows, has a relationship with."

"Is that safe?" I didn't want the demon community coming after Dave for informing on them.

Clive tipped his head, brushing off my worry. "Dave can take care of himself. Now," he said, looking me over. "I assumed you'd take a shower, change your clothes, and yet here you stand, damp and wrapped in a blanket. Why?"

"I knew you were waiting. I didn't want to hang you up. I'm sure you've got other important vampy things to do."

"You are the only thing on my to-do list, and don't use that word." His face was dead serious, but his eyes told another story.

"Important?" I asked, all innocence.

He raised one imperious eyebrow. "You know the one I'm referring to."

"Things?" God, he was so cute when he was riled up.

Ignoring that, he looked down at my backpack. "Is this your overnight case?"

I studied it, as Clive was. The more I looked at the threadbare, decade-old bag, the more embarrassed I felt. "It's the only one I've got. I figured a grocery bag was out." Maybe this was a bad idea. "Am I confirming vampire prejudice if I show up carrying a beat-to-shit backpack as my suitcase?"

He picked up my backpack and shouldered it. "I apologize for asking." Putting his arm around me, he led me to the stairs. "Let's get you home and in a hot shower."

"This is my home."

"Of course."

RUSSELL AND THE SWANK SEDAN WAITED FOR US AT THE TOP OF THE stairs. The other vampires appeared to have scarpered, thankfully. This time, the window between the front and back seats stayed down as Clive and Russell spoke. Most of it was vampire business I didn't much care about, but then Clive said something about his bedroom.

"Wait. Aren't I staying in a guest room?"

Russell's eyes snapped to me in the rearview mirror, before his focus returned the road. A moment later, the dividing glass rose, cutting Russell out of the conversation.

"You can, if you'd prefer. I'd rather you stay with me so I can make sure you're safe, but I certainly won't insist on it." Clive tapped the intercom button on his armrest. "Russell, can you see to it that the blue room adjacent to my own is prepared for Ms. Quinn?"

"Of course, Sire," Russell responded.

"The blue room?" I felt like I was in a Jane Austen novel. *She may practice the pianoforte in the blue room. She will be in no one's way there.*

He shrugged. "There are too many rooms. They need to be identified some way and that one has blue silk on the walls."

Russell pulled into the circular drive in front of the mansion. Misgivings set my head to throbbing. The vampires hated me. What was I doing, willingly walking into their home and spending the night? This was not going to end well.

Clive grabbed my bag, handing it to Russell. The front door opened as we approached. The same butler guy from before bowed with a 'Liege' as Clive passed.

Clive went straight to the stairs but paused on the second step. "Have you eaten? Are you hungry?"

"Uh." I actually kind of was, but I had no idea if vampires ate. Clive never did when he came into the bar. He just drank a whiskey and left. They probably didn't have food in the house. "I'm fine."

He studied me a moment. "James, could you have a late supper brought up to the blue room for Ms. Quinn?" He didn't wait for a response before continuing up the staircase. We climbed to the third floor and then turned down a long hall, the walls a saddle brown Italian plaster. Tall windows lined the opposite side, rising up to meet the fifteen-foot ceilings.

"Aren't these a problem?"

Clive turned to me. "Hmm?"

I pointed. "Windows. Sun. Death."

He rolled his eyes, a grin pulling at his lips, as he directed me into the second to the last door in the hall. I gasped. It would have fit in nicely at Pemberley. It was huge, the walls covered in a periwinkle blue silk. The bed was enormous and canopied. The writing desk and nightstands were made of an almost dove gray wood. There was a sitting area near the floor-to-ceiling windows that overlooked the garden.

I ran to the bed and dove on a fluffy comforter the swirling hues of water. "Look at this!" I reached for the heavy velvet draperies that hung, tied to each of the four posts. Unhooking the curtain on one side of the bed, I slid it closed along a silent rail. The windows and sitting area were blocked from view behind midnight velvet. "I can pretend I'm sleeping at Hogwarts."

Clive grinned, watching me. When a knock came at the door, his expression sobered. I slid to the end of the bed, my arm slung around a post, as a man walked in, pushing a cart on which sat a covered plate and a glass of wine. He rolled my dinner to the seating area, transferring the meal to the coffee table.

"If there's nothing else, Sire?" The vampire didn't acknowledge me, didn't even allow his eyes to momentarily settle on me. I simply didn't exist.

Clive shook his head, and the vampire pushing an empty cart left, closing the door behind him.

I pushed the blue velvet aside and climbed down. Reality was smacking me on the nose with a rolled-up newspaper. I was the wet stray their master had rescued, the one they didn't want or trust not to soil the carpets.

TWENTY-FOUR

Wherein Sam Makes a Shocking Discovery

There was another knock on the door. This time when Clive opened it, Russell stood in the hall, my backpack in his hand. "Sire," he said as he passed the bag in. I was struck, painfully, with how that beat-up, ratty, old backpack was me, being passed about, a blemish in this opulence.

"If our visitors need to speak with me, they can wait until I get Sam settled." He turned his back as Russell bowed out the door.

I stared at him aghast and then said, "I thought he was your friend."

"Who?"

I pointed at the door. "Russell."

Clive appeared confused by the question, my change in tone. "He's my second."

"You said I could trust him with my life." Was this a vampire thing? Was aloofness a prerequisite?

"Yes." Clive waited for me to get to the point.

"You turned your back on him as he was *bowing* to you. I can't tell if that's some racist colonial bullshit or some vampire hierarchical bullshit, but either way, it's rude."

Clive looked completely taken aback. "I was rude?"

"People bow and 'liege' all over the place, and you take it as your due and sail right past them. What is that if not superior rudeness?" I picked up the blanket I'd dropped when I'd jumped on the bed and wrapped it around myself. "Maybe that's why all the vampires I've met have been pompous twats. It's a trickle-down behavior." The room had lost some of its luster. I missed my Slaughtered Lamb.

Clive reached out an arm toward me but didn't make contact. "Come sit down and eat. Afterward, you can have a hot bath." He gestured across the room. "Whatever toiletries you need should be stocked." He sat in a chair angled toward the sofa. "Eat while it's still warm."

Sitting, I searched his face, looking for anger or resentment, but there was nothing. It was as though I hadn't just insulted him.

Leaning forward, he pulled the dome off the plate. A bowl of French onion soup and a warm, crusty sourdough roll. The fragrance was mouthwatering and set my stomach to rumbling. Clive gave a small, secret smile at the sound.

"Sorry."

Leaning back and making himself comfortable, he asked, "For calling me a racist twat or for being hungry?"

Taking a bite of the roll, I said, "Being hungry."

He nodded. "Of course."

I took a spoonful of the soup and closed my eyes. It tasted every bit as delicious as it smelled. When I opened my eyes, I found Clive studying me.

"One of the things I enjoy about spending time with you is that all the old rules no longer apply. The dismissive behavior that offends you so greatly is expected by vampires. We are very much a hierarchical collective." He appeared lost in thought for a moment. "Perhaps because we came to be in parts of the world where monarchs and oligarchs ruled, we have unconsciously mirrored the power structure. I would guess that if vampires originated in the States, we'd behave quite differently." His expression softened. "You know, you're the only one who insults me, and yet I trust you implicitly and enjoy your company. Why is that?"

Shrugging, I took another spoonful and swallowed. "You're perverse?"

He nodded slowly. "Most assuredly." He glanced around again, as though seeing the room for the first time. "Do you like it?"

"What's not to like?" Was he kidding? It was a freaking palace.

"If you decide you'd prefer something different, it can be altered." His voice remained calm and neutral, but he seemed honestly concerned that I wouldn't like his house. "You're used to a view of the water, so I hoped you'd like this."

"I'm only here for one night. It'll be fine."

He made a non-committal sound.

We sat in companionable silence while I finished eating. Once I was done, Clive stood and beckoned me to follow. He opened the door to the bathroom, allowing me to go first. It was light and airy, white marble floors with walls the barest hint of blue-gray. Sea glass decorated the shower. Inexplicably, a lovely crystal chandelier dropped from the high ceiling and a chaise lounge resided beneath the window.

"Is that in case showering takes too much out of me, and I need a nap?"

Clive grinned. "I take no responsibility for the decorating." He glanced up at the chandelier. "I've always found that odd in a toilet, but I don't really spend a lot of time in these places, so how would I know? Indoor plumbing didn't exist when I was young, so it all seems strange when I stop to think about it."

He scanned the room for something and then opened a cleverly hidden door. "Your closet."

Moving closer, I looked inside. Another chandelier, mirrors, built-in wooden shelves and drawers, as well as bars for hanging clothes, I was pretty sure the closet was bigger than my apartment. There were clothes in the closet, too.

"Is this someone's room?"

"Yours. I thought I'd made that clear." The mocking tone made me smile.

Pointing to the clothes, I raised my eyebrows in question.

"Again, yours." It was there and gone in a minute, but I'd seen it. Clive was uncomfortable.

"My clothes are stuffed in my backpack." I'd agreed to come ten minutes before we arrived. How were there clothes for me in the closet?

"Yes. These are just a few things. I wanted you to be comfortable, to have what you needed. That's all." He stuffed his hands in his perfectly draped trousers.

"I can't tell if this is sweet or super creepy. Are there panties in there?"

He threw up his hands and walked out of the bathroom. "I have no idea. I asked that items be picked up for you, so you'd understand you were welcome. It isn't as though I picked out your underthings."

"Whew, that's a relief." I followed him out, tickled by his discomfort.

"I'll leave you to bathe and prepare for bed." He glanced around the room, as though checking to make sure everything was where it was supposed to be. "I have a meeting downstairs. If you need anything, use that phone by your bed. Dial 0. Someone should always be manning the phones. Ask for Russell. He'll come help you." He reached out and cupped my face with one hand, his thumb brushing over my cheek. "It makes me very happy to have you here."

Grinning, I squeezed his wrist. "Thanks."

He held my gaze a moment, expression unguarded, and then he left. I watched him go, and then grabbed my backpack and returned to the bathroom. After a ridiculously luxurious shower, with multiple shower heads and a steam bath, I opened my backpack and pulled out the sweats I slept in. They'd always seemed good enough before, but now, sitting on a marble counter, they looked sad.

Tightening the bath sheet I'd wrapped around myself, fresh from the warming rack, I wandered into the closet. Telling myself I was only curious, I opened a drawer. Bras and panties in a rainbow of colors were lined up in neat rows. I wondered whose job that was. I checked the sizes and was disconcerted to see they were correct.

"Okay, I guess I'm doing this." I dried off and pulled on a pair of blue panties. When in Rome and all that. I opened another drawer and found a set of sea-green silk pajamas. I said an internal apology to my crappy sweats before donning them. I felt like an idiot playing dress up, but they were lovely and who would know?

I locked the door because, well, vampires, turned out the light, and climbed into the sumptuous bed. I considered closing the draperies around the bed so my Hogwarts fantasy would be complete, but I couldn't get past the thought of being pulled into a vision and no one knowing. If Clive stopped in after his meeting, I wanted him to know I was trapped, to see me slack-jawed and staring into space. Not that slack-jawed was a good look for me.

The visions were horrific. I'd had some success veering from the path they wanted me on, but it wasn't enough. If I couldn't get myself out, I at least wanted some control over what happened to me in them. Clive had a huge library downstairs. Maybe he had something on lucid dreaming or strengthening the mind.

Positive I could find the library again, I went to my door, unlocked it, and ducked my head out. Silence. I waited a few minutes just to make sure. I'd need to make it down two flights of stairs without anyone noticing. I wasn't too optimistic. Checking to make sure my pajama top was buttoned up to the collar, I headed out.

Barefoot, I padded silently down the hall to the top of the stairs. Nothing. I jogged down a flight and then stopped to assess again. Still nothing. Where the hell was everyone? Tiptoeing down the last flight, I slowed as the stairs opened to the foyer. That butler guy James was probably lurking somewhere close.

Deciding sprinting was the better strategy, I ran for it. Down the last steps, around the corner, down the hall and through the double doors. I held my breath as I closed them quietly behind me. Waiting, I listened intently for any sound. Nothing.

Breathing a sigh of relief, I turned to the library. Moonlight illuminated much of the room, and I had excellent night vision, so even as I reached for the light switch, I thought better of it. I didn't want to call attention to myself.

I walked to the shelves, looking for books on psychology. I eventually found them on the second level. It was a huge section, which made sense considering how much vampires like to screw with people's heads. I found two titles related to lucid dreaming. I grabbed both before descending the spiral staircase to the library's main floor. There were chairs and a sofa, but I went straight back to the window seat. I found the copy of *Jane Eyre* lying right where I'd left it last time. Clive promised he'd leave her be. I couldn't explain why, but it tightened my throat to find her waiting for me.

Climbing into the window seat, I found a throw to snuggle under, and then I began to thumb through the books, looking for strategies on taking control while dreaming. Unfortunately, most of what was written didn't apply to what was happening to me. I was skimming a chapter on mapping the mind when I heard the doorknob turn. Adjusting the curtain, I tucked my feet under me, effectively hiding myself. As long as no one walked over here, I wouldn't be seen.

"What room is she in?" The voice, a low, angry hiss, made me flinch.

"Blue." A different voice said.

"Well, isn't that cozy?" Disdain dripped from his words.

"Why now, when we have guests? I overheard one of their nocturne talking with their human assistant about our Master's dirty little secret."

"He's obsessed with the dog."

Shit. Shivering in the sudden cold, I looked over my shoulder. The window at my back looked out over the moonlit garden. I peered into the night, searching for movement, and was distracted by the waxing moon. It was almost time.

"He'll make us a laughingstock."

"Worse. They'll think we're weak. Ripe for attack."

They were quiet for a moment, footsteps moving from the door. Moon at my back, enemies at the fore, I shivered, the feel of fur bristling under my skin. No, no, no. Changing would take time and make noise. I'd be vulnerable to the ones who wanted to hurt me. That was not an option. Hands fisted on my thighs, I pushed the wolf down.

"We have to save him from himself."

The voices were closer now. Tucking the blanket and book behind me, I readied myself to fight.

"He's meeting with Santiago in the study. Do we do this here, when it's obvious it was one of us?"

"We stage it, so it doesn't look like one of our kills."

"Why not just snatch her while he's distracted. We can dump the body where no one will find it."

A cold sweat broke out across my chest. How easily they plotted my death, and for no other reason than the embarrassment of Clive caring for a werewolf.

"I'm sick of thinking about the mongrel."

"We need to be seen going downstairs. No one was informed ahead of time that she was coming, so it's plausible we didn't know she was here. We make sure we're seen going into our rooms, and then we take the servants' stairs up. With the visitors to entertain, no one may even notice us."

Sharp pain in my palm. I unclenched my hands and watched

my nails transform. Short, unvarnished nails were thickening and lengthening to points. Claws. I'd never transformed early, never. What was happening to me?

"If he discovers it was us, it'll mean our permanent death."

"Then we better not get caught."

The door opened and closed with a quiet snick. Staring at the claws shooting out from my hands, I felt revulsion. I was a human or I was a wolf, not both at the same time. Was this what it was going to be like without my mother's necklace to dampen the wolf? Would I sprout fur when I got angry?

Horrified, I felt shame as I hadn't since I'd first turned, since my body had been taken out of my control. When I ran as a wolf, I made sure I was alone. I stalked deer and hunted rabbits alone. I hadn't had to reconcile that part of me because I hadn't had to share it. Everyone knew I was a werewolf, and yet I was still a secret.

Now, in a nocturne of vampires, I had weapons to defend myself. I should feel powerful and ready to fight. I knew that. But staring at my claws, all I felt was stomach-nauseating shame, my otherness glaring. I didn't want anyone—especially Clive—to see them, to see me as less than human.

TWENTY-FIVE

Mind the Claws, Darling

Where to go? What to do? I tapped my claws on the edge of the bench. The blue room was out of the question, unless I was looking to throw down with a couple of vampires. I could just walk out the front door and run for it, but I was barefoot in pajamas and I'd lost the protective cuff Coco had given me. My own mind wasn't safe or fully my own.

Moving silently across the darkened library, I opened the door, holding it ajar. I slowed my breathing and stilled my thoughts, listening intently. There. Clive's voice, coming from down the hall. He'd told me to call for Russell if I'd needed help, but as there were at least two vampires in the house trying to kill me, it seemed wiser not to let them know where I was.

Waiting, sure I was alone, I closed the library door after me and flew down the hall. Two seconds from door to door. I didn't breathe until I was in the room where I'd heard Clive's voice, my back against the door.

There was a moment of charged silence and then, "Sam? Is something wrong?" Clive was sitting behind a desk, a blue-suited man across from him.

The man turned. He had black hair and eyes, olive skin, and

an arrogant set to his handsome face. "Well, who have we here?"

Clive stood. "Sam is one of my people. If you'll excuse me a moment. I'll take care of this." He glided around the desk and made straight for me.

The other man stood, too. "Strange. She doesn't smell like one of us." His tone was smug as he looked me up and down.

"I am Master of this city. They are *all* my people," Clive said, his expression carved in stone.

"Yes, of course." The man walked toward us, clearly not intending to give us a private moment to talk. "Is this the scarred little wolf I've heard so much about? I must admit," he added. "She's more casually dressed than I would have expected for someone requesting an audience with the Master." Smirking, he leaned against the wall next to me. "Love the jammies."

Standing stiffly, I ignored him, my gaze on Clive, my hands balled at my sides, claws hidden. "I apologize for interrupting, but it's important."

The other man reached out a finger and ran it over my shoulder. "Silky," he breathed.

My jaw tightened, teeth elongating in my mouth. I slid my eyes to the vampire, assessing the threat. I wanted his blood between my teeth. I wanted it very much. A deep growl filled the room.

"Santiago, I'd suggest you step back. I'd hate for a visitor to have his head severed from his body." He looked down at the floor. "And I'm rather partial to this rug."

The vampire snapped to attention, his focus on Clive. "You dare to threaten me? *Me*?"

Clive's eyebrows lifted. "I'm not threatening anyone at the moment. I'm also not the one whose personal space you've invaded, nor the one you're touching without consent. I would think, given the reputation you say you have, you'd have noticed the six-inch claws, the mouth distended by a wolf's teeth, and the warning growl. Clearly, the one you should be worried about is the one in the silk jammies. Now, as Sam is at her breaking point, and I'd prefer you left the city alive, I'll ask you again to please excuse us."

Santiago's eyes flew to my hands. He stepped away with a forced laugh. "Fine. Fine. Take your time." He pulled out a phone and dropped back into his chair.

Clive ushered me out of the office and into the next door down the hall, which turned out to be a bathroom. I looked up. Yep, chandelier. His decorator really had a thing for them.

"What's happened?" Clive bent his head, trying to make eye contact but I was looking everywhere but at him, mortified he'd seen the claws, the misshaped jaw.

"I—" The word came out slurred, my mouth contorted. Tears rushed to my eyes, and I turned away from him.

He leaned in, his lips at my ear. "It's okay. Talk to me."

I tried again, speaking as slowly and clearly as possible. "I was in the library. Two vampires came in. They didn't see me. They started talking about which room I was in, how I was an embarrassment that made you look weak. They're planning to attack me in the blue room, kidnap me while you talk to that vampire, and leave my dead body someplace you'll never find." There was spittle on my lip. Cringing, I raised a hand to wipe it away and then remembered the claws.

"Sam." He turned me around and took my hands in his, lifting them to his lips. "You're beautiful, but more importantly, you're strong."

I rolled my eyes.

"A fierce warrior."

I chuffed a laugh. "Right. A fierce warrior who hides in window seats and reads Brontë."

He leaned in and kissed my neck. "My favorite kind."

"So," I breathed. "Are we just ignoring the death threats?"

"No, indeed. Russell is taking care of them right now." He kissed his way down my throat.

"How? It just happened. How does he know?" It was becoming very difficult to concentrate on killer vamps.

"I can communicate telepathically with my people."

I smacked his shoulders. "Get out!"

"I won't," he said, before nibbling on an earlobe.

"But then why the phone, the talking out loud?" *Shit!* Did that mean he could read my mind?

Leaning away, he took off his charcoal gray suit jacket and draped it over my shoulders. "It doesn't do to show off."

Giggling, I shook him. "Tell me the truth. Can you really do that?"

"Mind the claws, darling, and yes. When you told me what you'd overheard, I sent Russell up to your room to wait for them."

"Won't he need help?" I didn't want Russell getting hurt on my account.

"The day my second can't handle two vampires is the day I need a new second." He kissed my cheek softly. "Please don't worry." He tipped his head to the side, his gaze drifting. "Anton and Michael. How very disappointing."

"They said you'd kill them if you caught them." Please, let that have been hyperbole.

"So, they're not complete morons." He caught my look. "I can't allow two of my people to conspire against me. They not only disregarded my order to protect you, they actively tried to hurt you. No. I'm sorry if it causes you concern, but they will not survive this night." A few minutes later, Clive leaned around me to open the bathroom door.

"Sire. They are downstairs awaiting you." Russell stood in the doorway.

"Thank you." He glanced at me, presumably to make sure I'd heard him say 'thank you.' I guess that racist twat comment really got to him. "Could you please escort Ms. Quinn back to the library to get a book and then to her room." He sighed. "I'm afraid you would've been safer and enjoyed more sleep if we'd left you in your bookstore."

"That's what I said!"

Grinning, he kissed my forehead and stepped out of the bathroom. "Russell, I'm trusting you to protect her."

He nodded. "It would be my honor."

After Clive left, Russell and I walked down the hall to the library. He hit the lights as I went to retrieve the lucid dreaming books from the window seat. I detoured to the shelves before returning to Russell. I might look at that one on the power of the mind, as well.

"This used to be a ballroom." His voice echoed in the large room.

I grabbed the book I'd seen earlier, and then turned back to him. "A ballroom?" Looking around the grand library, I tried to picture it and couldn't. "I thought this was original to the house."

His lip twitched. "No, indeed. It was quite the grand ballroom. Very impressive. When the Master—"

"Quick question," I interrupted. "Does it bother you to have to call him that?" Because it was making me *super* uncomfortable.

A huge grin overtook Russell's face. I'd never seen him relaxed enough to do that before. "It grated for a century or so." Chuckling, he leaned back, his ear to the door. "I must admit, I heard you ask Clive if his turning his back on me while I bowed was some colonial racist bullshit and I laughed like hell. On the inside, of course."

"Of course."

He watched me for a moment, and then, seeming to come to a conclusion, spoke. "You've had a good influence on him."

Me? "He hardly ever spoke to me before all this let's-kill-Sam stuff started."

Again, he was silent a moment. "Clive doesn't personally visit the supernatural-owned businesses in town. That's what he has people for, and they only visit when there's a problem. Clive went to check on The Slaughtered Lamb." He smiled. "You. Every month for seven years. He may not have spoken, may not have even appeared to be paying attention, but he was. You have—I don't want to say soften, because he is every bit as ruthless and powerful as he ever was. He has, though, regained some humanity."

Looking around the library, he added, "So the very impressive ballroom was scrapped, and the library installed." A brilliant smile split his handsome face. "He may not have realized why he'd done it, but it was always clear to me. He was hoping to lure you here with books."

I wasn't sure what to do about that tickled feeling in my chest. "It's a really good lure."

"Isn't it, though? Come, let's get you settled in a room not filled with killer vampires."

"Yes, please."

True to his word, I was dropped off in a vampire-free blue room. I locked the door after he left. Thinking better of the flimsy lock, I dragged the writing desk over to barricade the door. It was surprisingly heavy, given the delicate design. I knew it wouldn't stop any of the predators in house. I just wanted an alarm, so I wasn't killed in my sleep.

Placing the books on the nightstand, I realized that the claws were gone, and my jaw no longer hurt. Huh. I tore open the bedding, just to make sure there wasn't a wolf's head or a severed finger or some other sick threat left for me. Thankfully, I found only soft, white linens. I climbed in and opened to a chapter on manipulating dreams. I may not be able to extricate myself from the visions, but I hoped to learn how to better alter one while inside it.

I was so engrossed in the book, I almost missed the strange, soft noise. I put down the book and slid the bedding aside, in case I had to move quickly. Straining, I heard nothing. Flicking off the lamp on the nightstand, I waited for my eyes to adjust and then slipped from the bed.

Once the room was dark, though, I noticed something interesting. There was a faint light under a panel in the wall. Why would there be light behind my wall? Visions of creepy spy cameras floated through my mind as I quietly approached the wall. Maybe it was a closet, like the one in the bathroom. There wasn't a conventional door, just a panel. Using that as my working theory, I tapped the wall at about the same height I'd seen Clive do it. There was a quiet snick, and the panel swung open, revealing a short passage to another room. A secret passageway! This place was awesome. Other than the killer vamps, of course.

I tiptoed down the dark passage, hearing a rustling in the next room. At the doorway to the new room, I paused. Why wasn't there a closed panel on this side of the passage, too?

Movement. And then Clive stood in the middle of the room, his shirt unbuttoned as he pulled it from his trousers. I must have made a noise, because his reaction was immediate. One moment unbuttoning a shirt, the next in a fighter's crouch, eyes vamp black, fangs out.

Well, shit.

TWENTY-SIX

Never Sneak Up on a Vampire

I shouldn't find Clive being scary super sexy, but damn. He straightened, his shirt hanging loose, and my throat went dry.

Hesitating and unsure, I went to him and reached up, my hand to his cheek. "I didn't mean to startle you."

He put his hand over mine and closed his eyes. "Apparently, both of us have had difficult moments tonight."

I dropped my hand, but he held on. We stood in the middle of his bedroom, hand in hand. His room was even bigger than mine, with dark wood and charcoal gray bedding. On the walls, he had simple, black and white ink drawings.

"So," I said, glancing back at the passage between the rooms. "Am I staying in the side piece's apartment?"

He choked out a laugh, shaking his head. "No."

"You sure? Because I recognize this set up from historical romance novels. The duke or earl or whatnot has his room with a door adjoining his lady's room. The set up makes for easy conjugal visits while keeping her out of his space."

"If you'll recall correctly, I wanted you to stay here with me. *You* requested a guest room."

"And got the side piece's room."

"There is no side piece room." Saying 'side piece' in an offended British accent caused me to snort-laugh. He rolled eyes that were back to his normal stormy gray. "Come," he said, leading me to his sitting area. "Would you like a drink?"

"Do you have chocolate milk?"

His face went blank. "No. I don't believe we do."

"Bummer."

Squinting, he directed me to the gray and black striped sofa. "Do you really want me to send someone out for chocolate milk or are you screwing with me?"

"Clive, the lack of trust hurts." Befuddled was an adorable look on him.

"That's what I thought. Would you like me to send down for a pot of tea?"

"Can you guarantee it will arrive spit-free?" Vampires wanted to kill me. I was pretty sure spiking my tea with bodily fluids was not an unreasonable concern.

Clive considered a moment. "Bottle of water?"

"Exactly. No. I'm fine," I said, as I smoothed my hand over the soft damask fabric.

He stood awkwardly for a second, noticed his shirt was undone, and began buttoning it.

"You don't need to do that on my account." The man's chest and stomach were works of art.

Relaxing, he grinned, pulling off the shirt and tossing it, before sitting next to me. "This evening has not gone as I'd hoped. I put you in danger while promising to keep you safe. And your hands," he reached over to hold one. "Had that ever happened before?"

I shook my head.

"I thought not. You looked terrified and were trying valiantly to hide it." He lifted my hand to his lips for a soft kiss. "Demons, drowning, and vampires all in one night."

"What's happening to me?" I leaned over and rested my head on his shoulder.

"I think you'll need to narrow down your concerns." He kissed my hand again and then held it against his chest.

I closed my eyes. "The magical fuckery. The lost necklace. The missing cuff. I feel like I'm fighting an invisible attacker."

"We'll figure it out. Coco is working on a replacement piece. We'll find whoever is behind this."

"Before I die?" I was so tired, I couldn't keep my eyes open.

I AWOKE COCOONED IN WARMTH, A STRONG ARM WRAPPED AROUND me. A moment of disorientation and then I recognized Clive's scent. My hand was on his chest, my head on his shoulder. How had I got here? The last thing I remembered was sitting on his couch, discussing my impending death. Now I was lying in bed with Clive.

His arm tightened around me, as he caressed my hip. Stomach fluttering, I froze. Was this really happening? Was my mind my own? *Please don't use Clive against me.* Nothing horrible was happening, so this might not be a vision. I grinned at the thought. Maybe I was just snuggling with Clive. I mentally high five'd myself.

He kissed the top of my head. "Go back to sleep. It's late."

"How did I get here?"

"I carried you. You've only been out a quarter hour."

"Oh." When he was holding me like this, the panic didn't surface. Scars invisible in the dark, I wrapped myself around the very hot vampire. Was this okay? He'd said he'd wanted me here all along. I was the one who'd freaked and wanted my own room. Cuddled up with him now, I had no idea why.

I wanted to run my hands over his sculpted chest. I wanted my lips on his, but a part of me also wanted to go back to my own bed, where there was no expectation, no pressure, no fear of doing everything wrong. I wasn't used to having someone to hold, someone to rely on.

Could I do this? Could I let someone in? And if I did, if I finally had a hand to hold in the night, how would I ever again survive without it? All I had to do was run my hand down his chest and he'd know I was awake and wanted him. That's all I had to do. And I was terrified.

"Shh."

"I didn't say anything."

"You're thinking too loudly."

Fuck it. I slid my hand over his broad chest, down his toned stomach. Soft skin over hard muscle, the man's body wasn't real.

"I'm Clive Fitzwilliam, and I approve this message."

I giggled as he slid down, so we were nose to nose. Our eyes met and held. The heat and desire in his gaze burned away my nerves, leaving me warm and achy.

"Are you pulling that vampy stuff on me?"

"No, and you know how I feel about that word."

"Stuff?"

He opened his mouth to respond, but I got there first, shutting him up with a kiss. Yes. This. Was it always like this? Or was it Clive? His hand slid down silk, pulling my leg over his hip. He deepened the kiss, his hand on my butt, pulling me closer. When did this bed get so hot?

I shoved at his shoulders, pushing him back. "Is this real? Is this happening?" I felt him hard against me. Part of me gloried that I had this effect on him. Part of me worried the trauma was too great, that I'd never be able to lose myself, that nightmares in my past would make me forever cold and brittle.

"If this isn't real, then I appear to be horribly defiling this poor, unsuspecting bed. The cleaning staff will whisper about it for decades." He kissed me softly. "What else is going on up there?" he asked while tapping my forehead.

"There's a lot of shit battling to be my top concern right now."

"Give me the top two combatants." He ran his hand down my back, holding me close.

"I'm stuck in a vision. Someone is using you—my feelings for you—to keep me believing and engaged until a herd of vampires attacks or a guillotine drops."

"We don't travel in herds and—"

"Flocks?"

He nibbled on my lower lip. "No. And I can assure you, there are no heavy blades installed in the ceiling or walls."

I studied the ceiling. "Are you sure?"

He looked up with me. "I was. Now I feel like we should move to the couch."

"Ha!" I punched him in the shoulder. "Suave, dream Clive wouldn't have said that. He'd have been all 'I will protect you from all danger with my wicked hot body. You are safe and should now get naked so I can protect you from the inside.'"

"I don't believe I care for this dream Clive. Although." He paused, thinking. "Dream Clive has a point. Let's get you naked, Sam, so I can protect you from the inside." He laughed, kissing my neck.

When I went for the buttons on my top, he caught my hand and kissed it.

"I was joking. You can stay all wrapped up until you're comfortable. Until you know without a doubt that this is real. I'm not going anywhere."

Biting my lip, I said, "I thought maybe we could try second base."

Clive furrowed his brow, clearly confused.

"You know, touch me up top. Second base." My face heated. I was an idiot.

"It seems I was grossly misinformed about the nature of baseball."

I let out a nervous laugh.

"And yes, I would very much like to try second base. You have, after all, already felt me up."

I relaxed, as he knew I would. Clive using slang in his proper British voice always cracked me up. I unbuttoned the top and slid out of it, before falling back into his arms. He held me as we stared at each other. I was making it too momentous. I was screwing it up again.

"Give us a kiss, Luv," he said in a Cockney accent.

Smiling, I did, and all the nerves and worries fell away. There was only Clive and me, and we were fine. No, we were amazing. We lost ourselves in kisses and touches until I had trouble breathing. With his mouth on me, I had trouble thinking.

Eventually, he settled me in the crook of his arm, and held my hand against his chest again. We were back where we started. "This is enough. Having you here with me is more than enough."

I sighed at the truth I heard in his words, at the care. I had no idea what to do with that realization, but it made me hopeful.

"You should know, I'm far less alert during daylight hours, but I can be roused. If you need me, wake me."

I nodded, my cheek against his chest. "Can all vampires wake during the day?"

"No. It's a gift of mine."

Whew. And in the perverse way in which my mind worked, as I thought about day walking vampires instead of the hot vampire lying next to me, I fell asleep.

WHEN I WOKE AGAIN, IT FELT LIKE I'D SLEPT HOURS AND YET THE room was pitch black. Oh, right. Vampire. I was on my side, Clive at my back, his arm tight around me. I checked my phone. It was almost noon, and there was a message from Owen saying he'd be by around noon to pick me up for work. Shit! I scrambled out of bed.

Back in the blue room, I texted Owen to let him know I might be a few minutes late and then jumped in the shower. Afterward, I ignored the backpack on the floor, diving into the closet for clothes. The jeans were tighter than I was used to but fit perfectly. I pulled a thin, long-sleeved sweater from a drawer. It was the same green as the silk jammies that I now never wanted to sleep without. I found socks and a new pair of running shoes in dark gray. Looking in the mirror, I realized I looked like me, just upgraded. Sam 2.0.

He was right about the bathroom. There were toothbrushes and paste in a drawer, even expensive hair stuff and ties. I blow-dried, braided, and was ready to go two minutes before noon.

When I reached for the doorknob of the blue room, I paused, afraid of what might be waiting on the other side. I had claws, though. They'd come out last night. I needed to have faith they'd be there when I needed them.

The hall was empty and dark, some kind of mechanized panel had dropped from the ceiling to block the windows. Now, I understood Clive's nonchalance over big windows and death by sun. Knowing Clive was the only vampire who could wake during the day didn't stop me from tiptoeing down the stairs, tensing at every breath of sound.

There was a light on in the foyer that created deeper shadows in the recesses of the hall. I stopped at the bottom of the stairs and strained to listen. Footsteps. Clive had said he was the only one who could be awoken during the day, and yet I heard footsteps walking toward me. The front door had a security panel beside it. The light was red.

I wanted to get the hell out, but did a red light indicate that the door was locked? Would I set off alarms? The footsteps were coming down the main hall from the back of the house. There appeared to be no attempt to hide the sound. I wasn't sure if that was good or bad. Now or never.

I bolted to the front door and threw it open. Not locked. No alarm. I breathed a sigh of relief and then heard, "Ms. Quinn?"

Standing in the open doorway, I looked back and saw a young woman with a mass of beautifully curly hair, wearing black trousers and a white blouse. She looked more like an admin than a killer.

"I'm sorry to stop you. I'm Norma, Mr. Fitzwilliam's personal assistant. I was asked to give you this." She handed me a black velvet box. "It was delivered this morning. The Master wanted to make sure you had it before you left the protection of his home." Nodding curtly, she turned and walked back down the hall. My nose identified her as fully human, which made sense. He'd need people to work during the day.

Brushing that aside for now, I focused on what she'd handed me. Opening it, I found a necklace. It was different from my mother's, but then again, my mother wasn't a jeweler. It was longer than choker length, but just, which meant it should fit when I shifted. I didn't recognize the metal used. It didn't burn, so not silver, but a lighter, brighter metal. The thin strands of metal were woven in a kind of narrow cage running the entire length of the necklace. Trapped in the cage were the same blue, purple, and black stones my mother's pendant held. It was delicate—exquisite, really—and I wanted it around my neck as quickly as possible.

"Diamonds?"

I looked up and noticed Owen leaning against the side of his car. "Better." I closed the front door behind me and made my way to him. "Your beau's sister made me a replacement necklace." I turned the open jewelry box so he could see.

Owen's eyes lit up. "Ooh. Damn, she does nice work."

"Can you help me put it on? The clasp looks tricky." Owen and I needed to play with it for a few minutes before we figured out how the multiple locking systems worked. Once on, this sucker wasn't coming off.

Owen secured it around my neck, and I breathed easy for the first time since all this began. "Soooo," Owen drew out the word. "Spent the night with Clive, huh?" He winked as he got in the car.

"How did you know to pick me up here?"

"Clive left me a message. And how did it go?"

"A couple of vampires tried to kill me. Good times." I dropped into his passenger seat.

He looked aghast. "Damn, woman. Can you never do things the easy way?"

Apparently not.

TWENTY-SEVEN

There's a Curse?

Once we were on the road, Owen wasted no time. "I talked with my parents last night about Schuyler. Mom said the black streaks in her aura showed up months ago. Some people have stopped going, opting to buy online instead. Mom and her friends take turns, one going and buying for the group. I guess someone asked Schuyler about it when the first black streak appeared. She said she was working through a complicated spell she'd found in an ancient grimoire. Mom heard that Schuyler herself had been shocked the black was there and unsure how she'd earned it. As time has passed, though, and the black spread, fewer people believe it was accidental."

"That's disturbing but not terribly helpful." Couldn't someone snatch that grimoire and find out what she's been up to?

"Pretty much what I said to my folks." He turned down a tree-lined road, mansions diminishing in size. "Oh! And I asked her about you. She said there's been talk about you for years. A small but certain group—of which my Mom is a member—has always believed that you carried wicche blood. Helena won't talk about you, but just the fact that you were living with her when you first arrived had them all buzzing."

Pausing at a stop sign, Owen glanced over at me. "Mom says you bear a striking resemblance to the Corey wicches."

I grabbed Owen's arm. "My Mom was Bridget Corey."

Owen shook his head. "She's always right. Hang on a minute." He tapped his phone, and the sound of ringing filled the car.

"Hello, Honey. Your father and I were just talking. When are you bringing George home for dinner?"

"Soon. I promise. Mom, I have Sam here with me, and she says her mother was Bridget Corey."

"I knew it!"

"Yes, we're all very impressed." Owen rolled his eyes at me, but the love and affection he had for his mother shone through.

"Hello, Mrs. Wong. I don't know if Owen already passed this along, but thank you for the dumplings you sent last week. They were amazing." Owen's mom had a soft spot for me, always sending me little Chinese treats through her son.

"No, no. They were a little gummy. Not my best."

"Best in the city, Mrs. Wong. Hands down."

"Thank you, dear." The pride was clear in her voice and it warmed my heart.

"Can you tell Sam what you know about the Coreys, Mom?"

"I wish I could tell you more, but there isn't much known. The Coreys are a very old magical family, but one that keeps to itself. There have been rumors for centuries, but no one really knows—"

"Rumors about what, Mom?" Owen stopped as a chain of small children, all holding hands, crossed the street. Two adults bookended them.

"Well, I wouldn't want to say anything that might... No one really knows, you see?"

"Spit it out."

"Dear, I wouldn't want you to believe anything bad about your family, and certainly not your mother... It's just..."

"You're killing us, Mom."

"Stop, Owen. This is serious. I wished you'd brought Samantha here instead of making me do this on speakerphone. Okay, there have been rumors for centuries, as I've said, that the Coreys embrace both light and dark magic. The wicches who practice white magic have been killed horribly—rumored again—by family members practicing the black arts. I never met your mother, dear, but if she was a close friend of Helena's, then I'm sure she was a good woman."

"Oh." I came not only from a family of wicches, but a family of homicidal black wicches? Figures.

"Now, you said your mother was Bridget, right?"

"Yes."

"I believe Bridget had a younger sister. I try my best to listen to the whispers on the wind, but I don't believe I've ever heard a name. Honestly, I wasn't even sure there were any Coreys this generation. They could easily have killed themselves off. I can't stress enough how secretive and hidden they are. I'll see what I can see, though. I have my ways."

"I know you do. Thanks, Mom. We really appreciate it. Someone has been fu—screwing with Sam, trapping her in visions, trying to kill her. We think it's a black wicche or a sorcerer, maybe even a demon. Any info you can give us would help us keep Sam safe, okay?"

The line was silent.

"Mom?"

"Oh, dear. I wish you'd told me this sooner. This could be it, the Corey Curse."

My family had a curse named after it? Of course, it did.

Owen slid me a panicked look. "Um, what are you talking about? What's the Corey Curse?"

"Haven't I been telling you? Coreys die in strange and horrible ways. Brother, sister, parent, child…they kill each other off. I don't think it's a stretch to say there are sorcerers among the black wicches."

"So…you think it's a relative who's trying to kill me?" I

didn't remember anyone on my Mom's side of the family. Which was, I suppose, proof Mrs. Wong was right. Someone had stolen memories of my Mom and my childhood. Who could or would do that if not someone close to her?

"I'm sorry, dear. I have no idea, but it seems like a possibility."

"Okay, Mom, thanks." Owen eyed me. "I just pulled up to work. If you think of anything else, let me know." He turned off the engine and squeezed my hand.

Owen and I opened The Slaughtered Lamb. Grim, my grumpy dwarf regular, was waiting at the top of the stairs, none too happy with me. The first thing I did, though, was pour a mug of mead and slide it in front of his stool, telling him it was on the house. He grumbled less.

Once Grim was as content as he got, I went into the kitchen to pull glasses from the dishwasher. Owen followed me.

"Changing gears, we haven't talked about the blood-sucking elephant in the room." He leaned against the counter, arms crossed, waiting.

I ignored him and kept unloading.

"New clothes?"

I shrugged.

"As I've had the misfortune to view the entirety of your wardrobe, I can confirm that these are new clothes, ones that actually fit you."

And then Owen was next to me, nudging me out of the way so he could help. "Come on, give. What's going on with you two?"

"Heck if I know." I let him take over and hopped up on the counter.

"The sweater is nice." He brushed a hand down my arm. "Soft. It matches your eyes."

Oh, I guess that was why it was the same shade as the pajamas. Huh.

"Did you sleep with him?" He was being careful with me.

"Sleep, yes." I was being an idiot. Talking about it made it real, and I wasn't sure I could handle real.

"Okay, let's back up and start again. Are you attracted to him?"

I nodded. At his raised eyebrows, I elaborated. "Yes. Very much so."

"Good." He grinned. "Does he feel the same about you?"

"Yes."

"No hesitation. I like that. It means he's made it clear to you." He studied me a moment and then just shook his head. "How old are you, Sam?"

I tucked my hands under my thighs, against the counter. "Twenty-four. Why?"

He pried one of my hands out and held it in both of his. "Have you ever had sex?"

"P'sh, of course." I tried to pull my hand back, but he held firm.

He softened his voice, "I'm not talking against your will, Sam. Have you ever engaged in consensual sex?"

"Why?"

"And there's my answer."

I pulled again, but he was surprisingly strong for a wicche.

"So, I would guess that you're pretty nervous, maybe even worried that you'll freeze up, or disappoint Clive?"

My throat tightened, and my eyes stung. I shook my head, looking away from him.

"Sam, honey, we all worry about stuff like that."

I turned and breathed deeply. No lie. He meant what he said. I cleared my throat, "*You* do?"

"Of course. In fact, I will bet you a large sum of money that Clive, who's older than all of us put together, is nervous about being with you."

I searched his face for the truth. "Yeah?"

He nodded. "The most important thing to remember is to relax. Clive cares for you. Don't hide from him. Don't worry about your stupid scars. He's a freaking vampire who's hundreds of years old. He's seen it all. A few scars? That's nothing."

Shit. "That's true. He has seen and done it all. I don't know what I'm doing. I'm going to bore and annoy him."

Owen threw up his hands. "How did you get that from what I just said?" He took a deep breath. "Clive cares about you. *You*, Sam, just you. Get out of your own head and enjoy it, okay?"

"Easy for you to say."

"Nope, not easy, but so very worth it." He reached for the clean glasses, but before he could pick them up, I pulled him into a hug.

"Sam Quinn willingly hugging someone?" He squeezed me. "You'll be okay. I promise." He gave me a kiss on the cheek. "Okay, let's get back to work before we piss off Grim again."

The afternoon dragged by. Tonight was the full moon, and I was itching to shift. I kept reaching for the new necklace, assuring myself it was there. Late in the afternoon, the bar phone rang.

"Slaughtered Lamb Bookstore and Bar, this is Sam."

"I missed you when I woke up."

Earthquakes and tsunamis collided in my belly.

"I'm told you were given your new necklace. Are you wearing it?"

"Yep. It's too beautiful, though. I feel weird wearing something so fancy every day." Although, I couldn't stop myself from touching it as I said it. "Do you know the kind of spells Coco put on it?"

"Yes. I asked her to spell it so that your mind was your own. There shouldn't be any more visions."

I breathed out slowly. "Thank you. How much do I owe her?" Because this thing must have cost a fortune. I wondered if she was okay with a payment plan.

"Coco has already been compensated for her work."

"Clive."

"Sam."

A silence stretched as I attempted to see both sides. "Okay. You're right that I don't have the money to pay for a necklace like this, but I'd like the price to be added to my Slaughtered Lamb bill, so I can pay you back over time."

"I *could* do that, but it brings me joy to do for you. Yes, I'm perfectly aware you can do for yourself. There is precious little joy in my life, though. Please allow me these small kindnesses as they brighten my day immeasurably."

"That was very trickily done." Now, if I say no to gifts, I'm stealing his joy. "Manipulative bastard, that's what you are."

"You mean that in a good way, yes?"

"I'm very conflicted about all this stuff you've given me."

"I understand. I, myself, am less so."

Sighing, I put it away. After all, I loved the sweater, and the jeans fit perfectly. I hadn't realized how often I must have pulled up my pants until I didn't need to do it anymore.

"I hope the sigh means that you have resigned yourself to my attention, at least for now."

"Looks like." The bar was starting to fill, and as the sun was going down, the itch under my skin became more pronounced. Soon, I would run as a wolf.

"Good. New topic. I know you need to run tonight and that you have your new protection, but I'd like to accompany you. The necklace hasn't been tested, and there is still a threat aimed at you."

Good point. "It's just—well, I'm not used to anyone seeing me as a wolf, especially not someone who knows it's me and not a big dog or a stray coyote."

"I see. Would it be better or worse for you to know that I have already seen you in your wolf skin?"

"When?"

"Darling, you transform every month. You've lived in the city for seven years. I believe most of the magical community has caught sight of you at least once. It's not as much of a secret to us as it seems to be to you."

"Oh." I looked around the bar at all of my customers. Friends, really. They knew but they still came, still chatted with me. They'd accepted me, and I hadn't even realized it.

"I have one more request, and it's a rather large one. Remember, though, it is merely a request. I care for you, quite deeply. Neither answer is wrong."

"You're kind of freaking me out right now." What kind of request had such a big build-up?

There was a soft chuckle over the line. "I suppose I'm freaking myself out, as well. It meant a great deal to me to be able to have you in my bed, to hold you while we slept. My request is that I be allowed to stay with you tonight. In your home, as mine has proven to be problematic."

"Oh." No other vampires. Just the two of us. And the wolf strong in my blood, helping to quiet the fears that plagued me. "Okay."

TWENTY-EIGHT

Time to Shed This Skin

Later, when the bar was close to empty, I found Dave sitting on his usual stool and reading a book. He glanced over and checked his watch. Closing his book and shoving it in his back pocket, he said, "Okay, everyone out! Full moon. Sam's closing early tonight."

Everyone scurried out. "Thanks. They moved faster than usual."

He smirked, shaking his head. "It's called fear and I like it." He paused a moment, head tilted to the side. "Everyone's gone. Have a good run." And he jogged up the steps, leaving as well.

Turning off most of the lights, I walked behind the bar, sat on the counter, and willed the wards closed to everyone but Clive. Back to the wall and my knees pulled up to my chest, I watched the swirling water in the moonlight and willed the hypnotic rhythm of the waves to calm my racing heart.

When Clive walked down the stairs, my heart lurched. He stopped, finding me in the dark, and then approached slowly, his gray eyes luminous in the fog-filtered light.

"I'm sorry I wasn't here sooner." He flicked the fingers of one hand thoughtlessly, elegantly. "Random problems that needed to be dealt with."

I nodded, nervous and unsure.

"Hiding?" Clive leaned against the bar, watching me.

I shrugged, "Yeah."

He sat up on the counter next to me. "You do realize that nothing need happen tonight." He grabbed a hand that was clasped around my knees and pulled it to his mouth, kissing it.

"What if I suck?"

Clive's eyebrows rose, "Pardon?"

"What if my body turns you off? Or if my insides are too scarred to feel anything? What if I do it all wrong and you don't like me anymore? I couldn't handle it if you—" My breathing was coming faster; my voice was breaking. "I think we need to just forget all of this." I nodded, agreeing with myself. "We'll be friends. You can visit in the evenings and sit right over there." I pointed to his table. "We'll talk about books and movies and be friends forever. Okay?"

"I'm afraid I can't do that."

"Why?" I heard the wolf's whine in my voice.

"Because you are a physical ache in my chest. Every time I see you or think of you, I want nothing more than to pull you into my arms and never let you go." He smiled. "Most friends don't experience that sort of compulsion. Russell hates it when I try to cuddle him."

I exhaled a laugh, knowing I'd been beat. "Well, that's a stupid reason."

"Perhaps, but it's the best one I've got."

I jumped off the counter and headed toward the kitchen. "Fine. Let's get this over with, but if the whole thing is a fiasco, don't say I didn't warn you." I reached out to push the kitchen door and found myself swung around in Clive's arms.

"I don't think you're going into this with the right attitude." His mouth descended on my own in soft, maddeningly light kisses. He nibbled on my lower lip, before feathering kisses across my cheek. I felt his tongue trail down my neck, his fangs teasing me. I shivered and pulled him closer.

"Better." He found my mouth again, crushing me, his kisses hot and urgent.

I wound myself around him, one hand buried in his thick, soft hair, the other trailing across his broad chest. I heard his growl of approval, my hand sliding lower. When I reached his belt, I stopped. This was becoming too real.

"Chicken," he said before devouring my mouth again.

He was teasing. I knew he was, but I couldn't. It was too much. White noise filled my head, the metallic taste of bile in the back of my throat.

And then it all changed. Clive was cradling me against him, a hand rubbing my back as he murmured soothing sounds in my ear. Heart racing, I couldn't take it in, but I knew I was safe. Eventually, the white noise receded, and I heard his words.

"…wait until the end of time for you. There's no hurry, no pressure. You deserve love, Sam. You deserve it all. When you're ready."

I nodded, my forehead rubbing against his neck in a way that helped settle my raging mind. "I need to shift," I said against his chest.

"Then let's do that."

I looked up and found my pain reflected in his eyes. He hurt for me and I didn't know how to fix it, didn't know if it was mine to fix. Throat tight, I nodded and took his hand, leading him into my apartment.

"No one has ever seen me do this." I wasn't sure if I could shift while someone watched.

"Would you like me to wait elsewhere?" He was all soft, careful tones, and I hated myself for prompting it, for being so emotionally scarred that touch terrified me.

I wanted—needed—to be a partner, not a fragile pet who required tending. It was time to shed this skin, to feel my claws and fangs, to rejoice in my strength. I needed that very much right now.

"You can stay." I tried not to think about it as I pulled off my sweater, tossing it on the couch. His body was gorgeous. Mine was less so. He needed to know that. The jeans landed on top of the sweater. Breathing deeply, I undid my bra and slid down my panties. Once naked, I knelt on the floor. Magic surrounded me almost at once, singing through my blood, calling to the moon. My body began to change, my face elongating, my limbs sprouting with fur.

Afterward, I lay panting, recovering from the change. Tensing, I sensed eyes on me. I'd forgotten. Clive sat in a chair, watching me, his expression one of affection rather than disgust. I stood and shook, approaching him slowly.

He held out a hand. "May I?"

In answer, I stepped forward, ducking my head under his hand. His fingers sunk in, and a shiver ran through my body. "You're stunning. In both forms, absolutely stunning." He slipped a hand around my neck and found the necklace. "Good. It still fits. And you're right. It's lovely." A grin tugged at his lips and he said, "We probably should have discussed this sooner, but how about if you do what you normally do, and I'll follow along?"

My tongue lolled out the side of my mouth, ready to run. Sliding out from under his hands, I went to the bookcase, hit the lower shelf, and stepped back as it swung out to reveal a tunnel. I took off running without a backward glance. I could hear Clive behind me, but I had the advantage of knowing this tunnel like the back of my hand.

It was a short run, only a few miles. I emerged out the back of a massive monument in San Francisco's National Cemetery. The cemetery was thirty acres, filled with trees and wildlife. The rows of headstones made it difficult for anyone passing by to see a wolf.

Like the entrances to the bookstore, this was a magical opening. To the rest of the world, it looked like the back of a huge, black monument. If you were to run your hand along the stone, it would feel solid. When I touched, it yielded. I couldn't speak, so I thought *Let Clive use this entrance, as he needs*. I hoped that worked.

Apparently, it did, as Clive stepped out a moment later. I raced up and down the rows, zooming this way and that, as Clive leaned against the monument and watched, a smile on his face. I circled around behind him, intending to catch him off guard, but when I crept around the back of the monument, I found the spot he'd been standing in empty. Where did he go? I sniffed the ground, looking for his trail and found nothing.

A soft whistle sounded from above. And there he was, standing atop the ten-foot memorial. I sneezed, a strange scent in my nose, and took off running out of the cemetery. Clive ran like he had wings on his feet, easily keeping pace with me. We descended a slope and crossed a deserted road, leading to the stables. The horses knew my scent and didn't fuss much. Tonight, though, I had an unknown vampire with me.

As we got close, the horses neighed and stamped. I didn't want to upset them, so I veered to the south to a larger open area we could play in. The grass was high. Clive stood in the middle of the meadow, his arms crossed as though bored and waiting me out. I stalked him like a lion on the Serengeti. When I crept close, his scent filling my nose, I pounced and ended up sprawled in the dirt. Where the hell did he go? Searching, I found him thirty feet away, checking his watch. Bastard.

Slinking through the tall grass, I moved with the bending stalks, mirroring the waves created by the wind. There. Just ahead. A shadow passed over the moon, and I sprung. He was gone, and I was eating dirt again. He was close, though. I couldn't see him, but I felt him. Executing a flip I hadn't realized I had in me, I pounced on shimmering air and knocked a smug Clive on his ass. Laughing, he hugged me to his chest, and I settled in, content with my prize.

Clive lay back, one arm beneath his head, the other around me, fingers in my fur, as he gazed up at the moon. "It's a good night," he said, his voice relaxed.

A horse's neigh had my ears twitching.

Clive tensed beneath me. "Do you hear it, too? A kind of deep thrumming in the ground. Almost like..." He was up in a blink, his hand on my head as I stood alert at his side. "Someone's coming. Go!"

We raced across the field, arrowing our way back past the horses to the cemetery and the monument. Leaving the tall grass, I was bowled over and knocked off my feet by a heavy wolf. Snarling, I circled. Never again. I didn't care what I had to do, but I would never be at the mercy of another wolf.

He sprang and I launched myself straight up, snapped my jaws around his throat and shook him violently. His neck snapped as I slammed his body to the ground.

"Run, Sam. Don't stop. I'll be right behind you."

We ran. Off to the west, I heard the horses neighing again. Clive fell back and came up on my other side, so he was between me and the stables. I could smell it now, too. There were more wolves with us tonight. As we ran, Clive pushed me further east so we would be as far from the stables as possible while still running for the cemetery.

Wolves bayed to the west. They were closer than the stables now. They'd scented us, as well. I ran as fast as I could, but the wolves were pounding toward us from the side. Our paths were about to intersect. I doubted we'd make it to the monument before being overtaken.

A golden-eyed wolf with a rangy, brown body charged out of the underbrush to the west. He was coming straight for me, his scent hitting like a sledgehammer. Randy. He leaped in the air. I skidded to a stop and then Clive was flying over the top of me. He seized the wolf and flung him into the nearest tree. I could smell blood, hear a whine, and a scrabble of claws on dirt, but Clive wouldn't let me stop.

More wolves circled, looking for a weak spot. As they attacked, I ran to Clive's side, claws tearing open the fur of those in my path. We carved our way through them and didn't stop.

We were just rounding the last row of grave markers, when a wolf dove at Clive. As Clive grappled with one, another skulked up behind him. The strategy had changed. They were going to take Clive down first.

I barreled into the wolf, tearing a chunk off his ear. I had his neck in my jaws, my teeth sinking in, blood on my tongue. They would not get past me. The wolf yanked away, leaving fur between my teeth. I sprang back to stand at Clive's back, a deep growl of possessiveness rumbling through my chest.

A reddish-brown one tried to slink by me, but it wasn't happening. I wouldn't let them draw me away. When he was close, I pounced. Claws longer and sharper than I'd ever seen them tore through his muzzle and down his flank. Blood gushed from the wounds, and I gloried in it, grateful I had weapons to protect my own.

"Sam, go!" I looked back and saw dead and dying wolves piled all around us.

The great, black monument was close. I charged for it, knowing Clive would be at my heels. I dove through the entrance, skidding to a stop in the tunnel. Clive didn't follow. I paced the narrow tunnel. Where was he?

A few minutes later, he stepped through, and I snapped my teeth. He crouched down, and I went to him. "I had to make sure no more were coming. I didn't mean to worry you." He rubbed his hands through my fur. "I also needed to call Russell to take care of the bodies. A pack of dead and dying wolves in the city will set off alarms."

I pressed my cold nose to his ear, making him flinch. And that's what he got for worrying me.

"Come on, let's get you home."

I trotted in the lead, down the dark tunnel, unaware the night was far from over.

TWENTY-NINE

Wherein Sam's Anxiety Has a Drink in the Bar and Leaves Her the Hell Alone

We made our way back down the tunnel towards my apartment. The bookcase was still open. I trotted in and collapsed on the carpet, exhausted. Magic filled the room, and I was back in my human skin. Clive stepped in and closed the bookcase.

I squinted one eye open and studied him. "Are you hurt?"

Crouching, Clive ran a fingertip over my shoulder. A scar ran across my chest and over that shoulder. Instead of avoiding it, his finger brushed right over the top, as though it didn't matter. "Of course not. My only concern was you. You may be fierce, Sam, but you are still far more breakable than I am."

Feeling conspicuously naked, I scrambled up off the floor and rushed to the bathroom. "Be right back." I took a shower and then slathered on nice-smelling lotion. While brushing out tangles in my hair, I accidentally caught sight of myself in the mirror. My green eyes were too large. They appeared haunted in the harsh light. I refused to look below my neck, refused to let the scars cow me tonight. My traitorous gaze went unerringly to the scar on my lower lip. I'd bitten myself the night of the attack. Unrelenting pain had caused me to bite through my own lip. The scar was faint, but I knew it was there.

I'd forgotten to bring in clothes with me, damn it. Wrapping the towel around myself, I shook off rising nerves. I'd just taken down wolves. I could walk ten feet across a room.

The quiet tap at the door made me jump. Tugging on the towel to make it cover more, I opened the door. Clive handed me an overnight case. It was black with an image of lush flowers standing out against the dark fabric.

"I wanted you to have a proper overnight bag. There are a few things inside I thought you might like here."

"Clive."

"Sam."

"Didn't we discuss you buying me things?" I loved the bag. I didn't want to give it back, but I felt weird about the gifts. I'd been on the struggling side of barely making it before San Francisco and The Slaughtered Lamb. I was now on the I-can-eat-and-cover-emergency-expenses side of making it, which eased the tightness in my shoulders, but gifts still made me uncomfortable. Although, if I was being honest with myself, this was the longest I'd ever lived in one place and that was due to Clive's original gift.

"I believe we did, and we decided that it was acceptable as it brought me joy." The grin on his face did funny, jumpy things to my stomach.

"That doesn't sound like me."

"You were distracted, so you may have missed a few key points, but you definitely agreed to gifts." He placed his hand on my shoulder and nudged me out of the way, while pulling the door closed.

"You were pulling a vampy mind trick on me, weren't you?"

He sighed. "That word."

"Trick?" I grinned, as the door was shut in my face.

I hugged the beautiful bag to my chest, before placing it on the counter and opening it. More silk jammies, though this time they were lilac. Underneath, there were more panties and bras. I tossed the towel over the bar to dry and slipped on the panties and pajamas. I couldn't help but run my hand up my arm, enjoying the softness.

I found two more sweaters, three long-sleeve tops in a supple knit that drew my fingers, as well. Beneath those items, two more pairs of jeans and a pair of black trousers. There was something hard beneath the pants. I dug down and yanked it up. A black ankle boot. He'd given me a pair of shoes to wear with the black pants, since the only footwear I owned was running shoes. The man didn't miss a trick.

Smiling to myself, I brushed my teeth, gave my hair one last pass, and checked out my reflection. My eyes were less haunted, and my scars were covered. He'd seen it all and hadn't shied away from me. I blew out a quick breath and opened the door.

Clive was sitting on the bed. When I appeared, he rose. "You look beautiful. That color is lovely on you."

"Thanks."

"My turn," he said, slipping past me into the bathroom, a black leather overnight case in his hand.

I had just enough time to freak out and then calm down before the water turned off.

When the door opened, he came to me, slipping a hand down my arm before holding my hand. "May I stay?"

Nodding, I leaned into him. Strong arms crushed me. His mouth took mine with a ferocity I met and returned. I waited for the panic to set in, for the sweating and nausea to overtake me. They didn't. It was just the two of us. My fear—a usual third wheel—had decided to sit this one out.

Clive made a purring sound in the back of his throat. It should have made me laugh, but I felt an accompanying purr in my chest. I hadn't realized he'd been dancing me across the floor, until I felt the bed at the back of my knees. "Just full of vampy moves, aren't you?"

He picked me up and threw me across the bed. "That word." He sounded disgusted, but he couldn't hide his grin.

I giggled uncontrollably, propping myself up on my elbows

so I could watch what he did next. "Wait a minute. Are you wearing jeans? And how am I just noticing this?"

Knee on the bed, he instead straightened, posing. "Do you like them? I changed after the shower. They're my first pair."

Oh my God, how cute was he? "How is this your first pair? Aren't you older than dir—"

"You? Yes, I am." He shrugged. "Vampires are formal creatures. We don't do blue jeans."

"You do."

"I do *now*."

He unbuttoned his dress shirt and pulled it free from his jeans, before crawling up on the bed. He caged me in without touching, arms braced on the mattress, body held above. And then he slowly lowered his head and kissed me and kissed me.

I could do this. I ran my hands over his chest, down his abdomen. The purring sounded in his throat again, and I smiled against his lips. I broke for air and said, "I have an idea."

With a gleam in his eye, he flopped down next to me. "Do tell."

"I've been thinking. Maybe, if you'd be willing, you can lie down and not move. Let me be the one who touches…" I didn't know how to explain it.

"Yes. I like this idea. Consider me your boy-toy. We do whatever you want and nothing more."

My stomach fluttered at the thought. "Really? Anything I want?"

"Anything at all." He tore off his shirt. "Within reason. Don't set me on fire or stake me through the heart. Omitting that, I'm all yours."

I sat cross-legged and studied the man before me, from his heart-stopping face, down his strong, muscular body, to his— "You have nice feet."

He looked down, nodding. "Yes, I've always thought so."

I giggled and he glowed, watching me. I could do this. I reached a trembling hand and touched soft denim, his leg beneath. The fingers of my other hand ran down his stomach, tracing the lines of his abdominals. I heard a harsh intake of breath, but he didn't move. I could see him straining at his button fly, but still he didn't move.

Feeling more confident, I leaned forward and placed a kiss in the dip at the base of his pecs. I heard a slow exhale. I could do this. I swung a leg over and sat on his thighs. I waited for anxiety's claws to rip holes in my lungs, but she was staying on the sidelines. At a guess, I'd say she was in the bar with a bottle of tequila.

The scent of his arousal filled my head, making me want things I never thought I would. Bracing my hands on his shoulders, I tipped forward, dropping soft kisses up his stomach, over his chest, at the notch in his collar bone. I ran my hands over his broad shoulders. Clive watched me, his heart in his eyes, as I made my way past the fear to find him.

My gaze dropped to his jeans. I could do this. Fearsome, not fearful. I reached for his waistband, unbuttoning his jeans.

"Thank God," he said in a low, restrained voice.

I snorted a laugh, unsure but willing. I popped the button fly. His erection pushed at the black, silk boxers. With trembling, tentative fingers, I brushed down his length. His body jolted, but he restrained himself, hands fisted at his side.

I stepped off the bed and grabbed the legs of his jeans, pulling them off easily. He watched me, his eyes heated.

I touched the waistband of his boxers and then hesitated.

"Leave them on for now."

I nodded, more comfortable with that. I climbed back on the bed and straddled him. I let my fingers play across his stomach and chest, before leaning down to kiss him.

"Can I touch you?" He whispered.

I nodded. My heart was beating so fast, I was afraid I was going to stroke out.

"Where?"

"I don't know," I breathed.

He sat up and cupped my face in his hands, kissing me softly, reverently. His fingers slid down my neck and over my shoulders, pulling me close, as his kisses meandered over my cheek and along my jaw. When the tips of his fangs grazed my throat, I shivered in anticipation.

His hands found my breasts as his kisses drove me insane. I reached for the collar button of my pajama top, wanting to feel his hands on me, needing his skin on mine.

"Let me this time," he said, kissing my body, scars and all, as he exposed it. A moment later, my top was dropped by the side of the bed. He leaned back, his hands skating over my skin, his eyes feasting on my body. "Exquisite."

It should have embarrassed me, would have if I hadn't heard the absolute truth in his words. His hands settled on my hips, his thumbs sliding back and forth over my stomach and under the pajama waistband. In his gaze, I was seen. I was accepted. More, I was treasured.

"Clive?"

"Hmm?" His gaze traveled up and met mine.

"Will you make love to me?" I could do this.

Before my next breath, he had our positions reversed, most of his weight on one side, his head propped in his hand, his other hand resting between my breasts. "We will if that's truly what you want, but there's no hurry. No finish line, remember. We can touch and kiss until we've had our fill, and then we can sleep, wrapped in each other." He rolled my necklace back and forth. "That sounds perfect."

I sighed. "It does." I ran my hand through his thick hair, over his brow, down his nose. My fingertips and brain cataloging and memorizing. I'd felt the change and instinctively knew what it meant. I needed to store as many sense memories as possible. Wolves mated for life. Clive was mine. I hadn't accepted it when I'd first felt my heart open to make a place for him. He wasn't a wolf. I wanted nothing to do with wolves ever again, so I'd assumed I'd be forever alone. Maybe, when I was feeling stronger, decades in the future, I'd eventually take lovers, but there'd be no mate because there'd be no wolf.

Vampires didn't mate for life, like werewolves. He'd move on, but I never would. And so, I needed to save as much of him as I could for the long life I'd live after he'd left.

THIRTY

The Good, the Bad, and the Ugly

I ran my thumb over his bottom lip, along his strong jaw. "I'm ready."

His answering kiss was soft and sweet, a cherishing kiss that brought me to tears. "Shh," he said against my lips. "You can change your mind. At any point. If pleasure turns to panic, we stop. Yes?"

I nodded.

"Good." He took it slow, dragging open mouth kisses down my body, over my breasts and stomach. When he reached my pajama bottoms, he paused, waiting.

I ran my hands through his thick hair and nodded.

He slid them off, before resuming his kisses. His lips and tongue drove me over the edge. When he settled his mouth at my core, I had a moment of nerves, but they disappeared the moment he touched me. Hands fisted, forcing myself not to yank that beautiful hair, I rode the onslaught. Gasping for air, heart hammering, I realized I'd found a new best way to die. The pressure built and built, and with a moan, broke over me. I was a quivering, shuddering mess, and still Clive didn't stop.

Once my limbs were under my own control again, I tapped his head with a murmured, "Clive?"

He looked up, eyes vamp-black, fangs extended. "Yes?"

"Could you come back up here?"

"I'm a little busy. Could I get back to you in a few?"

My laugh ended on a groan when his tongue gave one last swirl. He kissed and nibbled and licked as he moved north, spending considerable time on my breasts. When his mouth fused with mine, I thought my heart would break free of my chest. I wrapped my arms and legs around him, never wanting to let go, and realized he was still wearing his boxers.

I broke the kiss. "You seem to be overdressed for this next part."

He smiled and kissed my chin. "There doesn't need to be a next part if you're not ready."

I put my hands on his face and drew him in for a soft kiss. "Clive, you are my world. And, yes, there does need to be a next part."

Clive stilled at my words, his eyes swamped with emotion. "Truly?"

"Yes. I know you have more sexy time vampy skills. Let's see 'em."

His head dropped to my shoulder. "That word."

"Skills?"

He plucked at a nipple. "Not that one." His eyes gleamed. A second later his boxers were gone, and his fingers slid between my legs. I arched my back, echoes of the last orgasm still reverberating through me. His hand moved, and he settled between my legs, arms braced beside me.

"Still with me?"

"Of course," I answered without hesitation.

He pushed into me, his mouth at my neck, his hand on my breast. I tensed. I didn't mean to, didn't want to, but he felt it.

"Look at me. Touch me. Stop thinking. Feel what I'm doing to you."

He licked my neck before running his fangs down it. I shuddered, and he slid out and slammed back in. He bent down and swirled his tongue over my nipple while his fingers slid between my legs again. He worked my body like a virtuoso. Gripping his biceps, I clung to him, breathless. Wanting only Clive, I exalted in the connection and collected memories—the feel of him, the sound of his voice as he rumbled in my ears, the way he was able to make me feel whole and loved—for when he was no longer here.

The intensity built, my body straining. When it came, Clive was there with me, sharing the moment. I clung to him, my true north.

Rolling on to his back, he took me with him, holding me close as I curled into him. My racing heart slowed, and I grew sluggish with sleep. I was drifting away when I felt a gentle kiss on my brow. "Sam?" Clive's voice was like a breath, my name an exhalation. I didn't respond. Breath required no response. "I…" He sighed and then kissed the top of my head.

Embracing Clive, I'd found home. I awoke later to the sound of buzzing and then Clive's voice murmuring in the background. When he threw the bedding back and stood, I forced my eyes open.

"You're leaving?"

"Sorry. Go back to sleep. Russell called. He's dealing with sticky diplomatic issues pertaining to our visitors. It also sounds as if my own nocturne isn't happy about last night."

What happened last night? Oh, right. Killer vampires. Like that was my fault.

"I need to go deal with it." He already had his jeans on and was buttoning up his shirt. Once it was tucked, he put a knee on the bed and leaned over to give me a kiss. "I hate leaving." He checked his watch. "I doubt I'll get back before sunrise. Whether things settle down or not, though, I'll see you tonight."

"Okay." I kissed him again, and then snuggled in for more sleep.

I AWOKE WITH A START. SOMETHING WAS WRONG. CHILLS RAN DOWN my spine. My wards were being destroyed. Each felt like a flash strobing in my brain. The magic was being ripped out of me.

Someone was coming. I heard the muffled thump of many feet running. Closing my eyes, I reached out, testing what was left of each connection. The tunnel. They were coming up the tunnel.

I sprang from the bed and dressed, diving into sweatpants and a sweatshirt. I refused to be at anyone's mercy, naked and defenseless. Not ever again.

The bookcase slammed open in the living room, books went flying as footsteps thundered into the room.

"Find her." I knew that voice. It was Randy.

I raced silently on bare feet to the hidden doorway into the bookstore. Someone walked into my bedroom as I slid through the passage, closing the bookcase behind me. I stilled and listened. Were they still together or had they spread out?

"It reeks of vampire in here. She's a freaky little wolf."

"I don't care what she fucks. Find her." Crashes sounded through the wall from my bedroom.

"Lookey what I found." A second later, glass shattered again and again, liquid splashing. It sounded as though someone had found my baseball bat and was demolishing my beautiful bar.

I ghosted through the dark to the last free-standing bookcase. I crouched down and jumped, landing on my toes and fingertips seven feet up, on top of the case. I'd never make it past them to the tunnels or stairs. I had to wait them out. I stretched out flat, trying to disappear.

"Where the hell is she?"

Someone was kicking displays, knocking books from the shelves. I froze, not wanting any movement to give me away.

"Turn on the lights, you morons!" Randy's voice boomed in the bookstore.

Bright lights flicked on, taking my invisibility with it. Now all I could do was pray they didn't look up.

Randy strode past bookshelves. "Did you check the storage rooms?"

Light footsteps danced down the stairs. "Well?" asked a female voice.

"She's not here," he said.

"You are as stupid as you are handsome. Of course, she's here. It wasn't easy to lure the corpse away, but we did. With any luck, he'll be pointed in the wrong direction when he finds out, and he'll eliminate his second for us. As for Samantha, she's here and cowering. All alone. Aren't you, dear?" she pitched her voice louder at the end for my benefit.

Heels clicked on the floor. "Just like your mother. She hid, too. Even with that disgusting wolf father polluting your blood, you still take after your worthless mother."

"Well, where is she?" Randy asked.

"Shh, I like to play with my food." Her tinkling laugh made my skin crawl.

Cornered, my mind raced. How would I survive this? I couldn't fight multiple wolves and whatever she was, not and live. Any movement would call attention to myself. I knew she was trying to get a rise out of me but staying put was a different kind of trap.

"I can't believe how much trouble you've been. How have you been slipping out of my spells? From all accounts, you're a weak excuse for a wolf with no magical powers. You're an embarrassment to the name Corey. Sometimes the family tree must be pruned to ensure that it flourishes in the future." Her voice was getting closer.

Movement and then, "Take your men and go. She and I need to have a little chat. I'll let you know when she's ready."

"You sure?"

"You doubt my ability to deal with one weak wolf? Do you need a reminder of what I'm capable of?"

"No. I just—come on, guys. We'll wait up top."

Footsteps shuffled away. I took advantage and leapt to the

next bookcase, landing silently on my toes. I caught a glimpse of men walking through the bookstore doorway, under The Slaughtered Lamb pub sign. I leapt again, landing without a sound and then slid down to hide prone across the top of the case.

Heels clicked past my hiding place, towards the corner I'd been in only moments before. I popped up and leapt twice more. If I dropped to the ground here, I might be able to make it through the bar and out a tunnel before she found me. I slipped over the side, hanging from my fingertips a moment before dropping lightly to the floor.

"Samantha, you've been such a disappointment. Werewolf father. Vampire lover. You're a cesspool, befouling ancient magical blood. Your very existence offends me." Her voice sounded from the back corner.

I took my chance and ran for the doorway. Electricity shot through my body. Pain, unendurable, unrelenting pain tore at me with knife-sharp claws. My brain fractured, sharp pieces grinding against one another, organs frying. Blood trickled from my nose and ears.

As I convulsed in agony, the click of heels approached. A woman leaned over me with my mother's face. Tears ran from my eyes, pooling in my ears. I was dying, and she was watching with mild curiosity.

"Do you remember your Auntie Abigail?"

A memory flashed in my mind, seeing those same eyes but through water. I couldn't breathe. I'd kicked my little feet, splashing in the bath as she held me under. Her voice was muffled, but I remembered. "You should never have been born. Abomination."

My mother came up behind her younger sister and smashed her over the head with a vase. When Abigail slumped to the side, my mother pulled me, choking, from the bath. She stuffed a few things in a bag, and we were running, the first of many late-night escapes.

"Oh, you do remember me. That's lovely." She smiled and

my blood ran cold. "I have another memory for you," she said as her fingers flicked.

I'm blindfolded and struggling, arms straining over my head, cuffed. The silver burns. My screams are nothing but breathy croaks. Slick, sticky blood runs down my body, dripping off my toes. The tickling of fur—he's changing again. And all at once, the smell hits me. Years of nightmares and I'd never identified my torturer. Abigail knew. She'd kept him hidden. Made him faceless. Made him every man.

Randy. Barely teenaged Randy had tied me down as he cut me to ribbons. Teeth tore. Claws ripped. Nauseating scents clogged my nose. Liquid washed over my abdomen and legs, slashes burning anew. The long, serrated blade slid through my sternum as Randy began to carve. Horrific memories and long-ago wails echoed in an endless loop.

"She's done," Abigail called up the stairs. "I'd hurry, if I were you. She won't last much longer. Do what you will, because it ends tonight."

She stepped over me and left as feet pounded on the stairs again.

Randy leered down at me. "Hey, Princess, did you miss me?"

THIRTY-ONE

It's a Hard Rain

It was raining glass. The electro-shock had ended when my aunt left, but the damage had been done. Glass shards fell, screeching in my head. It was hard to hear anything over the cacophony. Randy loomed, his mouth moving, but I didn't know what he was saying. Tall men and a woman gathered around. I'd been found. It would all start again. My pain would be used to power my aunt's spells. I couldn't fight, couldn't move. Paralyzed, it rained glass in my head as my torturers salivated in anticipation.

Randy hauled up my slack body. My skin crawled at his touch. He threw me over his shoulder. My eyes were as disconnected as the rest of me, so as he climbed, I had no choice but to stare at the frayed back pocket in front of me. My mind shied from what was about to be done to me. I wished I could see the bookstore and bar one last time, to say goodbye to my Slaughtered Lamb. Instead, my head and arms bounced against his back in time with his steps. Mine was an ignominious end.

Wind, carrying brine and eucalyptus, hit my nose as he passed my obliterated ward. My brain was slowly dying while imprisoned in an unresponsive cage. Glass continued to shower in my mind as the world swung and tipped perilously. A second later, I slammed onto corrugated steel. Breath left my body. The full moon hung heavy in the sky, standing vigil.

Something rumbled to life, and the other man settled down next to me. The view changed as air trickled into my lungs. The moon remained my constant companion, as tree branches whipped by, streetlamps sliding in and out of focus. Truck bed. I'd been thrown into a truck bed. I wondered if Clive still had vampires keeping an eye on me. After last night, it was doubtful. How had a bookish bartender inspired so many homicidal impulses?

He cared for me, though. He'd said as much, and I'd heard the truth in his words. Death may be stalking me on glass feet, but I'd been cared for. I'd found a home and friends. That was more than I'd thought possible. I hoped, whatever was next—please, not Hell—I'd be able to hold that memory close.

The truck flew around a corner, and I rolled, slamming into the wheel well. I'd lost the moon. A dirty, leaf-strewn truck bed was a far less poetic ending.

Memories flashed, like fractured home videos reflected on falling glass. Glimpses of stolen memories. They hadn't been stolen because of my mother. That was incidental. It was my aunt who had erased herself, not caring if I lost my mother, as well. She'd been there, at my mother's funeral, raging that the name Quinn had been put on the stone. What had she said? She'd been standing on the grave, rage charring the ground at her feet. "...got rid of that dog...put his name on her stone? No! Corey and Quinn...abomination!" Her eyes were on me as she seethed, smoke rising from the newly laid sod. Lightning arrowed down from the sky, splitting my mother's tombstone between Corey and Quinn.

The truck took another sharp turn. The moon was back. The rhythmic thump of the tires on the road and the girders overhead told me we were crossing the Golden Gate Bridge.

I wished I'd had time to learn about magic. I would have liked exploring my Corey side. Not the psychotic branch of the family that produced my aunt, but the totally normal wicchey side. I wished I still had my mother's pendant with me, not just because it was all I had of her, but because it carried stronger spells. My mother knew exactly who she was protecting me from. Coco's magic was different, a dragon's magic that lacked a target.

Wait. Coco was connected to the necklace around my neck. Maybe... *Coco! Coco!* I repeated her name over and over. She'd once said she'd heard me screaming in her head. Maybe she'd hear me now.

Once over the bridge, they left the freeway and headed up into the hills. The deluge in my head had petered off to a drizzle. Words were starting to come through. "...left up here...that crazy bitch...ATVs...remember, she's mine first..." The man sitting in the back with me was talking through the cab window with the other two.

My head bounced against the metal of the truck bed as we turned off a paved road and headed up a gravel one. I'd lost the moon behind a forest of trees. My nose itched, and my hand was halfway to my face before I realized it was responding to impulses in my brain again. Twitching my fingers and toes, I prayed this meant whatever she'd done to me wasn't going to kill me.

I slid, feet smacking against the rear gate as the truck powered up a steep hill. The engine died, and both doors opened up. A moment later, Randy leaned over the side, and sneered, "Enjoy the ride?" Chuckling at his own joke, he plucked me up and threw me over his shoulder again. "They're over here, under the tarp."

Pretending to still be floppy and unmoving, I stole glances at who was with us. A man and a woman. The man smelled like the wolf who had chased me off the cliff and into the ocean, the woman I remembered from the Crypt night club. She was a member of the Bodega Bay pack. I knew it. She'd been far too keen when Randy's name had been brought up.

Randy scrambled up a hill and then dropped me on the ground. "Shit, this isn't even going to be fun."

"She's more Joe's speed," the woman said. "You like drugging your dates, right Joe?"

"Screw you." A boot shoved me down a short incline. I kept my body loose as I rolled, crashing into the base of a tree. My back hit the trunk. Flopping my head onto a mossy patch, I watched the men.

"It still counts, though, right?" Joe said.

"What?" Randy responded.

"You know. That wicche and her—" He whispered, "Friend. What we do to her still counts even if she isn't screaming and crying, right? We still get what she promised?"

"It has every time before. Why wouldn't it now?" Randy looked between the two of them. "Everybody gets what they want. It's a—whaddaya call it? A symbi—a relationship. We all get something. They get the fear and pain and blood. We get the thrill and the rewards. Relax. We're covered."

Randy dug into his pocket and extracted three keys, tossing one to each. They caught them on the fly with grins.

While they were distracted, I tested my muscles to see if they were working yet. Lying in pine needles meant I couldn't move without being heard, so I tensed each muscle group, looking for minute movements, internal flexing. I'd regained some control, but not all. At this point, if I tried to stand, I was sure I'd fall.

Joe, closest to a dark bulk hidden beneath branches, pulled off a tarp revealing three ATVs. Each of the wolves pulled a three-wheeled motorbike out from under the tree.

"Keep an eye out on the way to the cabin. It's still a full moon, so the Bodega pack could be out."

"Nah, boss. They're probably sleeping by now," the woman said.

"That'll make our lives easier. When we get close to the cabin, you two park the bikes and shift. I want you circling. If you see or smell anything, howl. I doubt anyone will even notice she's gone before noon tomorrow, and by then, there won't be much left to find."

There were appreciative chuckles from the other two.

"Just in case, though, keep watch. I'm going to be busy getting reacquainted with our party favor and I want to know if some hero's about to crawl up my ass."

"You got it," Joe said as he swung a leg over the ATV.

I didn't know how he was planning to transport me. My body, as far as he knew, lacked the tension needed to sit. A moment later, he turned and watched me, speculation clear in his eyes. Had I done something to give myself away? *Coco!*

Doing my best to control my breathing, I kept my gaze fixed on one spot, and willed my body to betray no resistance. He'd make a mistake. At some point, he'd toss me aside, and I'd escape.

He picked me up and threw me back over his shoulder as he sat down on the ATV. *Shit*. He wasn't throwing me over the seat. He'd feel it. If he barreled down a sharp incline, and I braced, he'd feel it. If he cornered around a tree, and I adjusted my weight, he'd feel it. He'd know I was regaining feeling and strength. I had to let self-preservation go. Whatever happened, I couldn't react.

Tree branches slapped at my legs, tangled and pulled my hair, but I didn't flinch. Randy's arm pinioned my legs to his chest. He took a downslope turn, and I slid off his shoulder. My head hung inches from a wheel kicking up rocks and dirt, and still I didn't react.

He took his hand off a handlebar to pull me back up. The ATV hit a tree root and jolted, flipping sideways. I was thrown down a hill, rolling into a ditch filled with vines and shrubs. I heard Randy swearing on the path far above. This was it.

Popping up, I swayed a moment, muscles cramping. I found

my balance and ran. Randy yelled for the other two, who were ahead of us when he crashed. Sprinting up the gully, I heard the whine of engines slowing and turning around. Three. There would be three hunting me in a matter of minutes.

Up or down? I could follow the side of the mountain down, away from them, and try to find help. Or, I thought with a shiver of anticipation, I could run up and hunt *them*. Long, razor-sharp claws shot out. My jaw reshaped itself, making room for enormous fangs. Fuck hiding. I was not prey.

Sprinting up the incline, I dodged behind trees, keeping to the shadows. The full moon was setting, but the night was still bright with its light. Shadows abounded. I'd use that. They were talking, Randy pointing to the spot I'd hit in the gully. The ground was covered in vegetation. They hadn't realized I was no longer down there. While they planned, I kept to the shadows and hit the path, a hundred yards past where they were standing. I shot across, into the forest on the other side and circled back around. The two men did a kind of slide-jog down the side of the hill to search the ditch. The woman stayed with the bikes. She'd be the first to die.

Padding silently on bare feet, I came up behind the woman from the Crypt. She was leaning against the side of an ATV seat, eyes focused on the activity in the gully.

"Do you see her?" Randy's snarl brought a smile to my lips.

"Are you sure this is where she fell?" Joe asked.

"Where the hell else? The ATV is right up there. You can see the wheel hanging over the edge. This is where she should have ended up. Cam!" He shouted. "Do you see anything?"

"Yeah," she mumbled. "A couple of morons fumbling around in the dark." She crossed her arms. "No!" She shouted back. "Come on," she said to herself. "Find her already. I sharpened my knives special for this party."

Stepping up behind her, I stared down at my claws, grateful to have them. They gave me power. They gave me choice. My body was my own, and no one else's. There would be no party tonight. Leaning forward, I slashed my claws across her neck, cutting to the bone. When she slumped to the ground, blood gurgling, beginning to pool, I felt no remorse. She had it coming.

Two of the ATVs still had keys in them. I took both. Randy's bike may have flipped, but he was smart enough to grab the key. I got halfway across the path and then dropped to the ground, crawling to the edge and peering over.

Joe was on the other side of the gully, looking down the side of the mountain. "You sure she didn't keep going? She couldn't move to stop herself."

"Shit, I don't know. The ATV spun. I went one direction. She went the other." He studied broken branches, sniffing the air. "Cam!" he shouted. When there was no response, he looked up the hill. "Dammit, Cam! I'm talking to you." He turned to Joe. "Will you see what her problem is this time, then ride north. Look for tracks."

"Sure, but what are you gonna do?"

"Track her scent. I can smell her right here. There's a broken branch right there. Maybe she crawled while we were talking."

"I thought she couldn't move." Joe sounded strangely nervous.

"Man up. She'll be more fun this way."

Joe nodded, glancing around before dipping back through the ditch. When he began to climb the hill where I was waiting, I scooted back and then sprinted to where I'd left Cam. I needed a good spot from which to attack. Glancing up, I noticed a thick tree branch hanging over the path. Joe would check on Cam. I knew where he'd be in a minute. Now or never.

Crouching down, I jumped as high as I could and easily landed on the branch. I almost overshot it and toppled right back off, but I caught my balance and waited. Joe came over the rise a few seconds later.

"Cam? Where—Shit!" He ran to the body and checked for a

pulse, his fingers coming away drenched in blood. "Fuck me," he whispered.

I dropped from the tree, claws out. Landing on his back, arms crossed, I was already raking them in opposite directions against the back of his neck, taking his head completely off. Blood spurted as it rolled away. Two down.

THIRTY-TWO

In Which the Princess Saves Herself

"What the fu—"

I spun, claws out, and slashed Randy's face. He must have circled around behind me.

Shock rocked him back on his heels. Half his face was shredded to the bone, blood gushing from the wounds. "How?" He lurched forward, jaw clenched. "I'm the Quinn heir. I'm Alpha! You're nothing but trash. Used and dumped."

There was a crazed glint in his eyes. He didn't seem to care about his face. It was the long, razor-sharp claws that shot from my fingertips that had him unhinged. I glanced at his hands. They were a man's.

"I'm Alpha!" He pounded his chest. "Me!"

I edged to the side, keeping my weight on the balls of my feet. "What's the matter, Junior? Can't you do a partial shift, too?" He had at least six inches and fifty pounds of pure muscle on me, but my ability to shift isolated parts of my body had incensed him beyond reason.

"Not possible," he sneered. "It's some kind of illusion." He glanced around, wariness making him stiff. "Switching sides, Abigail?" he shouted.

While he was distracted, looking for my aunt, I tore at his

chest. My claws caught on his rib cage. I'd pierced him, but I couldn't complete the swing. He grabbed my wrist in his iron grip and yanked me forward, while the massive fist of his other hand sped toward my head, and then there was nothing.

PAIN. FIERY PAIN RADIATED DOWN FROM MY HANDS. HEAD pounding, I blinked my eyes open. Randy. I'd been caught, arms handcuffed over my head, hanging from a high branch. Blood dripped on my head from my mutilated hands. I kicked and twisted, my arms burning. Silver. My body felt like it was on fire. I couldn't change while silver was touching me. He'd improved his methods.

"No weak little bitch is gifted with Apex Transformation. No way in hell. No more claws for you. Now," he said as he shoved me, causing me to swing from my burning wrists. "Once I kill you, I'll inherit it."

"Pretty sure that's not how inherited traits work, dipshit." I scanned our surroundings. We were in a small clearing surrounded by dense woods, with a run-down shack tucked in a corner. The ATV was parked near the steps of the hovel, the front door hanging open.

"Nice place you got here." I refused to show fear. My stomach was quaking, my heart racing, but my expression was stoic as hell.

He grinned, a wholesome, all-American smile that masked unspeakable depravity. Fear fluttered in my mind. Memories of what he'd done to me seven years ago cycled through my brain. Ignoring the whimpers of my subconscious, I sneered.

The sky was lightening. Dawn was near. Nothing looked or smelled familiar. Wait. I pointed my nose toward the shack. Faint, I just caught it. Abigail and…vampire.

"You were my first. Did you know that? In a shack just like that." He ran a finger over my cheek.

"I'd hope so, you psycho. What were you, thirteen? Fourteen? You must have started killing neighborhood animals at an early age if you'd worked your way up to torture and rape in your early teens. Quite the prodigy." I continued looking everywhere but at him. He didn't deserve my attention.

The punch was fast. Head knocked sideways, my bell rung, blood trickled from my lip. I was making him crazy. Crazier. *Coco!*

His charming smile had flattened, eyes cold and hard. "Big talk for something that shouldn't even exist." He ran a finger through the blood on my lip and then licked it clean. "I love the taste of abomination in the morning."

"Been chatting with my auntie, have you?"

A split-second of shock raced across his face and then he was laughing, doubled over wheezing with hilarity. "That bitch is your aunt?" he gasped. "What the fuck did you do to her to give her such a hard-on to kill you?"

I stared him right in the eye, channeling my fledgling inner badass, and said, "She fears me." I turned up my lip in a smirk. "Like you do."

Glaring, he spat, hitting the chest of my sweatshirt. "If anyone around here should be afraid, it's you."

"How's your face?"

The rage was instantaneous and was hidden just as quickly. He prowled around me, grabbed my arms, and pulled down hard against the cuffs.

Fire burned up my arms, but I sealed my jaw shut. He'd scrape no cries, no screams from me.

He breathed hot in my ear, causing my insides to cramp. "Big talk, little wolf. Hiding in your bookstore. Fucking your vampire. So special. So smart."

I couldn't respond, teeth welded shut as the fire continued to rage in my body.

"Pretty stupid, if you ask me. Still haven't figured out who I am, have you?" He let go of me and stalked back around, waiting for a reaction to whatever bombshell he was about to drop.

Expression bored, I waited for it.

"We're family, Sam."

Mind and stomach rebelling, I forced boredom into my voice. "Is this going to be a 'Luke, I am your father' speech? Because, no."

"We're cousins. Your daddy and my daddy were brothers. *Are* brothers? Which way do we say it when they're both dead?" He poked me in the chest, and I swung back, arms awash in pain again. "Got your attention, didn't I?"

As far as I knew, my father only had one brother. "You're Marcus's son?"

"Damn straight."

"Strange he never claimed you then, huh?" Anyone this insecure needed that knife twisted.

"Mick was his favorite. I was just an accident from a woman he once fucked in a bar. Didn't even know he'd left her pregnant. Quite a surprise when I shifted the first time and killed her and her asshole boyfriend." He chuckled. "Good times."

I wouldn't give him the reaction he craved. My expression betrayed no shock nor sympathy, no disgust. Boredom, that was all he'd get from me.

"She'd let enough slip over the years. I was twelve. Mom was dead. I knew his name was Quinn and that he owned hundreds of acres in the Santa Cruz Mountains. I hunted for weeks as a wolf, following the scent of other wolves. Eventually, one led straight to my daddy." He laughed without humor. "Wasn't too happy to see me, that's for sure."

"Maybe because he knew you were a budding psycho killer." I felt no twinge of sympathy. None. That probably didn't speak well for me, but lots of people have it rough. They didn't torture and kill to stave off feeling angsty.

"Not budding. Weren't you listening? I was already a killer. So, he let me move into one of the cabins, be a part of the pack.

Not the main house, not for his bastard son. I wasn't real family. Just a stray he took in."

Was anyone looking for me yet? *Coco!* Maybe Clive had come back to my bed, after all. Maybe he was already looking. How dire was your situation when you were hoping for an invasion of vampires?

"A few years later, who do I meet in the woods? Abigail. Said if I fucked you up, she'd make me Alpha. Next day, Marcus is claiming you as his niece to everyone. But, shhh, no one tell her what we really are." He scoffed. "Fuck that. I showed you." He ran his finger over my cheek again. "I showed you real good."

"Damn, you are one chatty villain. Is this part over yet?"

He pulled a long, serrated knife from the sheath at his waist. He held the knife up close to my eyes, making sure I knew pain and blood would be my world before I died. Chuckling, he said, "Not so brave now, huh?" He ran the flat side of the knife along the exposed portion of my stomach.

"Marcus wouldn't shut up about you. So special, our Sam. Quinns are one of the original wolf families. With your wicche blood, he just *knew* you'd be special. Something we'd never seen before. So proud of you. Just like Mick. Next Alpha, our Mick." His smile made my knees weak. "I didn't get to finish before you ran off. Mick had followed your trail to the cabin. You should have seen the look on his face when he found me and my knives." He cackled. "Priceless. No more Mick in my way."

Grabbing my face, the knife still clutched in his fingers, he said, "And when I'm done, no one will ever see you again." He shoved my head back and then used the tip of the knife to trace the infinity symbol he'd carved above my wrist seven years ago. "Always. I'll always be better. Always be stronger." A leer took the place of petulance. "Let's get this party started." He gripped my breast and squeezed.

Anger, sharp and scalding, consumed me. I kicked out, making him stagger back. He grinned, rolling the knife in his hand, low light reflecting off the razor-sharp edges. Dawn was breaking. He cut my sweatshirt down the middle, the blade tip slicing through old scars, down my chest and stomach.

Never. Fucking. Again. Something broke inside of me. Rage consumed me, willing my wolf to the fore. Sam was gone. My brain was a snarl of disconnected thoughts and emotions. I let the wrath boil over.

And I remembered, all at once, how I'd escaped seven years ago. A hand had gripped a knife, plunging it through the air towards my heart. Fur had covered my body, jaw elongating, limbs transforming, claws shooting out from newly formed paws. I'd shifted between one heartbeat and the next for the first time. Scrambling out of the ropes holding me, I had dived at Randy, my claws slashing down the side of his face. Fear jumped in his eyes and he ran.

I'd chased him out of the shack where he'd been keeping me. Outside, he tore off up a path. A woman stood at the top of the hill. I had a moment to be outraged she hadn't tried to help, and then a shockwave reverberated through my brain, dropping me to the ground.

Abigail had stolen my memory of shifting to defend myself. She'd wanted me to view myself as beaten and afraid. It made me easier to kill. That shit was over.

Randy stood before me now, eyes glassy with sadistic pleasure. Claws ripped from my toes, as I pulled myself higher using the handcuffs. Arms burning, my legs pistoned up, claws slashing Randy across the face and down his chest.

His blood-soaked shock fed me. My paws slid through the handcuffs as I shifted completely. He moved back, hands clutching his chest, and I moved forward, stalking my prey. When he turned and ran, I exulted. My muscles bunched and I leaped, landing on his back, driving him to the ground. My claws dug in as I lunged for his neck.

He was transforming, fur in my mouth instead of skin. I closed my jaws tight and shook, trying to break his neck. I tasted blood. Felt his heart speed. He was mine.

He bucked, trying to dislodge me while he completed his transformation. His wolf was much bigger than mine. He threw me off. I skidded in the dirt ten feet away and circled. One of us was dying today and it wasn't going to be me.

A shadow moved across the clearing. Randy looked up and I dove for him, ripping him open down the side. He bit my shoulder as his back leg went out from under him. He fell in a heap, scrabbling, trying to get up. The shadow flew across the clearing again. If something else was coming to kill me, it could get in line.

I pounced, my jaws tight around his neck. He twisted out of my grip, snarling and lunging. Backing away from his snapping jaws, I held his gaze, enforcing my will over his own. His foot lifted, hesitated, and then dropped. I moved closer, battering against his power, dominating him.

When his head dropped, submissive before the dominant, I lunged, my teeth sinking through his neck to hold him in place. My claws ripped down his chest, opening him wide.

Something huge landed in the clearing. The ground shuddered with its weight, but I ignored it. I was not letting go until he bled out, until his heart stopped.

When I heard his last shallow breath, I released his carcass and turned to face the new threat. A massive, dark shape was silhouetted against the sky. Wings rose, blocking all light, and then settled again. My hackles rose.

Bright red eyes locked on mine as huge, razor-sharp talons dug at the ground. Dragon. I should have been scared but couldn't find it in me. I stared in wonder as he loomed over me. I saw a glint of something shiny beside the dragon's head right before Owen popped up.

He slid off the dragon's back, approaching cautiously. A wing whipped out and wrapped around Owen, protecting him from me. Owen's eyes took on a dreamy, faraway gaze.

"It's her! George, let go. I'm fine." Owen batted at the wing before the dragon released him. "Are you okay?" He made his way to me. "Did he hurt you?" He glanced at Randy's mangled body. "Did you do that?" he whispered.

I didn't need fangs and claws with Owen. And like that, I was standing in front of him. He gasped. I'd changed at the speed of thought. I looked down at myself. Naked, bloody, covered in dirt and clumps of Randy's fur. Angry, red welts ringed my wrists.

I almost laughed at the horrified look on Owen's face. "Got a shirt I can borrow?"

He began to pull off his tee and then stopped. "Wait. I like this shirt." He turned to the dragon. "Can Sam borrow yours?" I'd have sworn the dragon rolled his eyes. "It's just a basic white tee. You have a dozen of them." The dragon's head rose and fell. "Thanks!" Owen shrugged out of his backpack and dug down into it, coming back out with a rolled-up white tee. He waved a hand, and the dirt and fur disappeared. He threw me the tee. It fit fine but was too short. I yanked down on it, trying to cover up my lady bits. He laughed, the bastard. "Trust me, George and I couldn't care less."

"Yes, but I *do* care," a deep, familiar voice grumbled.

Owen and I jumped. Clive stood motionless in the clearing, rage and pain lining his face. His gaze traveled over me, lingering on my wrists and the blood blossoming through the tee. Dave walked through the trees, glanced at all of us, and headed straight for the shack. Clive, on the other hand, went to what was left of Randy, studied him, and then stared at me, pride glowing in his eyes. "Well done."

THIRTY-THREE

Little Shack of Horrors

"Demon," Dave said.

We all turned to him as he stood in the doorway of the shack.

"Do you know which one?" I asked.

He shook his head. His skin lost its brown glamour and turned its natural dark red as he walked in. "Multiple deaths in here. It's been cleaned up, but there's blood trace from…five to seven."

Clive and I had followed, waiting at the open doorway to watch Dave but stay out of his way. The shack looked old and dirty. There wasn't much to it. A rickety table and chairs sat in the corner. A bare, stained mattress lay in the other. Studying the setup, I wondered if the ones waiting their turn sat over in that corner watching.

My stomach revolted. I reared back, racing around the corner to the nearest tree and heaved. I had nothing but bile and spit in my stomach, but it couldn't stop convulsing. Was that the party he'd planned? Big, greedy eyes taking it all in, leering at the scarred, naked wolf, waiting to be the next to make her less than human, to make her a thing to be used and thrown away.

A hand settled on the back of my neck, calming my stomach.

Straightening, I found Clive, handkerchief in his hand, wiping away tears I hadn't realized I'd been crying. He clutched me to him, my head in the crook of his neck, as tears continued to flow, sopping the collar of his shirt. I'd killed my rapist. I'd stopped him and his friends from ever taking another person into that shack to make them nothing, disposable. We are—none of us—disposable.

Clive held me so tightly it hurt.

"Ow."

His grip loosened. "I have an overpowering need to kill the men who took you, who wanted to—who would have taken you away from me forever. But I can't, as you already have."

Sniffling, I said, "I'm kind of a badass."

"Dave was very impressed with the beheading."

"Damn right. He should remember that the next time he thinks about giving me any lip." I felt Clive's chest shake and knew we'd be okay. My kill count had gone from zero to…we'll go with between a few and a lot in the last twelve hours, but I was still me. And they had it coming.

"In your dreams, Sweetheart." Dave walked around the corner, saw us, and paused. Instead of coming closer, he leaned against the side of the shack. "I don't recognize the demon's scent. I certainly don't know them all, but I know the high-ranking ones." He gestured to the front of the shack. "This doesn't seem like demon shit to me. My vote is for a sorcerer calling up one of the lower-level demons for an exchange of blood and power." He looked at Clive. "There was a vampire in there."

Clive's body tensed. I knew he wanted to investigate the cabin, but he also wanted to stay with me. I made the choice for him, extricating myself from his arms, taking his hand, and walking back to the cabin.

When we got back to the doorway, he murmured, "You can wait out here."

"No, I can't," I said, and walked in. Breathing deeply, my

brain began categorizing the scents. There'd been a long period of disuse when the one-room hovel had served as a nest for various animals. I smelled opossum and badger, rat and raccoon. Many had taken their turn in this cabin before humans had reclaimed it. Randy? Yes, his scent was all over the room.

I stepped closer to the mattress without looking at it and inhaled again. Blood. Sex. My nose couldn't parse out the blood into individual scents as Dave's could.

"Randy, Ethan, Joe, Cam, and one of the wolves from the cemetery," I said as I stepped out of the shack and breathed in clean air.

"Two," Clive said. "And Leticia."

"Who's Leticia?" I didn't remember that name.

"One of mine. You saw her. She was one of Ethan's guards. I thought she was better now." He shook his head. "The unrest, the visiting vampires, the scheming. It all makes sense now. She must have been planning her revenge for years."

"Revenge for what?" I asked.

"Étienne. He disregarded my orders because he hadn't agreed with them. You almost died as a result."

Fucking kelpie!

"I delivered his final death. Leticia was Étienne's mate."

I flinched at the word.

"What is it?"

"Nothing. It's just...you said mate. I thought vampires didn't mate, not like werewolves."

"I don't really know, never having been a werewolf. We can and do have mates when we choose. For us it is a true partnership, a companion with whom to spend eternity. We experience no biological imperative to procreate, so that is taken out of the equation. When we chose a partner, we perform a binding blood ceremony, and it lasts until our true deaths. Why?"

"Someone..." I glanced at Owen, who grimaced. "I just heard that you guys didn't do that."

Clive glanced at Owen, as well, before focusing back on me.

"I'd prefer if you have questions about vampires, that you come to me. I've been one longer than all the people in this clearing—" He paused. "Than most of the people in the clearing combined have been alive."

Wait. Who else in this clearing was super old?

"As I was saying, after I delivered Étienne's true death, Leticia raged. It was to be expected. Some mates cannot move on and must be given their own true death. I believed this was the case with Leticia." He gave a barely perceptible shrug of one shoulder. "And then she started to get better. I remained wary for a few years, but she appeared completely restored to her former self."

"Because she'd put her plan for revenge into motion," said Dave.

Nodding, Clive replied, "That would be my assumption, as well."

"That explains why I keep getting a hint of vampire in odd places, like Schuyler's shop. But how do they all fit together? Randy and the wolves, Leticia, and Abigail? How would they even know each other?"

"Who's Abigail?" Dave asked.

All eyes were intent on me. Right. I hadn't told them that part yet. "Abigail is my mother's younger sister. According to Owen's mom, there is a homicidal strain of black wicches in the Corey line. She said they're a really old and powerful wicche family, and that white wicches sometimes die at the hands of their relatives."

I looked at Clive. "She's the one who's been trapping me in those visions."

Clive took my hand. "How do you know?"

I went back over the night in my head and tried to put the events in order. "You were called away to make sure I was alone."

Clive's eyes turned vamp black.

"Not Russell. I heard her talking about you killing him for what they'd done. They laughed about it."

The black bled from his eyes and his hand relaxed on mine. "Go on."

"My wards were torn down and wolves busted in through the tunnel we'd used earlier. I hid on a bookcase in the bookstore—"

"On it?" Owen interrupted.

"I got jump." I grinned. "Anyway, my auntie sauntered in and started ordering people around. When I tried to run, I got slammed with electricity. It broke my brain."

Clive looked at me sharply. "Meaning?"

"It felt like it was raining glass in my head."

They all stared for a moment. "Brain hemorrhage?" Dave asked.

"Well, that might explain why blood was dripping from my nose and ears."

Clive's grip increased to just this side of broken bones.

I caught his eye and said, "I got better. When my brain was raining—or bleeding or whatever it was doing—I remembered something. My aunt had been at my mother's funeral. She was raging because the name Quinn had been put on my mother's headstone. She was super pissed about a high and mighty Corey 'befouling' the family line with werewolf blood. Apparently, I'm an abomination. Which, I think, explains why she's been trying so hard to erase me."

Dave snorted. "Your family is as fucked up as mine."

"True dat."

"The question is, though, did Abigail's attack backfire?" Clive asked.

Dave nodded. "My thoughts exactly. She tries to kill Sam and ends up unlocking memories." Dave studied me. "They could come back on their own. If you want help rummaging around up there and finding them, let me know."

I didn't have to think about that one. "Yes, please. Do you know someone who can help me?" I needed those memories in order to protect myself and the people around me. Before this was done, I had a feeling I'd be joining a long line of homicidal Coreys.

"Me," Dave said.

"You what?" Had I missed something?

"I can help you find your memories, *if* you stop making me do bullshit chores like picking up people's dirty dishes. I'm not a fucking busboy."

"Really?"

"Yes, really. I hate that shit," Dave said.

"No, I mean about recovering my memories. Can you really do that?"

He shrugged. "We'll find out, won't we?"

Feeling better now that I had a way to recover what Abigail had stolen, I turned my attention to the elephant in the room and his boyfriend, Owen. "You brought a dragon." I stood in awe. "He's incredible."

"Don't I know it. Coco said she heard you calling her name over and over."

"It worked."

"It did. She ran downstairs to the shop and put her hands over the metal and stones she'd used in your necklace, trying to open a link. She did, figured out where you were, and told us where to look."

"Sam?" Dave stood next to the handcuffs I'd been trapped in. "These are silver." His voice betrayed confusion and more than a little speculation. "They're still locked and there's fur caught in the hinge." He grinned. "You shifted while touching silver."

"I know. I was there." I shrugged. "I was wicked pissed. I guess that overrode the silver."

Crossing his arms over his chest, he shook his head, grin widening. "That's not a thing. Wolves can't shift when they're touching silver."

Everyone in the clearing was staring again. Their scrutiny was making me itch. "Well, clearly some of us can."

"He's right," Clive said. "The studies on this have been conclusive."

Tension skated up my spine.

"It's going to be fun to see what else that wicche blood of yours allows you to do that other wolves can't," Dave said.

Clive exchanged a look with Dave and nodded.

"New question," Owen piped in. "Do you have a black wicche on retainer who can overpower this Abigail?"

Clive tore an assessing look from me, answering Owen. "Possibly. We'll need to see who our allies are. Speaking of which, thank you both for coming so quickly."

Owen eyed Clive and almost bowed. I could see his body twitch as though he wanted to. Instead, he nodded and pointed at the bloodstains on the tee I was wearing. "I don't have healing magic like my sister, but I can try."

"I've got her," Clive said. Owen retreated back to George, leaving Clive and me alone.

I met Clive's concerned gaze. "More scars."

He reached up and held my head in both his hands, his thumbs skating over my sore face. "I thank all the gods and goddesses that you're alive." He leaned in and gently kissed me. "Besides, you know I think scars are sexy."

I choked out a laugh, grimacing in pain. And then it was gone.

Leading me a short distance, we disappeared into the trees. He pulled off George's shirt and studied my wounds. Blood seeped through cuts beginning to heal. Bruises bloomed along my ribs.

"Can I seal your cuts?"

"Knock yourself out."

Grinning, he dropped to a knee and lazily dragged his tongue up my stomach. I clenched, pleasure overpowering pain. I closed my eyes, my head dropping back as he licked every drop of blood, closing my wounds and making me desperate for him.

He breathed in, the scent of my arousal replacing the stench of fear. He rubbed his nose along my abdomen. "Soon."

Standing, he unbuttoned his shirt.

"Dude," I whispered, glancing around. "We're not fooling around with three people twenty yards away."

He smirked. "I'm giving you something to wear."

I snatched up George's tee from the ground. "This is fine. Look, it's already bloody. Your shirt is pristine and probably costs more than my whole wardrobe."

"That's not saying much."

"Hey."

"Hush," he said while putting my arms through the sleeves. His eyes were vampy black, but his touch was gentle. "Wolves aren't the only ones who respond to scent. You're not walking around in clothing carrying George's scent." He was careful not to brush against my freshly scarred skin while buttoning the shirt. Breathing deeply, he said, "Much better."

Hmm, I guess I was going to have to start learning vampy stuff. How often did he feed? Who did he feed on? Was it sexual? Because I was not down with him getting blood with a side of hand job from random folk, from anyone. Questions for another day, though.

Releasing a sigh, I led us back to the clearing. "I still can't believe it. A real dragon. Right there!"

I felt Clive's hand go around my waist, unerringly finding a part of me that didn't hurt. "He *is* hard to miss."

I moved closer to George. "Can I touch?"

George blew air out of his nostrils and nodded his head.

In his dragon form, George was breathtaking. He was huge, dark green scales glinting in the early morning sky. The talons on his feet were almost as long as my legs. His tail snaked out into the forest, too large for the small clearing. The poor guy probably had trees jabbing him all over. He lowered his head so I could see him better. His eyes were a bright, glowing red. They should have been terrifying, but his kindness shone through. I leaned forward and kissed him.

"Thank you, George," I whispered against his jaw. I checked over my shoulder. Clive and Dave were talking near the shack. "You guys get to see a shirtless Clive. Your day's looking up."

Owen grinned, then turned and whispered something to George. It looked as though the dragon blushed.

The sun crested the tall trees. "Clive!"

He spun, eyes black, fangs extended.

"The sun." I pointed up, in case he didn't understand the emergency.

He gave his head a quick shake. Eyes gray and fangs gone, he grinned while Dave chuckled.

"I don't understand. How are you out while the sun is up?"

"Do I sparkle?" he asked, causing Dave to snort a laugh.

"Ha ha. Seriously though, why aren't you dead?" He looked fine. Gorgeous, really. No scorch marks on his perfect skin.

"I *am* dead." He walked toward me, but there was a strip of sunlight piercing the clearing between us. Stopping right before the beam of sunlight, he winked and then turned invisible. A moment later, he was standing in front of me, dropping a kiss on my nose.

"Thank you for the concern, but I'm fine."

"Some kind of vampy trick, huh?"

He held my gaze, joy alight in his eyes. "Something like that, yes."

"I *knew* it!"

THIRTY-FOUR

The Aftermath and New Beginnings

My home was trashed. A river of alcohol had been soaking into the wood floors for hours. The etched mirror behind the bar was smashed. Jagged pieces of glass were everywhere. The bar itself should have been more difficult to damage, as it was constructed from thick slabs of mahogany. Damage it, though, they did. Never underestimate a riled-up werewolf.

A few of his wolves must have stayed to play when Randy, Cam, and Joe carried me off. Chairs broken, tables cracked, lamps shattered—the utter devastation made my throat tight. They didn't care about who they hurt. It was the id in unrestrained glory. They were the only ones who existed. Their needs and desires, the only ones that mattered. They took, defiled, and destroyed because they could. That wasn't the wolf coming to the fore. That was the human.

Holding in a sob, I ran my hand along the edge of the bar, wanting to comfort an old friend. My hand came away bloody, a fine dusting of glass fragments now embedded in my palm. Pushing through the door to the kitchen, I headed for the sink and found more destruction. Holding my hand under the faucet, I assessed the room. Appliances crushed, refrigerator doors hanging open, spoiled food cascading out onto the floor. Picking glass from my hands, I had trouble breathing, the hurt weighed heavily on my chest. I wasn't sure I could take much more.

Ignoring the sting in my palm, I made my way to my apartment. I'd felt less afraid facing a demon than I did my own home. Blowing out a breath, I stepped in. The stench made me gag. My couch had been shredded and used as a urinal. My books! A tiny gasp escaped before I locked it down. My books had been ripped apart, pages scattered, stories stolen. Little treasures I'd collected over the last seven years—nothing anyone would care about but me—were lying broken on the ground.

Steeling myself, I stepped into my bedroom. This was the main source of the stench. One of them had defecated on the bed. Drawers had been pulled out, clothing torn. The closet door was hanging off its hinge, boxes of books tossed around, and urinated on. Holes punched in walls.

I stood stock-still, stunned by the chaotic rage required to do what they had done. A fire would have been better, cleaner. I would have mourned the loss, but I wouldn't have felt violated, as well.

They'd slashed the overnight case Clive had given me. It was just a bag, and yet my heart hurt almost as much as when I'd seen the books. I picked up the beautiful, floral bag and hugged it to myself, grieving for my home of the last seven years.

"Sam?"

I turned to find Owen and Dave standing in the doorway. I didn't know what to say. My heart was breaking.

"Come out of there, sweetheart." Dave waved me to them. "You don't need to see this."

Tears streamed down my face as I went to them, Clive's bag still clutched to my chest. "Why would they do this?"

"People are fucked," Dave said. "I tell you this all the time."

"I'm sorry, Sam." Owen reached for the torn bag. "Honey, you don't need that. It's ruined," he said. "And you can stay with me until all this gets cleaned up and fixed."

"Actually, Sam already has a room in my home," Clive said. He strode up behind Owen and Dave, his eyes on me and the bag I still stupidly clung to. The bag had become more than a bag. It was something rare and beautiful that had been taken, abused, and left scarred. I couldn't drop it.

"You'll rebuild, right? The Slaughtered Lamb can't just close," Owen said.

"Fuck no. The assholes don't get to win." Dave studied the configuration of the rooms. "As long as you're remodeling, you should change whatever doesn't work."

"It all works," I said. "Worked."

"No way. That kitchen setup was shit. I want an island and an eight-burner stovetop. A double oven. And a pot filler over the stovetop."

"Now that you mention it, I've always thought the bookcases should be angled differently to make browsing easier," Owen added.

"Why don't you two go make a list while I talk with Sam," Clive said.

Once they'd left, Clive gently pulled the bag from my hands and placed it on the ground, before pulling me into his arms, into an embrace I needed like my next breath.

"We *will* rebuild. We'll gut it and start again. All traces of what they've done will be burned away. You are a phoenix, Sam. You rise from the ashes."

I swallowed the sob lodged in my throat. He was right. When my home burned at seventeen, I'd moved to San Francisco alone, with only the clothes on my back, to start again. This was my crucible and I would rise from the flames. Again.

Nodding, I stepped back, stood on my own and assessed the damage with clearer eyes. It was gone and I'd rebuild. Taking Clive's hand in mine, I adjusted my thinking. I wasn't alone anymore. We'd rebuild and we'd move on.

I PULLED AT THE COLLAR OF THE DRESS AGAIN. IT WAS PERFECT, gorgeous, but I wasn't used to my scars showing. I was still dealing with a hardwired compulsion to hide them.

Clive pulled my hand from my neck and held it. "You look beautiful."

"Yeah, yeah." I rolled my eyes while smoothing down the front of the dress. If anything around here was beautiful, it was what I was wearing. Owen and I had gone shopping, and when I saw this dress, I had to have it. It was a wrap-around of soft, thin cashmere. The color, though—I'd been staring at it all evening and the closest I could come to describing it was an antiqued peachy-brown. It was rich and warm, and I loved it. I didn't, however, love the V-neck or the fact that my legs were visible, but I was working my way toward Clive's opinion that scars were sexy. It would be a long and difficult road, but I was on it.

"Our first date," he said.

I snorted a laugh, because I'm lady-like. "I'm pretty sure we're doing this relationship thing backward. First date after the banging?"

Clive grinned, kissing my cheek. "Whereas, I believe we're doing it perfectly."

"Are we still talking about the banging?"

Clive laughed, a sound that made wings flutter in my chest. He didn't do it nearly enough. It was a source of delight and pride when I could prompt it.

The maître d' rushed over. "Mr. Fitzwilliam, I apologize for making you wait. Your table is ready."

Clive rested his hand at the small of my back as we followed the man through the restaurant. It was on the top floor of a building in the Financial District, with a wall of windows overlooking the city. The lighting was low, the carpet black, the walls almost as dark, but the tables were topped with stark white linens. What I loved about it was the illusion of privacy. Large floral arrangements in white, with accents of pale green, were scattered throughout the room, situated under spotlights. They glowed in the dim light and blocked the view of other tables.

The maître d' led us through the main dining area and down a short hall to a private room. I walked straight to the window and looked out. I felt like Batman, standing on a rooftop, surveying my city.

A moment later, Clive slid his arms around my waist and rested his head on my shoulder. The shoes I was wearing made us closer to the same height. "Do you like?"

I put my hands on my hips, superhero-style and said, "Yes, Citizen. All seems to be quiet in our fair metropolis this evening."

Tickling me, he kissed my neck. "They've brought the wine. Would you like to sit?"

Being unused to wearing anything but sneakers meant that, yes, I was ready to sit. Owen picked out the heels. He was right. They were gorgeous, but they also hurt like hell. I didn't know how women wore these things all the time. Women were frickin' warriors.

The chairs were upholstered in a tone on tone black jacquard that matched the carpet and walls. Two large urns with magnificent sprays of flowers sat to the sides. Clive held my chair for me and then was pouring us both glasses of a deep red wine.

I held my glass to the light. "This *is* wine, right?"

He held his glass toward mine, and we pinged them together. "To new beginnings."

Nodding, I echoed, "To new beginnings."

We drank. When he leaned toward me, I gladly met him halfway, leading with my lips. The kiss was soft and slow, promising everything.

Flustered, I took another sip of wine. "Which reminds me, do you guys eat? I've been living in your house for a few days and have yet to see anyone besides me eat."

Clive took a moment to answer. "Can we? Yes. Do we?

Rarely. Our bodies don't need it and sometimes process it poorly. It's easier not to."

Worried, I thought about the whiskey he always drank when he visited the bar, the wine in his hand. "Does it make *you* sick? You don't have to eat and drink to make me more comfortable."

Shaking his head, he said, "No. I'm one of the lucky few. I lost interest in it long ago, though. Before you came along and started changing things."

Stomach flutters. "So, how do you get what you need?"

He leaned in and whispered, "Are we talking in code?"

Grinning, I smacked his arm. "We're in a restaurant. I'm being discreet."

"Ah, of course. A paragon of discretion is our Sam."

"A-ny-way, back to my question." I pinned him with a look while I sipped my wine.

He stared back, one eyebrow raised. "You know what I am. Becoming missish, are we?"

Was he right? Instead of talking around it, I asked what I needed to know. "Is there sex involved when you drink their—" I glanced back at the closed door, before lowering my voice. "Blood?"

Brow furrowed, Clive studied me. "Come again?"

"I've read books, seen movies. I know all about your kind, mister. You can just forget about that kinky vampire crap if you expect me to stick around."

"This ought to be good," he mumbled. "Exactly what do you know of vampires?"

Granted, my knowledge came from popular fiction, but still. "I know you drink blood, and may or may not turn into bats—"

"Not."

"I know you can mesmerize women." God, I loved it when he joined in the silliness. It was as though a heavy mantle had slipped from his shoulders, if only for a moment.

"I could do that long before I became a vampire." He smirked. "Have you seen me?"

Snickering, I countered. "I know you can fly and that you're strangely fixated on Jim Morrison and coastal towns."

Confusion colored his expression for a moment before he rolled his eyes. "*Lost Boys* was not a documentary."

"Says you. I know your kind sparkles in the sun. Or turns to ash. Not sure which." I took a sip. "The learning curve on that one is pretty steep. Imagine that poor sap who went out into the sun, hoping to sparkle like a disco ball and instead burned to a crisp."

"In his case, we'd consider it a necessary thinning of the herd."

"Right?" I sniggered.

"But back to your original question. No, I don't have sex with the people I take blood from. Regardless of what you may have read, that's not a common occurrence. When we're having sex, do we take a sip? Possibly. But none of it is a given, other than needing blood to survive. At this point, I rarely drink from people. We have bagged blood we drink in glasses. We're not heathens."

Oh. "Okay."

"Can you live with that?" Clive slid his glass away and took my hand, grave expression back in place.

"Yes."

"Can you live with me?" His hand gripped mine, tighter than I'm sure he was aware. It was okay, though. I could take it.

"I *am* living with—"

"Permanently. Will you stay with me, Sam?"

"Oh." I thought about my home, about the life I'd led there for the last seven years. It'd been a good one. Did I want to give that up? Live with vampires? Be drawn into all their political intrigue and bullshit? Not to mention, I still had Abigail to deal with. Maybe a demon, too. My life was a mess. I looked into the eyes of the man I loved. Could I live without him? Probably. Would I want to? No. So…

"Yes."

Dear Reader,

Thank you for reading ***The Slaughtered Lamb Bookstore and Bar***. If you enjoyed Sam and Clive's first adventure together, please consider leaving a review or chatting about it with your book-loving friends. When you're a new writer, word of mouth means so much!

Love,
Seana

Acknowledgments

I have been blessed to have many intelligent, kind, and witty women in my life. They've been the ones to bolster and push, making every step of publishing a little less scary. They've been the ones to offer chocolate when the journey was rough. Luckily for me, they've also been the ones who understood the importance of a well-made cocktail (I'm looking at you, Roseann). So, to all the amazing women in my life, thank you!

The person who has read every iteration of this story is my incredible friend and critique partner C.R. Grissom. Thank you for the advice and cheerleading, and for never wavering from your absolute belief that Sam & Clive would eventually be published. So, in no particular order, here are the fabulous women who read, offering encouragement and feedback. Thank you to Barbara Kelly, Roseann Rasul, Norma Jean Bell, Tara Sheets, Christy Hovland, Kimberly MacCarron, Maichen Liu-Grossman, Sara Carvalho, Marlene Spector, Suzanne Miller-Moody, Amanda Lease, Mary Beth Allman, Carol Mack, Mim Ostenso, Monica Stoffal, and Elaine Watkins.

Thank you to my brilliant agent Sarah Younger at the Nancy Yost Literary Agency. Thank you for understanding and supporting my need to tell this story. Thank you to my wonderful editor Peter Sentfleben, who has the gift to give spot-on insight in the gentlest terms.

Continuing on a theme, thank you to my amazing daughters Harper and Grace, both of whom consider it a given that their mom is an author. Thank you to my dad who always asks when that book with the bar overlooking the ocean is going to be published. That one's his favorite. And a very big thank you to my husband Gregory for sharing my dream with me, and for the countless times we pondered which drinks should be paired with the reading of which books at The Slaughtered Lamb.

Want more books from Seana?

If you'd like to be the first to learn what's new with Sam and Clive (and Owen and Dave and Meg…), please sign up for my newsletter. It's filled with writing news, deleted scenes, give-aways, book recommendations, and my favorite cocktail and book pairings.

The Dead Don't Drink at Lafitte's
Sam Quinn, book 2

I'm Sam Quinn, the werewolf, book-nerd owner of The Slaughtered Lamb Bookstore and Bar. Things have been busy lately. While the near-constant attempts on my life have ceased, I now have a vampire gentleman caller. I've been living with Clive and the rest of his vampires for a few weeks while The Slaughtered Lamb is being rebuilt. It's going about as well as you'd expect.

My mother was a wicche and long dormant abilities are starting to make themselves known. If I'd had a choice, necromancy wouldn't have been my top pick, but it's coming in handy. A ghost warns me someone is coming to kill Clive. When I rush back to the nocturne, I find vamps from New Orleans readying an attack. One of the benefits of vampires looking down on werewolves is no one expects much of me. They don't expect it right up until I take their heads.

Now, Clive and I are setting out for New Orleans to take the fight back to the source. Vampires are masters of the long game. Revenge plots are often decades, if not centuries, in the making. We came expecting one enemy, but quickly learn we have darker forces scheming against us. Good thing I'm the secret weapon they never see coming.

Read on for a sneak peek.

The Wicche's Glass Tavern
Sam Quinn, book 3

Whether I've learned enough or not, the time has come. I need to face off with my aunt, the woman who's been trying to kill me ever since I was a baby. In her mind, I'm an abomination. My father's werewolf blood sullied the long, pure line of Corey wicches. Whereas, I think she's a total psycho who trucks with demons to get what she wants. Unfortunately, what she wants is my death.

I've put together the Fellowship of the Sam, with werewolves, vampires, wicches, a gorgon, a Fury, a half-demon, a couple of dragon-shifters, and the fae. It'll be one hell of a battle. Hopefully, San Francisco will still be standing when we're done.

And for something completely different...

Welcome Home, Katie Gallagher
This romantic comedy was my first book published. Remember, don't judge a book by its (truly hideous) cover.

Nobody said a fresh start would be easy

A clean slate is exactly what Katie Gallagher needs, and Bar Harbor, Maine, is the best place to get it. Except the cottage her grandmother left her is overrun with woodland creatures, and the police chief, Aiden Cavanaugh, seems determined to arrest her! Katie had no idea she'd broken his heart fifteen years ago…

Sneak Peek at THE DEAD DON'T DRINK AT LAFITTE'S

SAM QUINN, BOOK 2

ONE

Wherein Sam Understands That Hogwarts Letter Is Never Coming

I liked ghost stories as much as the next werewolf. I'd assumed, though, they were just that. Stories. Something to make your heart beat faster and your skin prickle with unease. Tales told by the fireside, evoking ancient, unnamed fears and causing our eyes to seek out shapes in shadows. Turned out I was wrong.

A colorless, almost transparent woman who seemed vaguely familiar glowed in the moonlight. She gesticulated wildly, blocking the dark path to The Slaughtered Lamb, my bookstore and bar currently under renovation. Silently shouting, eyes filled with urgency, she flickered in and out of existence. I moved forward and strained to read her lips, more concerned than scared.

Cold air chilled my skin, damp from running. I caught 'no' and 'vampires.' Mostly, I was onboard with that sentiment, but my boyfriend—a stupid term for a gorgeous British man who appeared to be about thirty but was actually hundreds of years old—was a vampire.

While I contemplated how I was supposed to refer to Clive, even in my own head, the woman shot forward and clamped a hand around my wrist. She was a ghost. I'd swear it, and yet I felt her cold fingers digging into my skin. Her filmy image became a shade more solid at the contact and I heard a whisper of words.

"They're coming! He'll be killed. Go!"

Understanding, without a doubt, she meant my manfriend Clive, I tore my arm away and sprinted the four miles to the vampires' nocturne in Pacific Heights. There was unrest amongst the vamps. One of Clive's people had recently shown herself to be an enemy, working against him, trying to exact revenge for a dead lover. Clive had been investigating, trying to determine if others in his nocturne were plotting a coup attempt. He'd routed out two with an allegiance to her but suspected there were more.

Dodging trees and startled rabbits, I raced through the Presidio, a fifteen-hundred-acre park that was a former military post. Why had the ghost looked so familiar? I couldn't put my finger on it. *They're coming,* she'd said. Emerging from the park onto Pacific Avenue, I had to slow to human speed. I was almost there, four minutes tops.

Rounding the last corner, I slowed at the looming wrought iron gates. The vampire standing guard gave me a strange look, but stepped out of the way, allowing me to speed across the courtyard. Before I had a chance to touch the door, it swung open, Clive's butler already there.

"Where is he?" I shouted, racing past and skidding to a stop in the foyer.

"Who?" he responded after a moment.

I knew the vampires hated me, considered a werewolf little more than a stray mongrel, but I wasn't putting up with his bullshit. Long, razor-sharp claws sprang from my fingertips as my eyes lightened to wolf gold. "I will shred you, you pompous ass! If anything happens to Clive, I'll be back to slice the smug off your face."

"Sam?"

I spun and there he was, burnished hair glowing in the light, chiseled features, cool gray eyes assessing me. The door closed behind me as Clive waited, amusement coloring his expression. Retracting my claws, a skill I'd recently mastered, I walked to him.

"You're okay?"

"As you see. Why did you think I was otherwise?" Taking my hand, he led me over a marble floor toward the library. "And how was your lesson with Lydia?"

My shoulders slumped. "Miserable." Lydia was my right-hand-man Owen's mom. She was a powerful wicche who had trained all her children. I was coming into my magic late in life, but we were hoping she'd be able to teach me, as well. So far, I'd proven to be a failure at all things wicchey.

He closed the door of the library behind us and waited for me to explain. I crossed the room to my window seat. He'd it built for me. It was mine.

"Tell me all about it and why you raced home looking for me." He followed, sitting next to me.

Studying him, I made sure he wasn't hiding an injury. "You're really fine?"

He kissed me softly, tenderly, until I'd forgotten all about my horrible magic lesson and the ghost who'd scared the crap out of me. "I am," he finally said.

"I don't understand what that was about then." That's what I got for believing random apparitions.

"Tell me what you were up to while I slept." He leaned back and pulled me to him.

"Before or after I ruined another of Lydia's pots?"

Taking my hand, he squeezed. "I'll have a new set of cook-ware delivered tomorrow."

"It's not for you to replace. I'm the one whose potion turned to a toxic sludge that hardened into volcanic rock." Thunking my head against shoulder, I continued. "Owen walked in, wondering what the horrible smell was, and I saw it. A look of horrified pity passed between Owen and his mom. I'm a failure of a wicche."

"Nonsense. We just haven't found your gift yet."

Snorting, I flopped back on the window seat cushions. "A kitchen wicche, I most assuredly am not. Owen and his mom even did this cool incantation over me to open up my powers and make them manifest. P'fft. That worked real well."

I'd learned recently that I, like my father and grandfather and many male grands before me, was a born wolf. I hadn't been mauled by a werewolf and turned. Well, I had been, but the reason I'd survived prolonged torture was due to the werewolf genes that my mother, a wicche, had kept suppressed with a protective amulet. The necklace had been stolen a few weeks ago. Latent talents had begun appearing. Or not, as the case was clearly becoming for any inherent wicchey skills.

"Just as well as I rarely eat, and kitchen magic would be wasted on me." Lifting my hand, he pressed his lips to my palm. "I still don't understand why you thought I'd been hurt."

Oh, right. "I was jogging home by way of The Slaughtered Lamb to check on progress."

"I wish you'd just borrow one of my cars. There are many and you'd be better protect—"

I kissed him quiet. "Nope. Those are your cars, not mine. I'm already living in your house while mine is being remodeled," I said, in reference to my small apartment in the back of The Slaughtered Lamb. "I even went along with you calling the fortune you spent on this necklace a gift," I added, patting the stunning, spelled replacement for my mother's stolen one.

This one didn't hide me, though, as hers had. It protected my mind from my psychotic aunt hell-bent on retroactively aborting me. My mother was a Corey wicche—a ancient and powerful family of wicches—who had fallen in love with and married a werewolf. My aunt considered that union a blasphemy and their daughter an abomination that needed to be destroyed. She'd been doing her damnedest to turn my own mind against me, ergo the new protective necklace around my neck.

"Hell, you bought me a whole wardrobe to make up for the crappy jeans and t-shirt collection I lost when the wolves destroyed my home. I draw the line at expensive sportscars I don't need. I have legs and I like to run. Werewolf, remember?"

"Vividly."

Smirking, I continued. "Anyway, I was jogging down the path to Land's End and ran into a ghost."

Clive furrowed his brow, studying me. "A ghost?"

"Yep. At first, she just flickered in and out, waving her arms. When I got close, she—" Like a flash, I remembered where I'd seen her. "She was the second wolf. The one I'd gone out into the ocean to rescue. When I got shot?"

"Yes. I remember." His hand convulsed around mine. "This was the ghost of the woman who had been murdered and dumped in front of your bar?"

"I think so. She'd been torn up before she'd been murdered and her body had been in the water for a while, so I can't be positive, but it *feels* right. Anyway, she grabbed my arm and said 'They're coming. He'll be killed.'"

"We'll come back to the ghost sighting in a moment. How do you know she meant me?"

I opened my mouth and then stopped. Huh. "No idea. She never said your name. Your face popped into my head and I ran back to save you."

"Thank you for that," he said, grinning.

I shrugged, feeling stupid for racing in, ready for battle, only to find everyone safe and sound.

"Back to the ghost," Clive said, rubbing his thumb over my knuckles. "Have you ever seen a ghost before, communicated with one?"

"Nope. First time. Maybe she was grateful I'd tried to help?"

"Perhaps."

A knock sounded at the library door. I tried to extract my

hand from his before one of his vampires saw us. They'd never show me the disdain they felt for me in front of Clive. They feared him too much. All bets were off, though, when Clive wasn't around.

He didn't let my hand go, freakishly strong vampire. "Come," he called.

Russell, his second, stepped into the room and closed the door. He was a tall, handsome Black man, who seemed born to the formality of vampires, until you got to know him. "Sire, I've just received a call from a visiting party from New Orleans."

"Have you, now?" He shared a look with me before focusing on Russell again. "Isn't that interesting."

"Sire?" Russell's dark eyes looked back and forth between us.

Clive rose from the window seat, pulling me along. Leaning over the coffee table, he swiped through a tablet until classical music was playing throughout the room and then motioned for Russell to move closer. "Sam was just telling me that a ghost waylaid her to say—and I quote—'They're coming. He'll be killed.'"

"Ghost?" Russell looked more confused than concerned. "A ghost told her?"

"Yes. When are they due?" Clive dropped my hand and began to pace.

"Tonight. Lafitte's people requested, quite politely, an audience with you." Russell spared me a wary look, before crossing to the fireplace to speak with Clive. "If you believe Lafitte is moving against you, we can get you out."

Clive turned an incredulous look on Russell. "You'd have me run and hide?" Shaking his head, he patted Russell on the shoulder. "No, old friend, that I will not do. We will meet the envoys, take their measure, and if they lift a hand against us, we will slaughter them all. Afterwards, we'll send their remains back to Lafitte in a box with a bow."

Russell glanced at me and then leaned in closer to Clive. "Sire, perhaps we should—"

"No. We let them come. I am very interested in who arrives, and even more interested to see if any of our own nocturne fight with them against us. Leticia has allies I've yet to ferret out. Tonight will let us know exactly who our enemies are." Patting Russell's arm again, he added, "Trust me. It's better this way. We'll know who stands with us and who has betrayed their oath."

Nodding, Russell conceded, "Yes. You're right." He held out a dark hand for Clive to shake. "I'll speak with Godfrey, but no one else. If the three of us can't take them out, it has been an honor to be your second."

Shaking Russell's hand, Clive said, "The honor is mine, my friend. If I don't survive the night, you know what to do."

"Yes."

"Good," Clive nodded. "Go then and prepare."

When the door closed behind Russell, I stalked over to Clive and drilled a finger into his chest. "What the hell is this 'if I don't survive' bullshit? You're not dying. And there are four of us, not three!"

Clive was shaking his head before I stopped talking. "No. This is vampire business. I won't have you hurt because of political maneuvering. Stay with Owen. He'll look after you."

When he tried to pull me close, I shoved him back. "That's who you think I am? The going gets tough and I need to be protected? Screw that! I'm not hiding anymore, remember? If there's a fight, I'm in it. The *four* of us are going to wipe the floor with those New Orleans usurpers."

Studying me, he shook his head. "I can't lose you. I won't. You're stronger, yes, but you're still learning."

"Clive." I moved forward, resting my hand on his chest. "I love you, but I will kick your ass if you ever say anything this stupid again." When he opened his mouth to respond, I moved my hand to cover it. "No. We're in this together. Whatever it is, we're together. Battling syphilitic zombies or moonlit strolls. Good, bad, or insanely weird, it doesn't matter. Partners, okay?"

He kissed my palm and then moved my hand. "Point taken. Are you sure you're up for a vampire bloodbath?"

"That's my favorite kind of bloodbath."

Shaking his head, he twined his fingers with mine. "Do the zombies have to syphilitic? Being zombies isn't enough?"

Shrugging, I swung our joined hands. "Seemed worse. So, we have visitors coming and I need to change."

Clive raised his eyebrows and looked down at my hoodie, threadbare jeans, and running shoes. "I like it."

"Nope. I need to score higher on the badass scale." Lifting our joined hands to my lips, I kissed his fingers. "You, Russell, and Godfrey go work out the battle plan and then let me know my part. I'm going to go dive deep into that closet you keep adding clothes to and find something that says, 'I will fuck you up and then giggle as I lick your blood from my fingers.'"

The Dead Don't Drink at Lafitte's
Sam Quinn, book 2, is available for preorder at your favorite bookstores!

About the Author

About Seana Kelly

Seana Kelly lives in the San Francisco Bay Area with her husband, two daughters, two dogs, and one fish. When not dodging her family, hiding in the garage to write, she's working as a high school teacher-librarian. She's an avid reader and re-reader who misses her favorite characters when it's been too long between visits.

She's a two-time Golden Heart® Award finalist and is represented by the delightful and effervescent Sarah E. Younger of the Nancy Yost Literary Agency

You can follow Seana on Twitter for tweets about books and dogs or on Instagram for beautiful pictures of books and dogs (kidding). She also loves collecting photos of characters and settings for the books she writes. As she's a huge reader, young adult and adult, expect lots of recommendations, as well.

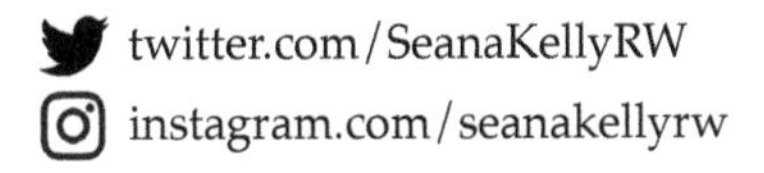

CPSIA information can be obtained
at www.ICGtesting.com
Printed in the USA
LVHW041547261020
669857LV00014B/1574

9 781641 971591